I'LL GET BY

PATTI GAUSTAD PROCOPI

Lavender Press
an imprint of Blue Fortune Enterprises, LLC

I'LL GET BY
Copyright © 2022 by Patti Gaustad Procopi

For information contact :
Blue Fortune Enterprises, LLC
Lavender Press
P.O. Box 554
Yorktown, VA 23690
http://blue-fortune.com

Cover design by BFE, LLC

ISBN: 978-1-948979-84-9
First Edition: August 2022

Praise for Please … Tell Me More

Beautifully written story, a must read, full of family trauma and humor. if you don't see yourself in it you will see your neighbor or relative. The story is very interesting it kept me turning the pages. The book flowed well, and was an easy read. The characters are well developed I wanted to read on to see what happened to them. I like the way it ended, very real to life. A book I would definitely reread a second time.
Mary Bush Shipko
Author of *Aviatrix*

A friend recommended this book to me and it did not disappoint. I felt like I knew the characters and hated to put it down after each evening after reading out loud to my partner. We can't wait to see what this author writes next!
Dana Cox
Amazon Review

Read it straight through - that's how good it is. This story explores the really important things in life weaving all the characters with each one's experiences together in the most beautiful way. Loved it!
Amazon Review

Patti Gaustad Procopi takes you on a journey of family, regret, guilt and forgiveness. There were many times when I felt like saying, "I know, right!" to a character's reaction to events.
I certainly could empathize with Rose's feelings. The book explores how easy it is to misinterpret other's words and actions. How a word said in anger or in a drunken stupor can affect a person for years. One thing is for certain, it brings home the importance of communication. Families that don't talk to each other, siblings that envy each other and individuals who hide their insecurities through alcohol, anger or withdrawal from society, may learn ways of coping if they would just talk. Talk to a family member, talk to a therapist, talk to a dead relative. It's all about letting go the voices inside.
For anyone who is looking for answers, this book doesn't have them, but it will help you understand the value of looking for them and asking. Use your voice, share your voice, and let go the past.
Sonja McGiboney
Author/Blogger
Jazzy Series

In loving memory of
My Parents
Jack and Marj
the original John and Evie

And to Army Brats everywhere
We lived the adventure

Prologue
The End and A New Beginning

I GOT MY DIVORCE PAPERS in the mail today. Hardly a surprise, but still a punch in the gut. I had made great strides in the last year, like a butterfly emerging from a twenty-year cocoon.

Until those papers arrived, I believed I had reconciled myself to what had happened but opening that envelope released all those painful and embarrassing memories again.

The surprise happened a year ago when my husband, Frank, and my best friend, Claire, announced to me and Chuck, Claire's husband at the time, that they had been having an affair and didn't want to wait any longer to spend the rest of their lives together. They were soulmates, and the universe had determined they needed to be together.

The most embarrassing part was Frank left me for my best friend. What a cliché! It made it so much worse.

So much more… humiliating.

But the worst part was losing Claire. In that moment when I needed a friend more than ever, I had no one. My friend, my confidant, had betrayed me. I loved Claire. I shared everything with her. And she left me. For a man I despise. A man she should have known was not worthy of her.

I told her all about my marriage. When Frank was at his worst, I turned to Claire. She'd listen, pour me a cup of coffee or glass of wine, and hug me. Give me a pep talk. And all the while, behind my back, she and Frank were together. She probably repeated everything I told her and they laughed about it together.

I have moved on, even moved to another town, but thinking about them sometimes still makes me burn in anger. I probably wouldn't have missed Frank or the marriage at all if I hadn't lost Claire as well. Surprisingly, despite the fact that he was a total jerk in all ways, I never suspected him of having an affair. Especially not with Claire.

I did not have a happy marriage. I should have pulled the plug earlier and not waited for Frank to dump me.

Why didn't I leave? Like most people in unhappy situations, I felt paralyzed, trapped. Plus, I had absolutely no resources. It's easy to tell someone to leave, but the reality is that the rent has to be paid and the lights kept on. Frank was a vindictive person who'd have made sure I didn't have a dime even if it meant starving his own children. Or he might have hired a lawyer to prove I was an unfit mother in order to take the kids away, not because he wanted them, but simply to punish me more. So, I hung in there for the sake of the children. Or so I told myself at the time.

I've been working on trying to move on. In the past, I blamed my parents and my husband for my unhappiness. We all are products of our past. I have come to appreciate that my parents were also the products of their childhoods. Just as their parents were. My ex, Frank, had a difficult and what could even be described as a bizarre childhood. We all have things to overcome. I needed to learn to "rise above."

"Rise above" was one of my mother's favorite sayings. She had a number of them. It was her equivalent of "don't let the bastards get you down," which was one of my father's favorite sayings. Mother believed if you kept your head up and didn't acknowledge the slings and arrows of misfortune, gossip, a bad haircut, or a bad fashion choice, you would be fine. My mother was the Queen of "Rising Above."

I have been the queen of regrets.

I have regretted my parents, my childhood, my marriage, many things I did or didn't do, my food choices, clothes I wore, money I wasted, horrible hairstyles, things I said, as well as things I wished I had said. "If only I had done X instead of Y," has been a constant refrain in my head.

What is that line from the Serenity Prayer? "Accept the things you cannot change."

I cannot change anything about the past and dwelling on it and punishing myself for all my poor choices is not helpful. I have spent this last year going over all the regrets one last time so I can lay them to rest. Forgive and forget.

1

Landry Parish, Louisiana

1917

MADELEINE LOOKED IN THE MIRROR, practicing various facial expressions. She turned her head slightly to the side and tried a winsome smile. Or was it a come-hither smile? Francois (Oh, please call me Frank!) said he felt weak in the knees when she smiled at him. She looked over her other shoulder, smiling again. Which profile was better?

Then she tried pouting. Charles said her pouts made him laugh because she looked so pretty, and she seriously had nothing to pout about. "You're beautiful and rich and every boy in town adores you. Why on earth are you pouting?" Then he would try to kiss her but of course she wouldn't let him. Sometimes she would let one of them kiss her but she liked to torment them before a little reward.

Standing up, Madeleine twirled around the room, imagining she was in the arms of one of her admirers, dancing. She could hear the music in her head as she spun around before falling on her bed. Looking up at the lace netting on her canopy bed, she told herself she could not survive until the weekend and the dance at the Blanchet's. She might die of boredom.

She might die of boredom at the dance, too. She loved to see what the other girls were wearing, hoping that no one's dress was prettier than hers. She had to be the belle of the ball or her evening would be ruined. And she enjoyed having a full dance card with all the boys vying for her attention. Still, it was one more dance in a lifetime of dances. Nothing of excitement ever happened. She would dance and talk to the other girls and gossip about the boys. A few of the boys might try to kiss her. And then the evening would end and everyone would wait until the next dance.

Climbing out of her huge bed, she walked over to the closet to check her dress choices for the weekend. She always liked to have more than one choice since she wouldn't make a final decision on what to wear until the afternoon of the dance. Her father and mother spoiled her and never said no to a request for a new dress. Or two. Sometimes they might suggest she have one of her older dresses cut down and remade but then she would use her charming pout and they'd laugh and give in.

Charles was right. She was lucky that she was beautiful, rich, and spoiled. Her father adored her. After her mother gave birth to five sons, the arrival of a daughter was a gift from God. The entire family doted on her, even her older brothers. The servants at the house adored her. Madeleine could be loving, and she charmed everyone she met. Until she reached the old age of sixteen.

Finished with school, she was expected to settle down and choose an eligible young man to spend the rest of her life with. Her father wasn't rushing her into the decision since he would have been happy to have her at home with him for many more years, but her mother was concerned that if she delayed too long, all the best choices would be snapped up and she would no longer have the entire male population of Landry Parish to choose from.

Though, in truth, she did not have the entire population to choose from since the pool of potential suiters was strictly limited to those who were in the same social class as Madeleine's family. Her father was a judge and came from a long line of judges and politicians. His name was Edward Butler Hebert. Her mother was Alphonsine Marie Villiers. Her mother's very French ancestors had arrived in Louisiana during the French Revolution, no doubt hoping to keep their wealth and their heads. They managed to do quite well, and the Villiers became one of the wealthiest landowners in Louisiana. Both of Madeleine's parents came from old money and could trace their roots back to wherever people liked to trace their roots in order to feel better about themselves and lord it over others who didn't know where they came from.

Each dance she attended was meant to winnow the field until she finally found the one. There were a number of boys she liked very much. Francois (Frank!), Charles (of course), and there was also Andre, Eduard, Christian and John. She loved writing her name over and over, adding the last names of each of these potential husbands.

Once during a rather long boring class at the Academy, a nun caught her writing these names on a piece of paper. She was given a firm smack on the back of the hand and told, "Your penmanship is lovely but your subject matter shows a frivolous nature. Best to pay attention to the lessons."

Still, while Madeleine liked all the young men who swarmed around her, professing undying love, there was something dull about them. They were all rich and would inherit their father's money and get boring jobs while she would be expected to sit home and have endless numbers of children and have tea with the other ladies in her social set. At least she would have servants to look after the children. Bored by the good boys, she wanted more out of life than a society wedding and children.

A sigh shuddered through her tiny frame. "I shall simply die of boredom. I want more out of my life than babies and dinners and tea parties." After she graduated from the Academy, she suggested to her father that she would like to go to college.

He laughed. "Seriously Madeleine, why would you want to go to college?

Are you honestly contemplating getting a job?"

"No, father," she replied, "not a dull job like yours." They both chuckled at that old joke about his job as a judge, which was anything but dull. "I thought I could study art and history and literature. Become more well-rounded. I already have all the social skills mastered but if one wants to move about in higher society, one needs to be able to converse intelligently on a wide range of subjects."

Her father paused to consider her idea. She could be right. With a good education, she might attract the attention of a man even higher up in society. Someone in the State Capitol or even a young man who had ambitions as a senator or ambassador.

Madeleine sent her application to Sarah Lawrence and was accepted on a probationary basis since she did not really have a portfolio of work like the other young ladies. She attended for only one semester. Unfortunately, she had never been a very dedicated student, and her lack of attention to assignments and deadlines proved to be her undoing. During semester break, her parents received a letter from the dean of admissions wishing her every success in life, but they could not offer her a place for the second semester.

Her parents never brought up her failure at college. Once home, she focused her attention on the usual events—dances and teas. She sighed. She was destined for something more. Something better. Something with adventure.

"It's rather difficult to try to change one's life, if others aren't willing to cooperate," she told her best friend Diantha, explaining that the administration at Sarah Lawrence had rescinded her admission offer. She'd been a bit shocked by the news.

"Was it hard? Is that why you didn't do well?" Diantha inquired sympathetically.

"To be honest, I don't really know. I enjoyed living in New Orleans far more than I enjoyed my classes, though it was nice not to be taught by nuns anymore. The professors even included men!"

Diantha tittered in response.

"But the classes were all rather dull. Not much better than the Academy. Why is learning such a bore?" Madeline studied her face in the mirror.

"I don't know. I would never have wanted to go to college. I couldn't wait to get out of school and get on with life," Diantha replied.

"What, if anything, has been happening while I've been gone?" Madeleine asked.

"Oh, the usual. The most exciting news is that Gabrielle thinks Anton is going to propose soon. It's all very exciting. She would be the first of our set to marry."

"Anton is going to propose to Gabrielle?" Madeleine asked incredulously. She had thought that Anton was smitten by her. She'd better focus her attention before all the young men turned to other girls. Her mother's fears might come true.

"Oh, there is a bit of news. Everyone has started to go to the town baseball games."

"Baseball?" Madeleine was even more incredulous over this bit of news. "Why on earth would everyone be going to see a bunch of sweaty men run after a ball? Sounds vulgar."

"That's because you haven't seen our local hero in action. Who cares about the game as long as you can look at him?" Diantha pretended to swoon.

"Who is this hero?" Madeleine was miffed to be out of the loop and that her friends had obviously found other pursuits while she was gone. She would have to catch up or be forever thought of as the formerly popular Madeleine Hebert.

"His name is Nappy Boudreaux, and he is very easy on the eyes. Kind of a Douglas Fairbanks look-alike but without the mustache. We're all going to the game on Friday night. You should come along and see for yourself."

Nappy stood on the mound, staring at the batter. It was his way of intimidating the opposition before he even pitched a ball at them. The stands were full of the hometown fans cheering his name. He wound up and threw the ball straight into the catcher's mitt as the batter swung and missed. He turned and bowed to the stands, smiling rakishly.

Nappy had come from a poor but decent farm family, which did not give him access to higher society. He had a stern, cold mother and a weak father. He had big dreams but no money. He worked hard at various jobs but couldn't get anywhere. Of course, there was no money for college, not that he would have wanted to go anyway. What he wanted to do with his life couldn't be learned in books. But he needed a leg up. He needed money. The one thing he had going for him was that he was a gifted athlete. He played ball for the town baseball league. He'd even been scouted by a pro team but nothing came of it.

The entire town was crazy about baseball and loved to go see Nappy pitch. All the girls thought he was a "dreamboat." Young, athletic, and good-looking, he seemed a bit dangerous and was rumored to be involved in various hijinks and misdeeds, which only added to his appeal. His prowess on the mound helped him get away with many pranks and bad behavior. He enjoyed the attentions of women of all social classes.

His given name was Stefan Artur Boudreaux. A fine name even though he was not from a fine family. When he started playing baseball, people began to give him nicknames. First it was The King, Le Roi. After a while someone said, "Oh no, he is so much more than a King—he is an emperor—the Emperor of Baseball." And the nickname got turned into Napoleon, the Great Emperor and Conqueror. Finally, it was shortened from Napoleon to Nappy. Nappy loved that nickname.

Maddie watched Nappy in action from her seat in the stands. Diantha had been right. It was easy to watch the game when Nappy was on the mound. After attending several games, she realized that she was a bit in love with the town bad boy and local hero. He made her pulse quicken unlike all those dull rich boys with impeccable manners.

"I think I should like to marry that Nappy," she told her brother Simon.

Simon was horrified. "He's a fine fellow and it's great to watch him play, but he has no money and no family name to speak of. He would hardly fit in with us."

Maddy didn't care what her brother thought of the idea. She wanted Nappy. She rather liked the idea of marrying an older man and creating a bit of a scandal in their dull town.

After the games, Madeleine began to hang around, along with many other young women, trying to catch Nappy's eye. It didn't take long for him to notice her. He began to single her out. She was very pretty, which helped pique his interest, but when he asked a friend who she was and was told that she was from one of the richest families in the area, he became even more interested.

Finally, he asked her on a date. Madeleine made up a story that she was going to a friend's house so she could sneak out and meet him. During dinner, he talked about his future. "I love playing baseball but it's not a career. I want to open a restaurant. My father was a fabulous cook, and I think I've inherited his talent. I want a place that everyone will flock to. I plan to call it *Nappy's*, obviously." He laughed about that. Madeleine was smitten. Here was a man who was going to make it on his own.

A few months later, Madeline told her parents that she had decided to marry Nappy. Her parents were aghast. They had devoted all their love and money on their daughter, hoping that she would make a perfect match with a son of one of their many friends. A match of equals. Not a match with a destitute older man who had a bad reputation as a lady's man.

Madeleine told her parents of her plans while they were gathered in the parlor of their beautiful old family home. Her prim and proper mother and upright father reacted with horror. They were momentarily speechless and then begged and pleaded with her.

She didn't give in to their entreaties. "I shall marry him or no one. You can prepare to send me to the convent if I can't have Nappy," she announced haughtily, before turning and storming out of the room.

Each of her brothers spoke to her and begged her to reconsider. Her mother promised her a trip to Europe, but she turned her head away and held up her hand to indicate she was not going to listen to anything they said. Her father told her that if she married this man, she would be cut off completely from the family. She didn't believe him. He had always given in to her before. This time he didn't.

Nappy thought that he had found his way to the top. Not only was Madeleine young and beautiful but her family was rich. When she told him her family said they would disown her if she married him, he was embarrassed and then angry. How dare they judge him?

His anger made him swear that he loved and adored her for herself, and he didn't care about her money. They would live on love until he found his fame and fortune.

They married in a small ceremony, not the grand wedding Madeleine had always envisioned. There was no write up on the society page. She assumed her parents would eventually relent. They didn't, and she soon found herself cut off from the society she had known. Neither her parents, her brothers, nor any of her former friends spoke to her. When they passed on the street, they turned away, avoiding all contact.

Madeleine finally realized that her parents had been serious. At first, she didn't care, despite suddenly living in reduced circumstances. She didn't have a housekeeper, a cook, or even a maid. She obviously had not thought this through very well. Soon, she began to see a change in Nappy. He had not married her for love. They were both disappointed.

Madeleine refused to hang her head and act embarrassed. She decided to make her own place in a new and changing world. When Nappy became rich, she could show them all. Her grandmother had left her some money, and Nappy used this money and a bank loan to open a nightclub. The nightclub was a great success. In addition to pitching a perfect game, he also had a head for business. Their new life of glamour began. It was the Roaring Twenties. Instead of garden parties and social teas, they had evenings of drinking, dancing, and hobnobbing with the other newly rich.

They married the year before Prohibition passed. There were rumors about Nappy running an illegal drinking club known as a speakeasy. He was never caught or charged but his cousin was the parish sheriff. By the time Prohibition ended, Nappy was quite wealthy.

This scandalized Madeleine's family even more. Her father was a judge from a long line of judges and due to his daughter's unfortunate choice, he was related to a criminal.

In addition to Nappy's suspected criminal activities, there were rumors about other women. Madeleine was confronted with the awful truth when she walked in on him and one of the maids in a guest bedroom. She ran to her room and threw herself on the bed and sobbed. Nappy never apologized.

Many women followed the parlor maid, though Madeleine suspected that she had not been the first. The long list included, in addition to their servants, the coat check girl at the club, the hostess, waitresses, and eventually, her friends. He drank heavily and began to abuse her, physically and verbally. She had no one to turn to and was too ashamed to admit her mistake, so she once again put on a brave face. She had a big house and servants, so what if her husband was a faithless, womanizing, abusive drunk.

She confronted him once about his behavior when he stumbled into their bedroom smelling of cheap perfume and gin. He sneered at her before slapping her across the face. The blow staggered her and she fell backwards. Nappy turned and walked out. Madeleine put her hand to her face. The slap stung. Tears filled her eyes. She had never been hit before in her life, other than a tap from the nuns.

Madeleine moved into her own bedroom. She tried to ban him from her bed but when he was drunk, he sometimes forced himself upon her. This was the greatest humiliation. Violated by the man who she once loved. She would lay in bed, staring at the ceiling, trying to will her heart and mind to block it out.

After one of these encounters, Madeleine discovered she was pregnant. They had been married for six years and she didn't think she would ever have a baby. Despite the fact that she despised her husband, she was thrilled to discover she was pregnant. She wanted a baby.

A small hope rose up in her. Maybe a baby would change everything. Maybe Nappy would fall in love with her again, and the baby would make them the family Madeleine had dreamed of. At the same time, she worried that it might make him worse. What if he abused her baby?

Building up her courage, Madeleine finally told Nappy that she was pregnant. She was relieved when he appeared to be thrilled at the prospect of having a child. "Well, it's about damn time," he said. "I was beginning to think you were too high born to be able to have a baby." He said this with great sarcasm. He often threw her supposed fine family history in her face. "I can't wait to have a son. Someone just like me that I can raise up in the business. An heir." Madeleine shuddered at the thought of a child who would turn out to be just like Nappy.

When he arrived at the hospital to see his son, Nappy was disgusted to discover his wife had given birth to a girl instead of the expected heir. "I assumed even you would be able to give me a son. Your mother had five boys and all you can manage is a girl." He stormed out of the hospital, throwing the flowers he brought in the trash.

Madeleine named her baby girl Evangeline Marie Boudreaux. When she came home with the baby, Nappy accused her of having an affair with one of those dandy boys that she had dated before she met him. She was stunned. *The way he runs around on me?* she thought. *He will not turn me into something like him.* Despite her husband's reaction to the birth of a baby girl, Madeleine was thrilled. *I will love you forever, my sweet baby girl.*

Two years later, Madeleine gave birth to a second baby. This time it was a son. The long-awaited heir, who Nappy joyfully named Stefan Artur Boudreaux, Jr. In a cosmic joke, the boy looked like a more effeminate version of his father. Stefan was terrified of the loud, masculine Nappy, choosing to spend time with his sister and mother. He was a delicate child who preferred to play quietly indoors. He did not like sports and cried when his father forced him to play baseball. Nappy's pleasure at having a son turned to anger and embarrassment.

Evangeline, "Evie," adored her little brother. They shared a passion for fashion, much to the disgust of their father. Evie asked her mother for a sewing machine at an early age, which was a surprise. People of their class had their clothes made, they didn't make them. Evie loved to design clothes and made outfits for her dolls and costumes for herself and her brother for their games.

Another interest that they shared was dancing. Evie and Stefan loved to dance together, often competing at dance contests at their father's nightclub. A visiting band leader once asked them if they were professional dancers. They easily won every dance contest they entered, sometimes traveling to other clubs outside their town to compete.

Sadly, Stefan was bullied and teased by the other boys at his school. Once Evie found him hiding in the garage, sobbing, with cuts and scrapes along his arms. He gazed at her, one eye turning an ugly shade of purple.

Evie cried as she hugged her little brother. "What happened?"

Between sobs the story came out. The abuse by the other boys. The name calling that had erupted into violence because Stefan finally tried to stand up for himself. Evie had been aware that the other kids said things about Stefan but she hadn't realized how bad it was.

Stroking his hair and wiping away his tears, Evie said, "We shall tell Mother and Father. They will talk to those boys' parents and stop this nonsense."

This brought a new round of sobs as Stefan begged Evie not to tell their parents. "Maybe not Father," Evie relented, "but we must talk to Mother. She'll know what to do."

Unfortunately, when their father came home that evening, he had already heard the news in town. "My son, the pansy! The nancy boy! That's what everyone is saying. I don't know how I can hold my head up in this town anymore."

Evie tried to defend her brother. "Those boys beat Stefan for no reason!" Her father's face darkened with rage, and Evie's mother shook her head, indicating that she should say no more. Stefan sat quietly, head down, staring at his plate.

Knowing his father loathed him made it worse. When Stefan was sixteen, he disappeared. They couldn't find him for days, but Madeleine and Evie held out hope he'd return. Finally, the sheriff knocked on the door to tell them Stefan's body had washed up on the shore of the river. He'd jumped off the bridge. They were devastated.

Stefan's suicide son broke Madeleine's heart. *It's my fault*, she thought. *I never stood up to Nappy. I should have done more.* Nappy appeared relieved to be rid of his son. At the funeral, he stood stiffly while his wife and daughter wept. He shook hands with the mourners, who offered their condolences but did not speak. He never visited his son's grave.

When Evie graduated from high school, she decided she wanted to go to college and study fashion design. She loved fashion but needed to get away from her father. Actually, she wanted to leave Landry and never see him again.

Of course, Nappy thought it was a waste of money to send a girl to college. Madeleine didn't want Evie to go to college either though she never shared those feelings with her daughter. She couldn't bear the thought of Evie leaving. Now that Stefan was gone, Evie was the only thing that brought joy to her life. Her first born. Her love. Her heart. Madeleine dreamed of Evie marrying and living in town, providing her with grandchildren she could love and dote on.

Instead of college, Nappy gave Evie a job as a hat-check girl at his nightclub. Why did she need a degree since she'd probably just get married and have babies? He hoped he could bring a future son-in-law into the business since he no longer had a son and heir.

Shortly after Evie started working at her father's club, she became engaged to the leader of the club's house band, Ben Miller, who was eight years her senior. Evie was not really "in love" with Ben, but he was a good man and offered her an opportunity to escape her home. Evie hoped for a quick engagement and a quicker escape. Nappy was pleased with the engagement since he too thought the band leader was a decent fellow who could join the business. He had no idea Evie planned to move far from Landry as soon as they married.

Madeleine did not want Evie to marry at such a young age. She wanted Evie to wait.

The sudden death of Stefan followed quickly by America entering the war put their plans on hold. Ben wasn't sure if he would be drafted or if he would enlist. Evie began to get exasperated with his wishy-washy behavior, worried that she was going to have to take charge.

Ben went to visit his parents in Chicago to discuss his future. Evie was annoyed not to be part of the conversation about what she was already thinking of as "their" future. She took a night off from work to hang out with her friends at Nappy's. With the world looking so grim, she needed a night to enjoy herself.

Nappy's club had become the popular weekend spot for the young officers from the local army post. They came to unwind and dance with the pretty town girls. With the war on, they wanted the distraction of music and fun. There was a young Second Lieutenant stationed at that camp who decided to go into town with his friends that evening. His name was John Smith, though he had been christened Einar Johann Gustaffson, Jr.

John's father was a complete failure at everything except for staying drunk and keeping his wife pregnant. By the time John turned ten, he had five younger siblings, including a baby. They lived in a one-room shack with a stove, sink and bed on the ground floor and a loft for all the children up above. There was an outhouse in the back yard. In the winter the wind blew through the flimsy boards while the children huddled together under threadbare blankets trying to keep warm. While Einar Senior was gone on his latest job hunt (binge), John's mother fell ill. The food had run out and they had no wood for the stove. He had no help and no resources.

One morning, John climbed down from the loft to find that his mother and the baby had died during the night. John knew they'd all die if he didn't do something. He told his siblings to stay in the loft and stay covered. He grabbed his threadbare coat and walked several miles to town to get help.

All kinds of agencies arrived to take care of the living and the dead. The Sheriff stormed around the small room muttering about what kind of man left a sick woman and a passel of kids alone with no food and no wood in the middle of winter. He declared he'd "happily shoot that sumofabitch between the eyes" if he showed back up. John never heard what became of his father. The children were all bundled off to an orphanage. John and his younger brother Harold were quickly adopted out to a farm family who basically wanted free labor. While not a loving home at least they had food and a warm place to sleep. John never knew what happened to his three little sisters. He hoped they were all adopted together.

He and his brother worked long and exhausting hours on the farm.

When John was thirteen, his brother was killed in a freak farm accident. Accidents often happened on farms but John was appalled by the callous attitude of the family, who acted as if one of the farm dogs had been run over. An annoying bother but not a big deal. They were more concerned about the inconvenience of having to go back to the orphanage to get another boy.

After the family went to bed that night, John decided it was time to strike out on his own. He packed up his few belongings, stole some food, and started walking. One day he stopped at a small farm. An old woman lived there alone since both her husband and son had died. She struggled to keep the farm going. She was nervous about giving food to tramps and hobos. However, this boy standing at her back door wasn't the typical homeless wanderer. He was a tall, handsome boy, blonde and blue-eyed, like his Norwegian ancestors. She knew in her heart she could trust him, and she happily offered a place to sleep and food in exchange for his labor. John was grateful to have a roof over his head and a hot meal.

Eventually, she let him move into her son's old room. She even gave him her son's clothes. She offered him a home. The first real home he ever had. Slowly he became like a son to her. He still had chores but she also made him go to school. While behind in his studies, he was smart and caught up quickly and graduated only a year late.

When the old woman first asked him his name, John thought this was his chance to completely re-invent himself. He'd always hated his name, since it had been his father's name as well. "My name is John Smith," he said, erasing his past completely.

Shortly after the new John Smith graduated from high school, the old woman died. She left him a little money and the farm. He sold the farm, moved into town, and got a job in a bank. He never imagined that he would be anything more than a simple farm hand. He was stunned to be living such a fantastic life. He planned to work at the bank forever, marry, and raise a big family. But far away on a small island in the Pacific Ocean, a surprise attack changed the world.

John, like so many others, quit his job and joined the army.

Evie saw him enter Nappy's that night. It was like a scene from a movie. The world stopped spinning and everything went into slow-motion for her. A spotlight appeared to shine on him as he walked to the tables near the dance floor. Everyone and everything faded into the background. It was only him. She declared him to be the handsomest man she had ever seen. When the group from the army post came over and asked if they could join the party, she and her girlfriends readily agreed. From the moment Evie and John met, they couldn't take their eyes off each other.

Evie floated home on a cloud. She climbed up into her mother's bed and said, "I'm in love. I met the man I'm going to marry and spend the rest of my life with." She flopped down on her back, staring up at the ceiling with a brilliant smile on her face.

Madeleine was rightfully confused. Evangeline was engaged. To a nice man at Nappy's club. What on earth could she be talking about? "I'm sorry, aren't you already engaged?"

"Yes," Evie admitted. She couldn't stop smiling. "I know. I'm engaged to Ben, and it will be difficult to break up with him. I don't want to hurt him. He's a fine fellow, but I can't marry him. I'm in love with someone else! I never knew what real love felt like."

Fortunately, Evie did not have to break Ben's heart. He called from Chicago to tell her he had enlisted and would not be returning to Louisiana. Evie wished him well and never mentioned she was seeing someone else.

Evie and John saw each other every weekend for the next six months. When John found out he was being sent to California to finish training before being shipped overseas, they decided to marry immediately.

Nappy did not want to give his daughter a big wedding. He said to

Madeleine, "He's a nobody. No name, no money, no job. And he wants to marry into my family? He probably heard we're one of the richest families in town and wants to get rich without working for it!"

Madeleine wanted her daughter to have the wedding she never got to have and so cajoled him into throwing a big wedding by appealing to his ego. "Won't everyone be envious when they see the kind of wedding you can give your daughter even in wartime?" That puffed him up and he went all out. They held the reception at the nightclub.

Nappy was mistaken about John. He didn't want Nappy's money. He hadn't even known that Evie was the daughter of the owner of the club until a few months after they started dating. John just wanted Evie. The thunderbolt that hit Evie that night had struck him too.

Evie didn't want her father's money. She wanted to leave and never see him again. Evie and John spent their wedding night at the finest hotel in town. That night was everything that they both dreamed it would be. The next day, Evie packed everything she could fit into her suitcases and left with John for California.

☙❦❧

Evie was excited. This was the first time she'd left her home state and she never wanted to return. When John shipped overseas, her mother suggested she come home to wait for him. Evie said she'd come back when her father was dead.

Madeleine knew she'd lost her daughter forever. Evie made plans with no thought for Madeleine, which hurt. She had devoted her life to Evie, loving her and trying to protect her from her father, but now all Evie cared about was getting away. Madeleine feared that Evie blamed her for what happened to Stefan as much as she blamed her father. Madeline thought about herself at eighteen and ruefully admitted the apple hadn't fallen far from the tree. She hadn't considered her parent's feelings either.

Evie moved into an apartment with several other young women whose husbands were also off at war. She got a job, waiting for the war to end and for her husband to return. Each morning, she woke with a prayer for him and said another when she went to bed at night.

At that time, the military sent telegrams to inform families of the death of a loved one. Evie received two telegrams. She almost fainted each time she got one. The first was to inform her that her husband had been awarded the Silver Star for bravery. The second announced he had been wounded and received the Purple Heart. Evie didn't care about the medals, she simply wanted to stop getting telegrams.

While Evie worried about her husband, another part of her believed nothing bad would happen to him. They were meant to meet and meant to marry. Did she actually believe that God had engineered World War II so the two of them could meet and marry? That seemed a bit extreme of God to annihilate millions of people worldwide simply to bring two people together. But Evie had an interesting way of looking at the world.

Finally, the war ended and John returned to California. After an amazing reunion, he told Evie he didn't want to work at a bank or pursue another career. He wanted to stay in the army.

He'd been afraid that she wanted to return to her small town and have him work for her father. She'd been afraid he'd want to go back to either the town he came from (awful) or her town (worse). They were both relieved to find out that neither wanted that and both were thrilled at the idea of him staying in the army. The army life suited them perfectly. They could be nomads, moving from place to place and party to party.

John and Evie didn't want children. They had endured miserable childhoods made even sadder by what happened to their siblings. Evie was totally devoted to John, and he was totally devoted to her. There was no room for anyone else.

Salaries, even for officers, were not huge. But they had everything they needed. The army provided them with a house. Evie saved money by sewing her own clothes. She also had an entire wardrobe of fashionable clothes. At the club on weekends, she was the envy of the other wives and the darling of the men.

After ten years of marriage, Evie began to feel unwell in the mornings. She had nausea and couldn't keep anything down. She went to the doctor, who examined her and began to laugh. "Goodness, madam," he exclaimed. "You're pregnant." She was horrified.

She went home and told John. He was equally horrified but after some consideration said, "We'll just have to make the best of it."

2
Virginia, 1953
Making the Best of It

MAKING THE BEST OF IT was how my mother described her feelings at discovering she was pregnant. She told everyone that, even me.

My mother shouldn't have had children. She obviously didn't want children. Children only brought sorrow. She wanted a life of loving my father and having him love her. She wanted a carefree life with her at the center of everyone's admiration. She had a wonderful, happy marriage, and that's all she wanted.

What is the secret to happy marriages? My mom told me it comes down to marrying the right person, but how does anyone know if the person they fall for is the right one? My father could have easily been a con artist looking for a woman with a lot of money. He could have scoped out the situation and discovered she was the daughter of the owner of the nightclub and made a big play for her. She got lucky. According to her, she knew from the minute she saw him he was the one. It happens. Unfortunately, not to most of us and certainly not to me. Though truth be told, when I met Frank, he did seem pretty darn perfect.

For my Mom, it was a good thing Dad was her everything because she really had no true friends. People were immediately attracted to her because she was pretty and vivacious. She was well dressed, made up perfectly, and always smiled and laughed. She was a great dancer and the life of the party. But after a while, her girlfriends realized she really didn't care about them at all. She made all the right facial expressions and said the right things, but it never went deeper. Moving every one to two years worked out perfectly for her because by the time people began to understand her, she could blow an air kiss and move on to the next group.

Like many women of her generation, my mother's clothes always had to be perfect. She never left the house unless she was completely put together. She gardened in a dress and make-up because someone might see her. But teaching fashion to her daughter was not a priority. She never took me to stores except for the obligatory back to school shopping. I was allowed to get three new dresses each year. She always bought me a winter coat two sizes too big so it would last for three years—one year it was too big, one year just right and one a little small.

The women in my mother's family had beautiful names. My mother was Evangeline, my grandmother Madeleine, and in the family tree there was an Alphonsine, Elenora, Julia-Rosa, Margarette, and other lovely names that would do a princess proud.

When choosing the name Jane, it was as if she tried to find the simplest, plainest name ever to give me. It couldn't be shortened to a cute nickname. And it was only made worse that my last name was Smith. My father might have thought John Smith was the finest name he had ever heard but I thought Jane Smith was the worst name ever.

The nickname Plain Jane stuck and was often used by cruel schoolmates.

I was born in an army hospital. My mother loved telling the story of what a horrible experience that was. I guess not just giving birth but the hospital itself. I overheard her tell someone all the nurses there were a bunch of dikes. I didn't know what that meant, though I could tell it wasn't a good thing by the way my mother said it. "Dikes," with the Evie Eye Roll. I looked up "dike" in the dictionary and found out a dike was a thick wall built to stop water from flooding low-lying land. It didn't make sense to me. Maybe they were thick, unattractive women? My mother was not fond of unattractive people.

Mother went on to say the day after she gave birth, one of those awful nurses came in and dropped a pile of diapers on each of the mothers' beds and said, "Make yourself useful. Fold these diapers."

My mother looked the nurse in the eye and said, "I am not here to do your job. I just gave birth. Fold them yourself." And she rolled over to take a nap. The other women were in awe of my mother.

I don't remember much about the first four to five years of my life. I have impressions and vague memories like dream sequences. I had one such memory of flying through the woods with light sparkling down on me through the trees as I zipped along. I shared this memory with my mother, and she told me it was probably when we lived in Germany and she took me to nursery school on the back of a bike through the forest between the housing area and the school. I was amazed by this story. I couldn't imagine my mother doing that.

The first strong memories I have are when we lived in a "civilian" neighborhood, not on an army post. It was like normal life. We lived in a house and had neighbors. Not to say we didn't have neighbors on post but this was different. I started school there. The school was a couple of blocks away and all the neighborhood kids walked there together. I made my first best friend when we lived here. Jeannie. I remember our games and dreams for the future.

We planned to be together forever and open a stuffed animal store. We both loved animals. She had a couple of cats and one of them had kittens. I remember lying next to the mother cat's bed and petting the kittens. They were so warm and sweet. They filled me with joy and happiness.

When they got bigger, I loved to hold them in my lap and let them sleep there, purring, while I stroked their soft fur. I wanted a kitten more than anything in the world. But my mother said no. We moved around too much, and it was hard enough to move a child.

My parents and Jeannie's parents were best friends. They played bridge together and had cookouts. After breakfast, I would pack a simple lunch and meet up with Jeannie. We played outside by ourselves. When we got hungry, we'd sneak into one of our secret spots—under a bush, or behind the garage, and eat our lunches. We were together until dinner time.

My parents didn't have money to spare. My mother had a strict grocery budget and there wasn't much money for extras. When the ice cream truck came through the neighborhood, it was sometimes difficult to scrape up a dime for a popsicle. It was the happiest time of my life.

We lived there for two wonderful years until my dad got promoted and we had to move. I remember our last dinner together. We were leaving the next day. Jeannie and I hadn't spoken to each other about my impending departure. I was so wrapped up in my grief at losing her. As we stepped out the door, my parents asked if I was going to say goodbye. Jeannie and I looked at each other and fell into each other's arms, sobbing. One of the reasons I was so bad at making friends was I couldn't bear the thought of losing someone I loved again.

Two things happened the summer we moved. It was the first time I spent the summer with my grandmother. Also, it was the beginning of the biggest change in my mother. As my father moved up in rank, she became even more remote and concerned about appearance and social standing. My mother often said, "Rank has its privileges but also its obligations."

3
Landry, Louisiana
1960

MY MOTHER NEVER VISITED HER mother after she married my dad. She wrote and called occasionally. I remember letters from her mother arriving in the mail. Noticing the return address, she'd glance up at my dad and say, "A letter from Ma Mere." My father nodded, not saying anything in response. I didn't know that "Ma Mere" was French for "my mother" and thought that she called her mother "Mamer" instead of Mother for some reason.

After saying goodbye to my best friend Jeannie and her family, we climbed into the car and drove off. I assumed we were heading to my father's new duty station. When we stopped for lunch, my parents told me that I'd be spending the summer with my grandmother. They tried to present this as a wonderful event to be excited about. Since no houses were available yet at the new post, it would be more fun for me to stay with her. Also, this was my opportunity to get to know my grandmother at last.

From a very early age, one of my constant companions had been a creature I called Nameless Dread, a faceless, formless blob living in the pit of my stomach. I often woke in the morning with this feeling that something terrible was going to happen. Nameless Dread has stayed with me ever since.

When I got older, Nameless was joined by voices I called the Greek Choir. In hindsight, they were all a version of my mother whose voice in my head constantly critiqued me on everything—my appearance, my manners, my social awkwardness, my shyness. The list was endless.

As my parents told me this news, Nameless Dread tied my stomach into knots. I stared at my plate, twisting my napkin into a ball in my lap. I was a painfully shy child. Talking to strangers, even sales clerks or librarians, was almost impossible for me. Speaking on the telephone to people who couldn't even see me was difficult. My parents knew this but they were leaving me with a complete stranger? For the entire summer? On top of saying goodbye to Jeannie, this was the worst thing ever.

We drove for two days. Louisiana was a different world. It was so foreign looking. Green and lush, like a tropical forest. Huge trees lined the roads, their massive limbs resting on the ground, covered with Spanish moss. Water everywhere, rivers and creeks that I learned were called bayous, wandering through what looked like a jungle. Mansions and shacks. And the heat. Stepping out of the car was like having a hot blanket thrown over you.

We finally arrived in the town where my mother grew up. She started pointing out things she remembered. "There's the road down to Nappy's." She looked at my father. "I wonder if it's still standing? It closed years ago. There's the road to my parent's old house. My childhood home… probably long gone and covered by ivy." She continued reminiscing as we drove.

After more twists and turns, we arrived at my grandmother's house. A small, brick one-story house. I was surprised since I expected something far more impressive. From the family stories, I had pictured a grand mansion with white pillars in front. The blinds were all drawn. My father thought no one was home. My mother said that it was to keep the sun and heat out during the day. We stepped out of the car and got hit by that instant smack of wet heat.

At the front door, my mother knocked and tried the knob. The door opened, and we stepped into the cool interior. Air conditioning made living in Louisiana more bearable. A woman, who I assumed was either my grandmother or the housekeeper, walked toward us.

"Just make yourselves at home," she said. I was terrified by my first impression of her. Gray hair lay flat on her head. No curl. No style. Her skin was quite wrinkled. A cigarette dangled from her lips while she spoke. This was the era when almost all women smoked. Even my mother smoked but only one or two in the evenings. Everyone thought it made them look glamorous. But this was far from glamorous. This woman wore baggy shorts and a big shirt. I was used to my mother always being well-dressed, made up, without a hair out of place. I was shocked that this woman was her mother. Worse—my grandmother.

My mother hadn't seen her mother for almost twenty years. They had only called and written to each other. My grandmother stopped, stubbing the cigarette out in an ashtray filled with cigarette butts, and reaching up to put her arms on my mother's shoulders, kissed her on both cheeks. My mother stood stiffly with her arms at her sides.

"I can see you don't waste much time on your appearance these days," my mother said, stepping back and staring at my grandmother.

My grandmother laughed. "Why bother? Not trying to impress anyone." My mother gave the Evie Eye Roll at that comment. I could tell she was upset that her mother didn't think that seeing her daughter and meeting her granddaughter for the first time was worth dressing up for.

My grandmother approached my father. She looked him up and down and said, "You're looking well." They didn't touch.

"Nice place you have here," my father said, looking around the small, dark room that stank of cigarettes.

My grandmother snorted. "Not quite the mansion you remember, huh?"

During all this, I tried to hide behind my father and be invisible. My mother took my hand, pulling me forward. "Jane, meet your grandmother." I hoped the earth would open up and swallow me. I couldn't imagine staying with this woman for the next ten minutes, let alone for the entire summer. By myself.

My grandmother bent down and looked me in the face. "So. This is Jane, my only grandchild."

My mother prompted me, "Hug your grandmother, Jane." Staring at my feet, I tried to make myself very small. I clutched Bear, my constant companion.

"She doesn't have to hug me," my grandmother said. "She doesn't even know me." This was said rather pointedly while she looked at my mother.

We were invited into the kitchen for lunch. I knew my mother didn't want to stay but since she was dropping me off for the entire summer, she felt obligated to at least have lunch. My grandmother had obviously gone to a lot of trouble to prepare a nice meal. Conversation was stilted. Everything my mother said was met with comments like, "You wouldn't know that since you haven't kept in touch." At last, the meal ended. My dad went and got my suitcase. My grandmother showed him the guest room. It was small but clean. At least I'd have a room of my own to hide in.

My mother announced that they needed to get on the road, as they had a long drive. My grandmother said nothing. My mother leaned over and hugged me. I stood there stiffly. When my dad patted me on the head and turned to leave, I grabbed him and buried my head into his stomach. I didn't say a word, knowing better but my entire being silently screamed, "Please don't go. Please don't leave me here." My father was embarrassed, and I hoped he might change his mind about leaving me. No doubt he had been looking forward to making a clean, unemotional getaway.

My mother peeled me off my father. "Don't be silly, Jane. You'll have a wonderful time with your grandmother."

We all walked to the front door, and my grandmother and I watched as my parents climbed into the car. They waved once, backed up, and headed out of town. I wanted to burst into tears but held them in. I was a master of the unshed tear.

I followed my grandmother to the kitchen and sat at the table while she cleaned up. When she was done, she suggested we move to the living room because it was more comfortable. We sat on the couch together, and she looked at me for a long while.

Finally, she spoke. "We're going to spend the next three months together. Time to set some ground rules. First, what do we call each other? I'll call you Jane, or do you have a nickname?"

I had always wanted a nickname. "No. Just Jane."

"Okay, Just Jane, what are you going to call me?" she asked. "To be honest, I have never wanted to be called Grandmother—too formal, or Grandma—too country. So, what do you think? Have you ever given me a name in your head? Thought of me in a certain way? I hope that your mother at least let you know I existed."

"Mamer." I said, looking down at Bear in my lap, squeezing him hard. If he'd been a real bear, he might have squealed in pain.

"Speak up girl! And look at me. What did you say?"

"Mamer. Doesn't that mean grandmother? That's what my mom always calls you."

She looked confused for a moment. "Oh, Ma Mére. 'My mother' in French. Well, I think I like Mamere. Yes. I like that a lot. That's what you can call me."

She looked down at Bear. I looked too, realizing he was rather pitiful. I had had him since my birth. At seven-years-old, he looked a bit worn. His stuffing had shifted into strange lumps leaving empty spots, he was missing an eye, and his fur had worn off in a few places. She reached and gently took him from me. "And what's his name?" she asked.

"Bear," I replied, worried that she'd want to throw him away like my mother often threatened

"Bear? I like that. Rather simple and to the point, though he doesn't really look much like a bear anymore, does he?" She looked him up and down before handing him back to me. "Maybe we could fix him up a bit? At least give him a new eye?" She smiled at me, and I smiled back. "Did you know that I gave you Bear?"

I looked at her in surprise. My grandmother smiled. "Yes, it's true. When you were born, I sent him to you. He was a fine-looking fellow then, but I believe he has improved with age and obviously, much love."

I hugged him tightly. Maybe my grandmother wasn't going to be so bad after all.

4

Mamere and Me

OUR SUMMER TOGETHER TURNED OUT to be the most interesting summer of my life. On the other hand, I was only seven, and since I didn't remember the first four, it didn't have much competition. Though if I compare it to all the summers since, I'd still say it was the most interesting summer of my entire life.

Mamere and I soon developed our daily routine. She got up early and had already smoked numerous cigarettes and consumed several cups of coffee by the time I got up around 8:00. I started drinking coffee that summer. I've never had coffee that good since. It was strong and black but made sweet and tasty by the addition of condensed milk and lots of sugar. We drank it out of tiny demitasse cups. I'd go to the kitchen and get a cup before joining her on the back patio. She'd nod a good morning as I sat down. She wasn't much of a talker first thing in the morning.

Our day began and ended on the back patio. Early morning, before the heat of the day came up with the sun, it was quite pleasant outside under the branches of a huge pecan tree. We listened to the birds singing as the temperature rose around us. In the evening, when the sun set, we sat out there again, contemplating our day.

That's what Mamere called it. "It's good to sit and think about your day and determine the best parts of it," she declared. "If there are bad parts, best to deal with that as well."

When we finished our morning coffee, we went inside for breakfast. Mamere always made me toast and eggs with a large glass of orange juice. At home, I usually got cold cereal. Then our day officially began. We'd split up, going to our rooms to get dressed. Mamere insisted that beds be made but that was no different from home. Then we'd meet up again in the living room.

First order of the day was deciding what we should eat for lunch and dinner. Mamere was a good cook, and I enjoyed helping her plan the meals. She even let me help with the cooking. My mother never let me help in the kitchen because I might make a mess.

At some point during the day, Mamere switched from coffee to gin. At first, I had no idea. I assumed it was water until I once accidentally took a swig, mistaking it for my glass. I choked and sputtered, trying to catch my breath. She snorted and said, "Don't drink out of my glass." Looking back, I am amazed at her ability to consume the amount of alcohol she did each day without falling into a coma by dinner.

She also smoked constantly. Sometimes she'd have a cigarette in her mouth and another smoldering in the ashtray in the kitchen and one in the bedroom, bathroom, or patio. She was the kind of smoker who lit a new cigarette from the butt of the old one, so she was almost never without one.

I feared that the house might catch fire and burn down. I went from ashtray to ashtray checking to be sure that the butts were all out and the ashes were cold, before dumping the mess in the trash. Mamere thought this was quite funny.

I can thank my grandmother for the fact that I never smoked cigarettes.

Early afternoons were devoted to a nap and Mamere's soap operas.

Mamere had a color TV, the first I had ever seen. It was her one indulgence. We'd climb into her big bed, pile the pillows, and watch her soaps. Another thing my mother never did. I'm sure she would have been appalled that I was watching soap operas with my grandmother since most of the subject matter was certainly not suitable for children—adultery, divorce, illegitimacy, lying, cheating, and stealing. The soaps were pretty tame, though, compared to the stories Mamere shared with me about my extended family.

We watched TV together propped up on pillows. Well, I watched, and Mamere napped. I asked her why she slept during her soaps. "Aren't you afraid you're going to miss something?"

She laughed. "Lord, child! It takes weeks or months for the plot to move forward. I could sleep for a year and nothing would have changed that much!"

After our soaps and naps, we had the rest of the afternoon for the weekly chores.

Mondays were laundry day.

Tuesdays we went to the grocery store. Mamere thought it was the quietest day to shop.

Wednesdays we went to the library. Mamere loved to read, and she instilled that love in me. We spent at least an hour looking over the books before we made our selections and checked out. Mamere sometimes pointed out books that she read at my age, suggesting but never pushing anything on me.

Thursdays were "beauty day". That was when Mamere went to the hairdressers to get her hair washed and set for the week. She must have been trying to annoy my mother by not having her hair styled when we showed up. I sat quietly reading magazines while she chatted with the hairdressers. They always offered to cut my hair, but Mamere said I looked perfectly fine just the way I was.

Fridays we went to the cemetery to visit the graves of my uncle and grandfather, her son and husband. I was surprised that she visited my grandfather Nappy's grave, but she said, "He doesn't have anyone else to visit him. It's my Christian duty." She'd neaten the grave sites, sometimes bringing fresh flowers to place in the stone urns, and sit quietly on a little bench by Stefan's grave.

We never stayed long at Nappy's grave. She'd put her hand on his gravestone and say, "How you doing you old S.O.B? (I didn't know what that meant but I gathered it was not a nice thing to say.) Burning in hell, I'm sure." That always made her laugh. Then she'd put her fingertips to her lips before touching the headstone again.

Saturdays were for visiting. Mamere had no one to visit and no one visited her except for her friend, Old Joe. So, instead of visiting people, we drove around town visiting places from the past. Out to the old homestead where she grew up. Past Nappy's old nightclub, now closed and falling down. Past the house where my mother grew up. It had not fallen down, it was still a grand mansion just as I had envisioned, with white pillars. I enjoyed those drives. Sometimes we drove way out into the countryside to visit old churches, graveyards, or other grand old homes.

One of my favorite places was the Academy of the Sacred Heart, a Catholic girl's school that both Mamere and my mother had attended. "It was a tradition in my family for the girls to be educated at Sacred Heart," Mamere said. "Nappy really didn't want to pay to send your mother here, but I shamed him into it." She laughed. "I told him that all the leading families sent their daughters here and wasn't he a member of the leading families? He really wasn't, but he certainly had enough money to send his daughter here."

The grounds were extensive and covered with ancient live oak trees. I loved those massive trees with their enormous limbs reaching down to the earth. When we came to one of the giants, I ran ahead to hide under the branches, playing hide-and-seek with Mamere.

I was much more animated with Mamere, asking questions constantly. She always knew the answers. "How do you know so much Mamere? You know about everything—trees, birds, history… everything!"

"I've lived a long time. You're bound to learn things if you're around for many years. When I was young, I was not a good student. I regret that. I was frivolous."

"What's that mean," I interrupted.

"I was only interested in clothes and boys and dancing. If I'd been a better student, I could have done so much more with my life. I went to college for a semester but didn't try hard, so I was kicked out. Remember that, Jane. Education is the key to a good future. Now, if I don't know the answer to something, I go to the library and find out. Most people could do that but they're too lazy or not curious enough."

I asked Mamere if I could go to the Academy since it was "family tradition." "Then I could stay with you all year."

She appeared to give that idea some thought. "I'm not sure what your parents might think about you living here permanently," she replied after a while. "And I'm not sure we could afford to send you. It's for rich people's daughters. It's even more expensive than when your mother went there. I don't believe your father and mother could afford the tuition. And sadly, I have no money."

I didn't tell her, but I was convinced my mom wouldn't mind me living with Mamere year-round or going to boarding school, but the money could be a problem. Mom liked to spend money on clothes and entertaining, not on me.

Sundays we went to church. "I know it scandalizes everyone that a divorced, twice-married woman comes to church and takes communion, but that's between God and me," she said defiantly.

Over time, she told me stories of the family. Her family mostly, though she did give me a bit of information about my dad's past. She had been alone for so long, she enjoyed having someone to talk to, especially someone who never talked back. I was a good listener. On our first day together, she looked at me carefully. "You remind me of my son, Stefan. He had that same way of sitting or being in a room that said, 'Don't look at me. Don't notice me.' As if you're trying to fade into the furniture."

I stared at her. What could I say? I was shocked that she saw that so clearly. I never wanted anyone to notice me.

After Mamere diagnosed me as being "just like Stefan", I was given a free pass. She didn't expect much from me. She was probably relieved. If I'd been wild, exuberant, or demanding and whiney, she'd have packed me up and shipped me off to wherever my parents were hiding for the summer. My personality suited her perfectly. I was always required to be polite and have good manners when we were in public and she'd introduce me to someone, but other than that I could be as quiet as I wanted.

When we sat together in the living room after breakfast, she talked. I learned all the stories of her life and my mom's and dad's lives. She filled in the very sketchy picture I had of my parent's past as well as my ancestors.

Mamere had no qualms about sharing some of the dark secrets that people usually consider unsuitable for a child. Which is why the themes of the soap operas were not very shocking in comparison.

She told me what she knew about my father's past, about his family and childhood. I had known nothing, not even that John Smith wasn't his real name.

From Mamere, I learned about how he lost his entire family. His brother Harold and his little sisters Volborg, Gurinna, and Marta. I thought about how Jane Gustaffson sounded. I wondered if he had wanted to name me for one of his sisters. Would I have been teased more if my name had been Volborg or Gurinna? Marta might not have been that bad, but Volborg Smith? It almost made me happy to be named Jane.

My absolute favorite thing to do with Mamere was to look at old family photographs. I sat quietly while she turned the pages of the albums, mentioning names and relationships. Often a photograph led to a long rambling reminiscence.

Some of the photos made her laugh, some made her angry, and some made her sad. My Uncle Stefan was a beautiful boy. Those photos made her sad.

Sometimes, I would point to a photo and ask a question or make a comment. I loved the photos of Mamere as a young girl and the photos of her parents. Her father looked every inch a judge, and her mother was so elegant in her old-fashioned clothes. There were many photos of Mamere in costumes looking rather dramatic, and she told me that she had acted in all the school plays and once dreamed about becoming a famous actress.

"I think I would have been a fabulous actress. I certainly had the attitude for it." Mamere laughed. Looking at the photos, I thought she had been beautiful enough to be a movie star.

My all-time favorite was a photo of my mother when she was about two or three years old. She wore a dress that looked like the petals of a rose and she was the center of the bloom. She had flowers in her hair and sat in a chair covered in roses. Initially, I thought it must be a picture of a fairy child. "Oh Mamere," I exclaimed. "This is the most beautiful thing I've ever seen. Who is this?"

"That's your very own Mama." Mamere smiled as she looked down at the photo. "She was such a good girl. She behaved like an angel, sitting still while the pictures were taken. She rather enjoyed being fussed over like she was a royal princess."

"She looks like a princess." I stared at the photo, wondering why people didn't have pictures like that taken anymore.

The photos of my mother always made Mamere smile, though I could tell they also made her a little sad. She'd get quiet and run her finger over the photo. "Your mother, she was quite the beauty. When she was born, it was the happiest moment of my life. I knew she'd go far." I wasn't sure if marrying my father qualified as going far but I guess it was better than staying in their small town.

The photos of my Grandfather Nappy brought out all kinds of emotions—anger, sorrow, sometimes smiles and laughter. I wondered if she still loved him a little.

When I saw photos of my grandfather Nappy for the first time, I said, without thinking, "Goodness, he looks like one of those old-time gangsters."

That comment sent Mamere into spasms of laughter. "Child, that describes him perfectly. He was a bit of a gangster though he skirted just this side of the law." She paused. "Well, maybe he veered over the line a few times."

She told me that she had thought about divorcing Nappy many times, even though it was a sin. She was very devout. It was the one thing from her past that she didn't lose or give up when she married my grandfather. Nappy refused to divorce her not because he loved her, but because he didn't want to look like a fool in front of everyone. No one was going to leave him. No one could say that his wife was not happy and satisfied.

After the war ended and life began to return to normal, she finally convinced a cousin of hers to draw up divorce papers. Her priest agreed to annul the marriage. "Nappy was angry about the annulment. I'm not sure why. He wasn't religious. He yelled, 'You've made our children bastards, including your precious Stefan.' That hurt but I wasn't backing down."

In the end, Nappy didn't even put up a fight. Mamere thought he was distracted by his new girlfriend. Mamere didn't care, she just took advantage of it. She didn't ask for anything. She just wanted to be rid of him. She got a cash settlement. He got the club, the house, and all the money that he had hidden over the years.

She put the money in the bank, which gave her a little security, and she went to work for the first time in her life. She was still a beautiful woman. I could see that from the old photos. She got a job traveling for a famous cosmetic company. The manager told her, "If people see your skin and think they can get that out of a bottle, we'll make a fortune."

In the meantime, Nappy married again. He had a young, beautiful wife, but he was getting old. One night, on his way home from the club, he was attacked in his driveway by two drifters. They had heard that at the end of each day, he brought the entire day's receipts home. They also heard that he was a feeble, old man. They were right about one thing: his age.

When he got out of his car, one of them jumped him, wrapped a cord around his neck, strangling him. The other began to beat him, trying to get the money. Nappy punched the thief in the face, breaking his jaw. The other thief yanked on the cord with all his might. Before my grandfather blacked out, he pulled out his pistol from his coat pocket. With all his remaining strength, he twisted around and shot the man behind him in the chest. He then turned back and shot the other thief, who was on the ground holding his jaw and screaming.

Nappy staggered into the house and told his horrified wife to call the police. When the police arrived, they found the two thieves crumpled on the cement floor of the carport. Miraculously, both were alive. They were thrown into the back of the police car and taken to the hospital. After they were patched up, they both made a full confession and landed in prison.

One of them told the police on the way to the hospital, "We heard he was a feeble old man."

"You heard wrong," the policeman responded.

My grandfather, of course, was not charged. However, he never fully recovered from the attack. He had a heart attack about a year later and suddenly became a feeble old man. His young wife was not happy with the thought of nursing an old man and she left, making up some excuse that she needed to go home to visit her mother. She claimed she'd be back soon. She didn't have any intention of filing for divorce. She believed that when he died, which she thought was going to be quite soon, she'd get all his money.

When Mamere heard what had happened, she quit her job and returned home. She moved back into her former home and started caring for my grandfather. She set him up in one a downstairs bedroom, and she moved into a small bedroom upstairs. Not the master bedroom. She shut that up. Of course, the entire town was completely scandalized but she didn't care.

She hired a nurse, and between the two of them, Nappy was well cared for. Every morning they got him up and dressed, settled him in his wheelchair and fed him a good breakfast. Then Mamere wheeled him outside to enjoy some fresh air. She ensured he had a healthy lunch and dinner. At the end of the day, she'd roll him back out on the patio, make them both a stiff drink, and they'd sit and talk.

"It was the best part of our lives together," she told me. I couldn't help wondering why she'd done that after everything he had done—the cheating, the abuse, the death of her son. But I didn't have the courage to ask, and I didn't know how to frame the question. In my heart, I thought that she always loved him even if he had only married her for her money.

With my grandmother's care, Nappy lived for another year. One night, he passed away quietly. She made all the funeral arrangements. It was a very well-attended affair. Nappy was still a legend in the town. The gossip about what might have been going on between him and my grandmother also drew in the crowds.

The shocker came when the young wife returned, wrapped in furs and carrying on as if the love of her life had just died. "She was a sight to see." Mamere laughed at the memory. "Walking down the aisle with a handkerchief held up to her face as if blotting tears. No one could take their eyes off her."

The crowds got the show they had hoped for. She flounced up to the front of the church to take center stage as the grieving widow, but Mamere was already in the seat of honor. Since the church was completely full, the young widow had to squeeze into a back-row seat. She was seething with anger but probably consoled herself with the thought of all the money waiting for her.

Unbeknownst to her, Mamere's cousin, the lawyer, had helped Nappy divorce his second wife on grounds of abandonment. Nappy had changed his will, leaving everything to Mamere. The second, now ex-wife, was furious to discover she wouldn't get a dime. This made Mamere hoot with laughter. "Little gold-digging whore," she said. (I didn't know what whore meant but I knew from Mamere's tone it was not a compliment.)

At first it appeared that the estate was enormous, but Mamere didn't end up wealthy. My grandfather had a habit of not paying bills. His creditors were afraid of him while he was still alive and had to settle with being happy to proclaim that they were Nappy's preferred suppliers. So, after all the bills were settled, my grandmother got less money but more than she had anticipated since she didn't know she was the beneficiary.

She was the rich widow. She sold the big house and the club, and bought herself the little brick rancher, ready to live the second half of her life happier than the first.

5

Life is Good... Maybe

$\mathcal{A}$T THE AGE OF SEVEN, I considered myself an expert on sadness. After all, I had just said goodbye to my one and only very best friend. But I really I learned about sorrow and tragedy over the summer as my grandmother told me the story of her life.

After Nappy died and Mamere inherited his money, I thought life had turned around for her. She certainly thought that was true at the time. I hadn't picked up on some obvious clues. The old car she drove. The rundown condition of the house.

One night, I woke up to use the bathroom. I walked through the dark house, not wanting to turn on a light and wake my grandmother. When I got to the kitchen, the light from the carport illuminated a shadow on the back patio. Terrified, I almost screamed, thinking it was a burglar. But something about the outline of the figure looked familiar. I snuck closer and peered out the window. Mamere sat, staring into the darkness. Tears streamed down her face. I'd never seen an adult cry like that. I cried like that, at night, alone in my bed, sometimes. But my mother never cried, ever. I thought it was the memory of all that she had lost: her son, her daughter, her husband. But it was worse.

My grandmother had been a happy child. "I was loved. Spoiled. Adored. My parents cherished me. They were strict but loving. I was the baby of the family and my older brothers doted on me. That love proved my undoing because I thought I could do no wrong. That I'd be forgiven for all transgressions."

She took a long drag on her cigarette, slowly exhaling the smoke, remembering a time long ago. "I foolishly thought Father and Mother would indulge me when I wanted to marry Nappy." When they didn't give in and didn't pay for her wedding, she convinced herself it was only temporary. When they didn't come around or accept her calls when she came by the house, the seriousness of the situation finally dawned on her. She had made a huge mistake.

She pretended not to care. She decided to act as if it was fine with her and that she had cut them off. When she began to grasp that the man "she could not live without" was every bad thing her father said he was and was abusive as well, she was too proud to return to her family and say, "I was wrong. Please take me back." She had made her bed and she was going to lie in it no matter how uncomfortable it became.

My grandmother had been thrilled when she found out she was going to have a baby. She stared up at the ceiling, watching the cigarette smoke curl around as she told me the story.

"I hoped it might bring Nappy back to me. That a baby would bring us closer. We hardly spoke by then. He had the club. I had a big house and a new car." She laughed bitterly. "Also, I hoped my parents would want to see their grandchild."

None of that happened. Nappy had never been particularly interested in children but became excited at the prospect of having a son who could be raised to be just like him and take over the business. "He had a shock when he got to the hospital and found out he had a daughter, not a son." I felt sorry for my mother in that moment.

My grandmother's parents sent a card congratulating her, but no visits were made or encouraged. Still, she had someone to dress and fuss over and love. Something to take her mind off her husband's bad behavior. My mother became her little ally against her husband. Mamere often went to sleep in my mother's bed when she feared Nappy would come home drunk and in a bad mood. As bad as he was, he was only verbally abusive in front of the children, not physically.

In the eyes of others, my grandmother had a glamorous life. Her husband was a celebrity. They always had the newest cars. She had fancy clothes and furs and jewelry. They had a big house with servants. They gave great parties. But it was all a sham. She had no real friends. The few she had soon ended up being seduced by Nappy, so she stopped trying. Her husband didn't love her. Even though it was her inheritance from her grandmother that funded his business, he never forgave her for being disowned and not giving him access to that top tier of society.

Nappy's death freed Mamere of all obligations. She looked forward to a simple life. Her life had taken a wrong turn, but she accepted that she had made a mistake and she vowed to put the past behind her. Mamere was able to mend fences with her family and see her father and ask for his forgiveness before he passed away. Her hope that my mother would visit her was in vain. My mom blamed her mother for Stefan's death and never visited.

Then she made the second biggest mistake of her life.

As we were looking through old photos one night, I came upon one of her with friends at a nightclub. They were dressed up and looked quite glamorous. There was a man in the photo I hadn't seen in any other pictures. He had dark wavy hair, a thin mustache and piercing dark eyes. Even my seven-year-old eyes saw that he was incredibly handsome. He looked like an old Hollywood movie star.

I pointed to him. "Who is that?"

She was quiet for a long time before finally saying, "Louis. My second husband."

Wow. I had no idea that she had been married a second time. My mother certainly never said a word about it, though maybe she didn't know.

Mamere didn't tell me anymore that night and I didn't want to press her for information. The story came out bit by bit over the summer.

Her "second life" as she called it, included a group of friends that she went out to dinner and parties with. One night at a club, one of her friends brought along a friend named Louis Fontenot. She said he was so good-looking that people turned and stared when he walked by. Men and women.

She'd had her fill of good-looking men. Nappy had been attractive, and how had that worked out for her? Not too well. Plus, Louis was about twenty years younger than her. What young man could seriously be interested in a woman her age?

She was friendly but remained cool and detached. He flirted with her shamelessly and declared his undying love. Finally, he told her that if she wouldn't marry him, he would have to kill himself because life wouldn't be worth living. She thought that was a bit dramatic but his passion for her poured out of him and over her like a hot wave.

He was attentive, showering her with flowers, love notes, and all the sorts of things that Nappy never did even when they were courting. For almost thirty years she'd been married to a man who gave her no love, except maybe in that last year when he was an invalid. Nappy had never sworn undying love and passion for her. Now in her fifties, this thirty-year-old Adonis claimed he wanted her above all the other women in the world.

So, she married him.

The stage was set for a happily ever after. He brought her breakfast in bed. Her interests were his interests. Little by little, he moved into every aspect of her life. Strangely, he didn't have a regular job. He said he was an investor. He spent a lot of time driving around looking for "opportunities." He claimed to have family money but most of it was tied up in his various schemes, so he had no ready cash.

She believed him. She never questioned his lack of money or refused his "small" requests for financial help. He was always apologetic and said he was keeping a list of the money she loaned him and planned to pay it all back.

Mamere bought him a new car because his was unreliable. His funds were being transferred from one bank to another or unavailable because of his "investments." He continually explained that the big pay-off was coming "next week or in a month."

He always made it seem like he didn't want her money. As he slowly wormed his way into her life, he talked her into putting his name on all the bank accounts "just in case" something bad happened, he could take care of her.

One morning, after the happiest year of her life, she woke to a silent house. There were no sounds of breakfast being made. She got up, put her robe on, and wandered through the house looking for her young husband. Glancing out the window, Mamere noticed his car was gone. Maybe he had gone to the store, but wouldn't he have said something to her before leaving? The house felt strangely empty. When she opened the closet door, all his clothes were gone. His drawers were empty. She looked in the small bedroom, and the luggage was gone.

There was no note. No explanation. She didn't know what to do. An hour later the phone rang, and she jumped up, sure that he was calling and she'd been worried for nothing. Maybe he had to make an emergency business trip. But it was the bank calling to confirm the completed transfer of money that her husband had requested. She jumped in her car and drove to the bank quickly, but it was too late. All the money was gone except what she had left in her checking account.

She called the police. She called the friend who had brought him to the dinner. He said that he didn't even really know Louis. He had met him at a party at the home of a mutual friend and assumed because he was there, he must be a decent fellow. Since he was a fun, personable guy, he started inviting him along to other outings and introducing him to friends. No one knew anything about him. The police said that they could find no records of a Louis Fontenot. But they did find information about a con man that matched his description.

The second biggest mistake of Mamere's life ended with her having no money and no husband. She was ashamed for being such a fool. She knew everyone was laughing at the silly old woman who thought that a young, good-looking man was in love with her.

Louis had only been after her money, but he ended up taking something far more valuable away from her. He took her last hope of love and of happiness. Mamere became a recluse. No one visited and she didn't go out.

My grandmother never stayed down for long.

Slowly, she began to go out again, not to clubs and dinners but to the library, grocery store, and church. She told me she enjoyed scandalizing the congregation. "Good Christians, my ass!" she laughed. "Bunch of hypocrites who like to sit in judgement on their fellow parishioners. Guess they forgot that 'judge not lest you be judged' thing from the Bible." Even though she had the marriage to Louis annulled, in most people's minds she was still a divorcee, even worse, a two-time divorcee.

"There's no fool like an old fool," she told me one night while we were sitting in the dark watching the lightning bugs light up the yard. "Don't forget that. You'll be old one day. I tell you all these things so you won't make the same mistakes I did."

She lifted her glass to her lips and took a long sip of gin. "Make your own mistakes, Jane. Always be original. I may be a mess, but I was always original." She laughed so hard when she said that, the gin came out her nose, which caused more hysteria and laughter.

When Mamere went out, she always fixed herself up. She put on her make-up. Fixed her hair and wore something nice. Not fancy, but clean and presentable. Made me wonder why she deliberately looked so bad when Mom and Dad showed up to drop me off. Probably to get under my mom's skin.

"Do you think I should wear my mink stole today?" she asked, laughing. I shook my head. It was way too hot for fur and I thought it might be a little much for the local grocery store. Right before we left, she glanced one last time in the mirror to make sure she had on a "face". She hid behind her regal face that had once been beautiful. Her look said, "Don't mess with me."

The first Queen of Rising Above.

6

Old Joe

OLD JOE WAS A BLACK man who could have been anywhere from sixty to a hundred years old. He was small and wiry with an ageless face. His skin was smooth except for the wrinkles around his eyes and mouth because he smiled and laughed so much. He was bald with wild gray bushy eyebrows above bulky black eyeglasses. The lenses were so thick it made his eyes look enormous.

Old Joe had worked for Nappy all his life, doing gardening, odd jobs, and pretty much anything that was asked of him. His father had worked for Nappy's father, and his grandfather had worked for Nappy's grandfather and so on into the past. There was a lot of history between Old Joe and Nappy.

He was the only one who appeared to have anything nice to say about Nappy. "I worked for him my whole life, and he treated me real good. I could always get a meal at the club, like a fine steak, not just scraps or leftovers. If I walked into the kitchen to cool off after a job, your granddaddy always said, 'Joe, sit down. It's hot out. Have something cold to drink. Don't work so hard.' He looked out for me."

"I guess that's how you got so lazy." Mamere shook her head and rolled her eyes. "You probably expect me to be cooking your meals, too."

"I ain't waitin' for that to happen," Joe replied, smiling at Mamere. "You not as nice as Nappy."

That sent Mamere into a fit. "Nice? Nappy… nice? As if!"

Joe would start laughing.

Along with Nappy's money, Mamere also had apparently inherited the services of Old Joe. He didn't seem to work for anyone else though there probably weren't too many people lining up to hire someone that old. He worked for Mamere more out of friendship and loyalty. I never saw any money change hands nor was there ever any discussion of payment.

Early every Saturday morning, I'd wake to the "swish, swish, swish" of the old push mower as he cut the yard. Mamere did not have a power mower. It was a comforting sound, that clickity-clack of the blades spinning around rather than raucous engine noise.

Old Joe finished the front yard before moving to the back where my bedroom was. When I'd hear him, I immediately jumped up, got dressed, and ran out to the patio. Mamere was already out there drinking her coffee.

When Old Joe was about halfway done with the back, Mamere called out, "Old Joe. Stop and take a break. Have a coffee or something cold to drink. You're too old to be working this hard. See, I can be nice."

Old Joe stopped what he was doing. As if considering her request, he'd take his battered straw hat off, pull a big handkerchief out of his pocket, and wipe the sweat from the top of his bald head and the back of his neck.

"Mizz Maddy, you sure one to talk about being old. You look at yourself in the mirror lately?" he replied, grinning. He'd put his hat back on and shove his handkerchief back in his pocket. "If you'd get me one of them power mowers that run by themselves instead of makin' me push this old thing around, I wouldn't be so wore out."

That made Mamere laugh too. "Not as old as you, Old Joe. You notice, my name isn't Old Maddy. Plus, where do you think I'm going to get money for a fancy new lawn mower?"

Smiling, he slowly ambled over to the patio and eased himself down into one of the chairs. He always tipped his hat to me and said, "Mornin' Mizz Jane. How're you this fine day?"

"I'm fine, Old Joe. How are you?"

"Gettin' older and slower. Used to be able to do both front and back before Mizz Maddy even got out of bed."

Mamere huffed, "Now that's a flat-out lie. I've always been an early riser." She pretended to be angry with him.

Old Joe would let out a big sigh and put his hat on the table. "I believe I'll take that cold drink now. You got any sweet tea?"

"Jane, run and get this old man some sweet tea with lots of ice."

I dutifully ran to the kitchen to fill up the largest glass I could with ice and tea before carefully carrying it to the back porch. I'd hand Old Joe his tea, before running back in to get myself a demitasse of coffee with lots of condensed milk and sugar.

Old Joe took one look at my cup and said to Mamere, "Why you lettin' that little girl drink that terrible coffee you make? You'll stunt her growth or worse. And when you goin' to buy some new comfortable chairs for out here? I'm tired of sittin' in these hard metal chairs. You make my life difficult with these chairs and that old push mower."

"Shows what you know, Joe. These are wrought-iron chairs. From It-lee. Very fine. Only the best people have them. I brought them with me from Nappy's house."

Joe took a big swig from his glass and wiped his brow again. "Just goes to show how foolish white folk are. Some salesman tells you that something awful is really fine and all the fine folk have it and y'all jump on board."

Mamere laughed and laughed.

Old Joe and Mamere carried on bickering and picking at each other and joking until he finished his tea. Then he slowly got up to finish the lawn.

One Saturday morning when Joe was taking his break, a large, gray tabby cat sauntered out of the bushes and plopped down in front of Mamere. He didn't meow. He just stared at her.

"All right, your majesty," she said, getting to her feet. "A little patience and I will soon have your breakfast ready."

She went inside. I was so excited. I didn't know Mamere had a cat.

"Is that Mamere's kitty, Joe?" I got out of my chair to pet him.

"Don't go near that cat, Baby Girl." Old Joe put an arm out to stop me from getting too close.

Mamere walked out with a dish filled with cat food. I wondered where she kept it. I'd never seen cat food in the kitchen.

"Joe is right. Don't touch the King." She walked toward him and set the dish down. He took a sniff and looked up at her with a disapproving stare. "I'm sorry it's not your usual lobster or filet mignon. It will have to do."

The cat, apparently named the King, gave her one last baleful look before lowering his head to the bowl and eating.

"Is he your kitty?" I asked.

"No. He is not my kitty." Mamere looked amused. "Cats are not like dogs. They don't belong to anyone. In their minds, they rule the world and people are just servants responding to their whims. King comes and goes as he pleases. He probably has a circuit of houses where he shows up expecting to be fed. He only comes here every seven to ten days."

"I always wanted a kitty," I said, looking sadly at the King.

"Cats are overrated as pets," Mamere snorted.

"'Specially that one," Old Joe chimed in. "It ain't no pet. He'd probably shred yore arm to the shoulder if you tried to mess with him."

"Stop saying bad stuff about 'my kitty.'" Mamere rolled her eyes at him.

"Yore kitty, indeed. He's 'bout as useless as that Louis boy. You sure ain't learned nothin' about men. You always pickin' the wrong ones."

They acted like an old married couple. At that time, I didn't understand the racial issues in the south. In the army life that I was used to, the dividing line was rank, not race.

One day, I asked Mamere why she hadn't married Old Joe instead of Louis since they got along so well and seemed like such good friends.

Mamere choked on her drink, which started a coughing fit. Old Joe laughed at both of us. "Lord child, you don't know much 'bout the world, do you?" he said when he managed to stop laughing.

Mamere finally got her breath back and wiped the tears from her eyes. "Oh my God, Joe, she's right! We should get married! It would be perfect. I married a man who was not my social equal, then I married a man who was young enough to be my son who stole all my money. The only scandal left for me is to marry a black man! What would they make of that at St. Christopher's? I'd love to see their faces when I walked in with my negro husband."

"That might be a momentary pleasure since no doubt I'd be run outta town on a rail or worse! Not to mention, it's against the law," Joe said.

Against the law? What was he talking about? "What do you mean? What's against the law? Can't you get married as many times as you want?"

"Yes, you can," Mamere answered. "However, in the state of Louisiana, you can't marry a black man. Or I should clarify and say, a white woman can't marry a black man."

I was speechless. I'd never heard of such a thing.

"Not to mention you might still be married to that Louis boy," Old Joe said.

"I am not! I had that marriage annulled on the grounds of abandonment, theft, cheating, lies, and all kinds of other legal mumbo-jumbo. Louis Fontenot wasn't even his real name so that hardly qualifies as a real marriage. I've only been married once, and I could even say I was widowed, not divorced."

"Well, Mizz Maddy, you can say anythin' you want, but it don't make it so," Old Joe added, jutting out his chin.

"Since I'm not legally married, what do you say? Should we take Jane's advice and get hitched?" Mamere smiled wickedly.

"I'm not sure your name would fit on a marriage license anymore. Madeleine Louise Hebert Boudreaux Fontenot. I don't see how you could squeeze in Landry at the end of that mess."

Mamere shot back, "That is not my name. I am not a Fontenot. Why do you keep making that my last name? My name is Madeleine Hebert Boudreaux. That's all." Mamere seemed a bit testy.

I interrupted their argument. "Is that your last name, Joe? Landry? Like the town here? Did your family settle the town? Mamere told me that the town was named after the Landry family."

"Oh Lord child. No! That's the name of the family who had the largest plantation 'round here so they got to name the town. They owned my people who took that name when they got their freedom. Don't have no idea 'bout my family's real last name. Could be Watusi for all I know. All the African names was taken away from black folk. Just one more thing they took." Old Joe spoke with a bitterness I'd never heard before.

I didn't know what to say. I had learned about slavery that summer on our drives around the Parish. Mamere explained how the rich plantation owners had owned slaves. "Even our family, Jane. It was a sad time in history." Still, I hadn't thought about Joe's family being slaves.

Mamere tried to change the subject to lighten the mood. "You didn't answer my question about getting hitched, Joe."

"No. I believe it's best we don't. I'd like to live out my life in peace 'n quiet. We already got people gossipin' about us. That should be enough for you!"

Mamere sniffed at the suggestion that she enjoyed having people talk about her. "They talk about me no matter what I do."

"Have you ever been married?" I asked Joe.

"No chile. Ain't never had that pleasure. Though listenin' to your grandma, I ain't sure I missed much." Joe finished his tea and stood up. "Best finish the yard. This heat makes everythin' grow too fast." He walked to the back of the yard and started trimming overgrown bushes.

Mamere and I sipped our coffee and watched him work as the day got hotter. After Old Joe left, we went inside. The air conditioning felt like jumping into a cool pool of water. I was still thinking about what I learned that day. Not legal to marry a black person? It was the strangest thing I'd ever heard.

Sadly, the summer ended much too quickly. I was surprised that I dreaded leaving Mamere more than I had dreaded meeting her. We had become like a real family over the summer, Old Joe, Mamere, and me.

When the last day came, they drove me to the airport. Mamere was spitting nails because she was so angry that my parents weren't driving to pick me up and instead had sent money for a plane ticket.

"She's only seven years old! A baby! I have to drop her off at a huge airport and let her fly alone across the country? Outrageous! I should have said, 'if you can't come get her than I am keeping her here!' That's what I should've told Miss Evangeline Fancy Pants."

"Now don't get all upset," Joe said as he drove to the airport. "It'll be fine. Jane's a smart girl. One of them stewardess gals will watch her all the way until she gets home and Mizz Evie picks her up."

"I don't care. Is it that hard for her to come and see her momma twice a year? Hell! Last time they didn't even stay the day. Couldn't wait to get away."

"Is this what it's about? Mizz Evie not coming to see you? Not about Baby Girl at all." Joe turned into the departure lane leading to the airport.

"No, that's not it." Mamere pouted.

"Sounds like it might be a little bit of it," Joe said.

"Is it too much to ask? For my daughter to come see me?"

"Well, you got the grandbaby. I believe you got the better end of the deal." Joe pulled up to the front of the airport. "I'll wait here. You take her to the airplane."

I stepped out of the car and stood waiting while Old Joe got my suitcase from the trunk. Joe bent down to look me in the eye. "Mizz Jane, it was mighty fine havin' you here this summer. You made a real difference. Mizz Maddie was actually nice with you here."

"Stop your nonsense. Jane, say goodbye. We have to get inside."

I looked up at Joe. My eyes filled with tears. I was afraid I was going to cry. Another farewell to a friend. I hugged him tight and mumbled goodbye.

"Now, don't go cryin' on me, Baby Girl. You'll start me cryin' and your grandma will surely be cryin' all the way home. It's just too much for an old man. I'm not used to all these women carryin' on."

I took a deep breath and stifled a sob. "Thank you for everything, Old Joe. I had a wonderful summer."

"I'm just sorry you had to spend yore summer with two old people, but you made us happy. Hope you'll come again." Old Joe patted my shoulder and smiled.

Mamere took me by the hand, and we went up to a counter where I handed over my suitcase and was given a boarding pass. We walked down long corridors and finally came to another counter. A young woman came over, took my hand, and pinned a piece of paper on my blouse with my name and destination on it.

"Don't worry. We'll take good care of her. She'll be watched over until we turn her over to her parents."

"You better take good care of her," Mamere said. "This is my grandchild."

Mamere bent down. "Jane, I am so glad we finally got to meet each other. I hope the summer wasn't too awful."

"I had a wonderful time, Mamere. Thank you. I hope to visit again."

The stewardess took my hand and we walked on to the plane. I tried hard not to cry. Since the plane was half-empty, they let me sit in first class. They treated me like a princess. I might have even enjoyed the flight if I hadn't been leaving Mamere.

7

Mamere Again

THE NEXT SUMMER, WE DIDN'T have to move for a change. Most parents were considering summer camp for their kids or a family vacation. My mother wasn't interested in spending money on summer camp for me. Since my first summer with Mamere went so well, she thought she'd give that another try.

My parents didn't consult me about what I might like to do, but I was thrilled when I overheard Mom speaking to Mamere on the phone making the arrangements for me to fly down for the summer. My parents were happy to find a place to stash me for three months, and I was happy to go see Mamere and Old Joe again.

Mamere was waiting for me as soon as I stepped off the plane. We walked outside to find Old Joe behind the wheel of Mamere's car. Mamere was furious at my parents for putting me on a plane again and Joe was shaking his head. Obviously, nothing had changed. They were the same. Same routine. Same cigarettes and coffee and gin. Same Old Joe. Same bickering. Same laughs. It was great.

One day, when we were looking through the old family photos, I said, "You know, Mamere, all these photos are a bit strange."

Mamere was confused. "In what way?

"Well, kind of stiff. Everyone is always dressed up and sitting up straight, staring at the photographer. And there are marks on them with the photographer's name. Didn't people ever have photos taken of just regular stuff?"

"What do you mean, regular stuff?" Mamere asked.

"People sitting around the backyard in shorts or cooking dinner? You know, regular stuff. All these photos are of special occasions like weddings and fancy parties and baby and school photos." I wasn't quite sure how to explain what I meant.

Mamere thought. "When I was young, only professional photographers had cameras. People got formal photographs for special occasions. It was expensive. And in the early days, you couldn't even move when you were having your picture taken or it'd be all blurry. So, people dressed up and posed for their pictures. Not like nowadays when everyone has those little Brownie Instamatic thingamajiggies and they stick them in your face and snap a picture when your hair is messed up or you just stuck a forkful of food in your mouth. Just awful." Mamere sniffed haughtily at the thought of having her photo taken without being posed.

Old Joe listened to us and laughed. "White folk are so particular 'bout their appearance."

Mamere narrowed her eyes at him.

The next Saturday when I came outside, Old Joe was already sitting and drinking his cold tea. "Been waitin' for you, Mizz Jane. Got you a present."

I was so excited. A present for me! It wasn't even my birthday or Christmas.

"You shouldn't be buying her presents, Joe," Mamere said. "You'll just spoil her."

"You the only one who gets to spoil her?" Joe asked.

Mamere didn't answer and Old Joe handed me a package. I opened it slowly. Inside was a Brownie Instamatic camera. I squealed with delight.

"Now you can take pictures of yore grandma that show her true side. Be sure to get one of her in her shorts while she's eatin'." Old Joe laughed at his own joke.

Mamere swung her arm out to punch him, but he leaned away from her. "You too slow Mizz Maddy. Old and slow."

That summer, I took lots of photos of Mamere and Old Joe. And photos of her house and all the places we visited. I especially loved to take photos of the grounds of Sacred Heart Academy. I planned to show them to Mom when I got home with the hope she might decide to send me there.

"Why do you want pictures of the library and the grocery store?" Mamere snorted, pretending to be angry.

"I want to remember it all."

"Planning to stop coming down to visit?" Mamere asked.

"No! Never." The thought of not visiting panicked me. "I just want the pictures to look at between visits."

When I finished shooting a roll, Mamere took it to the drug store to get the film developed. It took forever before the packet of pictures came back. Mamere always insisted on looking at them first so she could "tear up" the ones that made her look bad.

"Truth hurts," Old Joe said, hiding a smile.

My favorite photos were some I had taken one morning on the back patio. There was one of Mamere and Old Joe caught in a moment of complete joy. Old Joe's head was flung back and his mouth was wide open as he laughed uproariously. Mamere was bent forward with her hand to her mouth as if to stop the laughter from erupting, but her smile was wide behind her hand. When I showed that one to Old Joe and Mamere, they both grinned.

There was another one of Old Joe looking straight at the camera with that wonderful smile of his lighting up his face. My other favorite was one that Joe took of me and Mamere sitting together on the bench. I had my head nestled on her shoulder and she was looking down at me sweetly.

When I got home, I showed the photos to my mom and dad. Mom appeared quite interested in the ones I had taken of the town, the graveyard, the old homesite, and Sacred Heart. "I had forgotten how beautiful the grounds of the Academy were," she said, lingering over the photos.

"Yes. It is," I replied. "It would be wonderful to go to school there like you and Mamere did." I dropped my hint but Mom didn't bite. She was distracted by one of the photos with Old Joe in it. She held the photo closely and squinted to get a better look.

"Goodness," she finally said. "That looks like Old Joe."

"It is. He and Mamere are best friends."

My mother looked a bit shocked by that statement. "I can't believe he's still alive. He worked for my father, and I thought he was ancient then."

"He just looks really old," I said. "He claims he's the same age as Mamere and that he's always looked that way."

When I was ten, visiting for the fourth time, Mamere had changed a bit. She wasn't quite as feisty. She moved slower, and Old Joe seemed to be concerned about her but if he said anything she snapped his head off.

"Well, least-wise you could quit those cigarettes," he said.

"Sure. Good plan. I'll give up everything I enjoy."

"Don't you enjoy me 'n Jane?" he asked.

She just rolled her eyes at that.

At the end of that summer visit, Mother and Father finally drove down to pick me up instead of having me fly home alone. They even stayed for the entire weekend. I saw Mamere and Mom sitting out on the patio talking late into the night. I was so happy for Mamere that Mother had come to visit at last.

That year, there were more phone calls between Mom and Mamere.

Mom always let me say hello but I couldn't talk long. It was too expensive. Letters from Mamere also came more frequently that year. The letters always included a separate note for me which my mother handed to me as she read her letter. When she finished reading, she'd sigh. She glanced over at my father and he'd ask, "Everything all right?" In response, she gave a little shake to her head. Something was up, but I didn't ask.

At Christmas, I got a big box from Mamere. I usually only got a book, so I was curious to discover what she had sent. I could hardly wait until Christmas morning to open it. I ran downstairs and grabbed the box while I waited for Mom to make coffee. (I never drank coffee at home. It wasn't as good as Mamere's and my mother would have been horrified to find out I was already drinking coffee at my age.) After my parents sat in the living room with their coffee, I carefully and slowly opened the box to find Mamere's photographs. I shifted through them.

"What on earth are those?" Mom asked.

"Family photos of Mamere when she was young. Photos of you and your father. Your brother. People that Mamere knew. Her father and mother. Her grandparents. When I visit, we look through them while she tells me stories about her life."

"What an odd thing to send." Father looked into the box.

"Yes. How odd," Mother said, but in a way that made me believe she really didn't think it was odd at all.

"She knows I love these pictures, but what will we do next summer? We won't be able to look at them together," I mused, sorting through the box.

In February, Mother got a phone call. When she hung up, she came to my room. "Jane, I'm sorry. I have some bad news. There's been an accident, and your grandmother was killed."

Part of me was stunned but another part knew that something had been terribly wrong ever since I got the box of photos. "What kind of accident? What happened?"

"Your grandmother's been sick. She started feeling bad last summer. The doctor diagnosed her with lung cancer. I guess all that smoking finally caught up with her. She didn't want any treatment. She just wanted to live out her life but the doctor talked her into doing something which he said wouldn't make her feel bad. She said he lied. It made her feel so horrible, she couldn't live like that. Apparently last night, she was out driving in her car, ran off the road, and hit a tree. The police said it looked like an accident. It was dark and rainy."

"No! That's not right." I cried. "She never drove at night. Why would she be out at night? Where would she be going?"

"I don't know." My mom shook her head. "I don't think we'll ever know.

I asked her who had called to tell her. "The sheriff. I guess they found my number in her wallet."

"I wonder if Old Joe knows," I sobbed. "He's going to be broken-hearted."

"I'm sure the news will get around town quickly. That's the way things are in a small town."

The next day, my mother surprised me by saying we were flying down for Mamere's funeral. At the airport, we rented a car and drove to Landry. I wanted to stay at Mamere's house, but Mom said we'd be more comfortable in a hotel. I didn't understand that at all. I wanted to be back in my room at Mamere's.

The next day, we arrived at the church early. As we walked to the front, I spied Old Joe sitting in the very last row. I wanted to go over and hug him and tell him to come sit up front with me, but I couldn't stop because Mom had a firm grip on my hand as we walked to the front. The pews quickly filled.

Two women behind us whispered loudly as if they meant for everyone to hear them. "I can't believe Father Michael is allowing a suicide to be buried in the church."

"I know," the other woman retorted. "It is a mortal sin, after all."

My mother slowly turned around and fixed them with one of her famous withering looks. We didn't hear another word out of them during the rest of the service.

Father Michael gave a wonderful eulogy. "Madeleine was a good woman with a good heart," he started. He smiled out into the congregation. "She wasn't always the easiest person to deal with." That brought out some laughs and snickers. "Sadly, she had a lot of demons, but she always meant well."

At the graveside, Old Joe stood in the shadows. It wasn't right. He was her very best friend and he was hanging back. I ran up and hugged him and started to cry.

"No, Mizz Jane. Don't start, cause if you do, I'll start and I'll cry a river 'n wash us all away." He turned me back around to face the grave.

"Ashes to ashes…" the priest intoned as people tossed flowers into the grave.

When the service ended, Joe knelt down and said, "Goodbye, Baby Girl. I don't believe I'll ever get to see you again. It was a rare privilege to spend those summers with you. It was an honor to be your grandma's friend."

I hugged him long and hard. I never wanted to let go because he was my last connection to Mamere. As long as I held on to him, I could believe she was still alive.

He hugged me back. "It's time to go, Mizz Jane. I hope you remember me 'n your grandma. We sure loved you. You made her so happy these last few years."

Mom walked up and nodded at Old Joe. "Old Joe. Good to see you. I was surprised to hear that you were still around."

Old Joe grinned. "Been here forever, for sure. Good to see you, Mizz Evie. Take care of this sweet child."

Mom took my hand and nodded at Joe again. When we got to the car,

Mom told me to wait. She walked back to Joe, and they talked for a few minutes. On the drive into town, I wanted to ask Mom about what those women in the church had said about Mamere committing suicide. But I knew from experience that if Mom didn't bring a subject up, the subject was closed.

Mom explained that we had to stop by Mamere's lawyer's office to look over some paperwork. I sat out in the reception area while she talked to Mr. Dupont, the lawyer. As they walked out of the office, he said, "I'm sorry to be the one to tell you that your mother had nothing left. But if you let the bank take the house, at least you won't owe anything."

"I didn't know things were this bad," Mom replied as she shook his hand. "Thank you for your time."

It began to dawn on me that I wasn't going to move back and live in Mamere's house when I grew up. The house apparently did not belong to us anymore.

When we got to the car, Mom handed me Mamere's old leather black purse. "The police gave this to Mr. Dupont. Is anything in there?"

Mamere never went anywhere without her black purse. I found her wallet at the bottom and pulled it out. "There's her driver's license, library card, a card with a picture of the Virgin Mary on it, some other cards, and five dollars and some change. Also her keys, a handkerchief, and a tube of lipstick. That's all."

"Apparently that's your inheritance, Jane. Five dollars and a picture of the Virgin Mary." She rolled her eyes.

Mom glanced over at me hugging Mamere's purse. "Let's go by the house before they lock the doors on us." I was shocked that she had suggested it. "You might see something you'd like to keep to remember your grandmother. I asked Old Joe to meet us there. I think your grandmother would like to have left him something as well."

"Yes. Please. I'd like that." I was excited to see Old Joe again.

We pulled up in front of Mamere's little brick ranch house. It already looked sad and empty, as if it knew that Mamere wasn't coming back.

We walked around back to the patio. I sat in one of the wrought-iron chairs and looked at the backyard, remembering all the times we had spent there. "We should give these chairs to Old Joe," I told Mom.

She was confused. "Why on earth would he want them? They aren't even comfortable," she said.

I know, I thought and smiled.

Old Joe's truck pulled up, and a few minutes later, he came around the house to the patio.

"Jane seems to think you'd like this patio furniture, Joe?" Mom asked.

"Oh, she did, did she?" Joe replied, smiling at me. "I believe I just might. Sittin' on those chairs will remind me of all the times Mizz Maddie an' I sat here together."

Mom offered Joe the old push lawn mower and any tools out of the shed that he might like. Joe looked at me. "Shame she never got one of them fancy mowers for me. But I guess I'm used to this ole thing."

"I know Mother wanted to give you more for all that you did for her but there isn't anything left," Mom explained. "Is there anything you'd like from inside the house?"

"Thank you. But no. I'll leave that for you two." Joe took the lawn mower and tools and loaded them into the back of his truck along with the Italian wrought-iron chairs. He winked at me as he carried them away. After he had his truck loaded, he came back one last time and shook hands with us. "Mizz Maddie was one of a kind for sho'. The priest got that right. I'll miss her terribly." He looked like he was about to cry. He shook his head, smiled, and walked away.

Mom and I went into the house. She looked around in disgust. She just saw a bunch of old junk. I saw a million memories.

She handed me a box and told me to pack anything I wanted. In the kitchen, I carefully packed up the demitasse cups we drank our coffee from each morning. In the living room, I took her favorite ashtray to use for coins or jewelry. In my bedroom, I folded up the quilt from my bed. In a closet, I found a little glass cat figurine that reminded me of Mamere's kitty, the King. I wondered what would happen to him now that Mamere was gone.

I was surprised when I walked in her bedroom. Framed on the shelf over her bed were the photos I had taken of her, Old Joe, and me. It made me happy that she liked those photos enough to put them up in her bedroom.

I carefully added the framed photos to my pile. "I've packed what I'd like to keep," I said.

"Not much here." My mother looked around sadly. "You should have seen the house I grew up in. So grand. So many beautiful things."

My heart was breaking. I had lost Mamere and Old Joe. I had planned to finally get them to marry that next summer. But now it was too late. They'd never get married like they should have. Worse, I'd never see or talk to either of them again.

8
David

I OFTEN FANTASIZED HOW MY life would have been different if Mamere hadn't died. Knowing she was there supporting me, believing in me, and loving me would have made a huge difference. In her mind, I was perfect. My "negatives" were fine with her. She liked that I was quiet. "Too many people go through life making way too much noise. That's the way your grandfather Nappy was. 'Look at me! Look at me!'. He had to be the center of attention. I was that way too. Two people simply can't get along if they both want to be the center of attention."

If she had lived, I'd have moved in with her after I graduated from high school. My mother would happily have gone along with that plan. I often wonder if that had been her secret plan originally. But as it happened, my life took a drastic turn in my junior year of high school.

At the end of fifth grade, I was bereft, facing my first summer without Mamere. We moved again that year, which took up some of the summer. My parents decided I was old enough to stay home alone. I almost looked forward to school starting.

Sixth grade wasn't that bad. I actually made some friends. But when I started seventh grade, all the girls I knew seemed to have morphed into monsters over the summer. A group of girls in my English class who thought of themselves as the queen bees and rulers of the social scene singled me out to be their victim. We were reading *Lord of the Flies* and they started calling me Piggy. They cornered me in the hallways and gym class and even on the school bus, whispering in my ear what they planned to do to me. One time, they scared me so badly that I wet myself, which sent them into peals of laughter. They couldn't wait to spread that story around school. They called me Piggy Pee-pants and for the first time ever, I was sorry not to be called Jane. The other girls shunned me, afraid to be associated with a loser. They didn't want to be singled out either. I shut down completely and stopped trying to make friends.

I had no one to turn to. My parents would have just thought I was being silly, and my mother would have probably told me to "rise above it." I held onto Bear and cried in my bed at night, wishing Mamere was there to help.

I was so relieved when we left at the end of the year. That summer was spent moving and setting up a new house once again. My eighth and ninth grade years passed more easily as I continued to perfect the art of blending into the background. Then we moved again.

High school can be a terrible time for any teenager. It can be worse for military brats. In one move, a kid could slip from the top tier: the popular kid to the bottom of the social heap. However, moving did provide some kids with a chance to reinvent themselves. That is one of the advantages of moving often, the chance to change yourself, to be a completely different person at the next place.

I had so little chance of being cool, I never tried to reinvent myself. My best hope was to find a couple of people like me and coast just enough below the radar of the cool kids to escape bullying. Kids with no chance of being in the top tier simply tried to avoid being at the very bottom.

It is the hope and dream of every military kid to at least get to spend the final two years of high school in the same place. Luckily, I spent my last three years of high school in the same location. This was my dad's last post since he would be retiring. After thirty years of living all around the country, Dad picked North Carolina for his last duty station. Looking toward retirement, he and mom decided it would be a nice place to live, not too hot and not too cold.

My sophomore year passed in my usual quiet, shy, don't bring attention to myself mode, though I did find another girl with similar social issues, and we became friends of a sort. The year passed smoothly enough.

At the start of junior year, we added a couple of other girls to our group. We had sleepovers and complained about the popular people and how shallow they were. Our conversations centered on how lame it was to play sports, joking about kids who thought their deeds in high school could lead to fame and fortune. It's odd how people can bond over putting others down. In some ways, I was now no better than the girls who had teased and tormented me.

Though I spent time with this group, I didn't feel close to any of them. I had not had a soulmate kind of friend since Jeannie, all those years ago. Someone I could really connect with, share all my silly hopes and dreams with. Still, it beat having no one to spend the weekend with.

In the second semester of my junior year, my mother and I were out running errands and while looking for a parking spot, she noticed a bunch of kids walking down the sidewalk. They were obviously happy, confident, and having a good time.

After watching them go by, she turned and asked me, "Do you know those kids? They look nice."

I replied in a flat voice, "I know who they are, though I'm sure they don't know me. They're part of the popular crowd."

Mother was genuinely surprised. "Aren't you part of the popular crowd? I always was at school."

For the first time in my life, I spoke my true feelings to my mother.

"Me? Part of the popular crowd? Look at me. How could I be part of the popular crowd? Look at my hair, my clothes! If they noticed me, they'd just laugh at my appearance."

My mother turned and stared at me. Maybe for the first time in her life, she really looked at me. "Let's go," she finally said. "Our errands can wait."

The next thing I knew, we were at the hair salon where she got her hair done every week. She walked me in and said, "My daughter needs a new look. Give her whatever hairstyle all the girls are wearing these days."

An hour later, we walked out. I couldn't stop looking at myself in the mirror. I was transformed. My limp, lank hair was now shiny and silky and framed my face. Next, we went shopping. My mother said to the salesperson, "What are girls wearing these days? I want to get my daughter the latest styles."

We walked out with several new outfits. When we got home, my mother took me up to her room and sat me at her vanity. "Everyone has at least one good feature. The trick is to figure out what that is and play it up. You have very nice eyes, but they need to be brought out. You don't want to do too much or you'll look obvious. The trick is to make it all look natural." She played around with various jars and tubes and when I looked in the mirror, I saw a pretty girl for the first time in my life.

The next day, I noticed a difference when I walked down the hall at school. Girls were looking and checking out my clothes and hair. Even a couple of boys smiled at me. However, at lunch, sitting with my friends, I got nothing except negative comments.

"What's up with you?"

"What'd you do with your hair?"

Why are you wearing those clothes?"

And the worst comment of all: "You look like one of them!"

I tried to brush it off by saying it had all been my mother's idea and I was going along to make her happy. I almost had them convinced before

I made a fatal error. "You know what? I like the way my hair looks. I like having new clothes. This weekend, we could play around with make-up and try new looks on each other. Doesn't that sound fun...?"

It didn't go well. Apparently, what I had done was an act of betrayal. I had committed the ultimate sin of not staying plain and dowdy and trying to escape notice. I looked better but now I had no friends on the top or bottom tier.

A few days later, a boy stopped me in the hall. "Are you new here?"

I laughed. "No," I said. "In fact, we have a class together. History of Western Civilization? Mr. Gregson?"

"Oh yeah! You always sit way in the back and never say anything."

I was tongue-tied talking to this cute boy who was no doubt part of the popular crowd or on its edges. Waves of kids going to class flowed around us.

"You should move up. Sit next to me. I bet you're smart and you could help me. I don't like history."

"Sure," I said quietly, looking up and smiling at him.

Who could have guessed that a shopping trip with my mom for a new haircut, some clothes, and a little makeup would change my world? With my newfound confidence, I switched seats, learned to talk and laugh, and soon life became more comfortable.

That last year and a half of high school was the best time of my life. The best after Jeannie and my summers with Mamere. For the first time in a long time, I had a friend. A confidant. Someone who loved me as much as I loved them. David. And as young love goes... sex eventually follows.

"Save yourself for marriage," was my mother's constant cry. She regaled me with stories about meeting my dad. She told the tale as if it was one of the greatest love stories of all time. "I was a virgin when I got married," she told me. Along with, "When you meet the love of your life, you don't want to present him with used goods." And the best one of all: "Why buy the cow when the milk is free?" The message was clear—hold out!

I heard these stories so frequently that my eyes automatically rolled back in my head (behind my mother's back of course) the minute she started up with the "virginity tales," which always included the sacrifices that were made and how my mother saved herself for marriage. Of course, she and dad had only known each other for six months before they got married. Pretty easy to hold out at that point.

Nevertheless, the message seeped in. I was determined to save myself for the one love of my life. My physical relationship with David started slowly. We both had very little experience. In our first six months, we hardly made it past hand holding and kissing, though we were at the dangerous French kissing stage.

I thought David understood that I was waiting for marriage. But the more time we spent together, the more we experimented. From kissing, we went to petting (outside clothes), heavy petting (inside clothes) and finally to being naked together. It all was so innocent.

Then David started to push. He had all kinds of reasons why we should have sex.

We loved each other.

This was the ultimate expression of love.

He wanted us to become one, totally merging our bodies and souls.

Oh, how I wanted to hold out. I told him we should wait until we were married. Sex would be more meaningful once we were married but it became harder to resist.

One day, we were naked in bed, and David pushed himself up against my leg, groaning. He fell off with a gasp and a shudder and I was horrified to feel something warm and wet all over my leg and stomach. I jumped up and ran to the bathroom to wash off. I panicked, thinking I was pregnant. I knew I was the kind of person who could get pregnant just being naked with someone.

I told him that was it. No more close calls, no more naked petting and… no more anything!

David had other plans. One night, he picked me up for a movie date. When he passed by the theater, I pointed out his mistake. He looked over and smiled at me. "I've planned a surprise."

On the outskirts of town, he pulled up in front of an old motel. The kids at high school had nicknamed it the "Sex Shack". The concrete parking lot was crumbling and pitted with potholes. The paint was faded and the "Vacancy" sign had several letters burnt out so that it flashed "V*CAN*Y. I started to protest. He reached over, kissed me on the cheek, squeezed my hand, and said, "Don't worry, it's not as bad as it looks."

When we got to the door of room 14, he told me to close my eyes. He guided me inside and told me to wait for a moment. "Okay, you can open your eyes now."

Candles flickered on every surface. A soft blanket covered the bed. He had brought his record player from home and put on "our song," *Can't Take my Eyes off of You* by the Four Seasons.

He wrapped me in his arms, and we swayed to the music. He slowly started kissing me. I closed my eyes. We sat awkwardly on the bed, and he started undressing me. We were clumsy at first but it didn't take us long to figure it all out.

Surprisingly, once the deed was done, I wasn't upset. I believed that this was another confirmation of our love and the fact that we were going to spend the rest of our lives together.

The rest of our senior year was great. I was part of a crowd. David's crowd. They might not have been at the very top of high school society since that was reserved for football players and cheerleaders, but it wasn't skating the bottom where I had been. I wasn't close to anyone else in the group, but I had David, which was all I cared about. I didn't anticipate what was around the next corner. I assumed David and I would get married, though the exact time for that event was a little murky.

We graduated, with David near the top of his class and me somewhere in the middle. David's family, particularly his father, had great plans for him. As the only child, he had to carry on his family name and join the family law firm. David applied to many colleges, including the one in our town. We talked about it, and I thought he planned to attend the local college so we could stay together.

I hadn't applied to any colleges. My parents never planned for me to go to college. Neither one of them had gone to college, and they didn't see the value. My mother seemed to have forgotten her own wish to go to college. They suggested I go to the local community college where I could take courses in practical subjects like typing, shorthand, bookkeeping, something I could earn a living with while waiting to get married and then support a husband while he pursued higher education. Neither considered that a woman needed a career.

As long as David was close by at the local university, I was happy to go to community college. I had no ambitions. Or if I had, they'd been swallowed up by the dream of marrying David and having his children. Being a stay-at-home mom sounded great to me. As soon as he graduated, we'd get married unless we could convince our parents to let us get married sooner.

Looking back, I definitely assumed too much. That had been my plan, but it probably had never been David's. Or even if it had been, his father overruled him.

At his high school graduation party, he pulled me aside and told me that he would attend Wake Forest, not the local college. Up to that point, he hadn't shared with me that he had even applied to Wake, which was many miles and hours away.

I was stunned. Speechless. He kept talking, telling me it had always been his father's dream that he attend Wake for undergrad and law school. That's where his father had gone, and he wanted David to follow in his footsteps before joining his father's law firm.

"You'll be so far away," I managed to mumble. "It'll be like six or seven years before you finish law school." My voice shook as my eyes filled with tears.

"Don't worry, love," David replied, kissing my tears away. "It will pass in no time. You're my world. We'll write and phone, and I'll come home at least once a month. You can visit for football games and concerts and other fun things."

My face hurt from trying to smile back. I knew it probably didn't look like I was smiling. More likely I had a horrible grimace on my face.

Without knocking, his mother popped her head into the room and ignoring my tears and obvious distress, smiled brightly. "There you are, David. Come out and join the party. Everyone is waiting for you in the living room. Time to cut your cake and open your cards." She didn't include me in the invitation.

We walked out and I kept the smile plastered on my face. As David opened his cards and joked and laughed with everyone, his father watched me with a smug expression. In the last few months, he appeared less welcoming when I came over. I mentioned it to David, hoping for reassurance—instead, he made me feel worse. "Don't worry. He likes you. He's just concerned you might get pregnant, and we'll have to get married."

"You didn't tell him we're having sex?" I blurted out in horror.

"No, but I'm sure he suspects that we might be. He has my whole life planned out and getting married at eighteen is not part of his plan."

David laughed it off. I didn't think it was funny and it made me wary of his father. I felt as if we were in some kind of epic battle for David's soul and future. His father apparently thought I wanted to destroy any chance David might have for a bright future by having untold numbers of children and forcing him to marry me and work as the school janitor to pay for our one-bedroom apartment in the slums.

His mother hovered around David while he opened his cards, getting check after check from relatives and family friends to help pay for college expenses. At the end, his father walked over and handed him one last card.

"Hopefully this will be a big help as well," he said with a huge grin.

David opened the card, expecting another check. He let out a whoop and held up a set of car keys. Jangling the keys, he jumped up and everyone followed him outside to see his new car. He sat behind the wheel of the car, running his hands over the seats and dash and honking the horn. He jumped out and hugged his parents.

"You only get to keep it if you maintain good grades. You need to be at the top of your class to get into law school." His father smiled and looked at me triumphantly.

As everyone went in to continue the party, I stopped David and told him I had to go. Lying, I said my parents were waiting for me. He started to talk me into staying but a couple of his friends waved at him, shouting something about taking the car out for a spin later. I hoped to hear him say, "the first person in this car with me will be Jane 'cause she is the most important person in my life."

That didn't happen. He looked at them and back at me and gave me a quick hug and a kiss. "Come over tomorrow and we'll talk and go for a drive."

"Sure," I said and turned and walked away.

At home, my parents sat on the couch, reading. My mother looked up. "We weren't expecting you so early. Weren't you at David's graduation party?"

"Yes. Too much excitement. Too many people. I have a bad headache." I headed up the stairs, not wanting to talk.

"We're very proud of you," Dad said. "Let's go out for dinner tomorrow night to celebrate your graduation. Bring David. Later this week, you can go to the community college and look at classes for the fall. You should probably start looking for a part-time job, too."

"Sure Dad. That sounds great." I went up to my room and flopped down on my bed, trying not to burst out crying. David was going to one of the best universities in the state with his brand-new car, and I was going to have to get a job to pay for my own community college classes.

The next day, I was determined not to call David first or go over to his house. Let him call me. Let his dad see how much he cares for me. By lunchtime, I hadn't heard from him. I wandered into the kitchen. My mother was making a sandwich for my father.

"I didn't know you were still here," she said, cutting the sandwich in perfect triangles before placing a parsley sprig on the side of the plate.

Seriously? A parsley sprig on a china plate? Couldn't Dad eat a sandwich on a paper plate like the rest of the world?

"I assumed you'd be spending the day at David's."

"David has a lot of family over. I thought he might want to hang out with them. Maybe we can get together later."

I sat down and started eating chips out of the bag.

"Please serve yourself on a plate. Don't pick food out of bags with your fingers."

"Sorry." I took a plate out of the cabinet and served myself chips and made a sandwich. "I found out last night that David is going to Wake Forest instead of the local college," I said with my back to my mom. I hoped my voice didn't quaver and betray how upset I was.

My mother looked at me when I turned around. "He must have known that for a while. I wonder why he didn't tell you before?"

"I guess he didn't want to upset me, so he was putting it off. He wanted to go to school here but it turns out his dad had other plans. The local university isn't good enough, according to his dad. He wants David to follow in his footsteps, which means same university, same law school, same law firm."

"I'm sorry to hear that for your sake though I'm not surprised. His father is quite full of his own importance."

"His parents gave him a car for graduation. Hopefully, he can come home for visits often."

My mother cocked her head to the side. "A car. Oh yes. Has to show off."

David never called that day. My parents and I went out to dinner that evening without him. They gave me a card with some pre-printed sentiments on how wonderful it was to graduate from high school. They didn't ask where David was.

That summer slipped away much too quickly with David's departure looming. Each day that passed was one day closer to having to say goodbye. On his last day, I tried not to cry. I went to his house and watched him and his parents load all his things into their cars. His parents were driving up with him to Wake.

David couldn't hide his excitement about leaving. He almost forgot to say goodbye. As he climbed into his car, I called his name and he looked up, smiling sheepishly. He ran over and gave me a quick hug and a kiss.

"Call me," I whispered in his ear. He smiled and nodded before returning to his car. I stood alone, staring after him until he was long out of sight.

The next couple of years ground slowly along. I became lonelier and more miserable, while David became happier and more involved at school.

We talked twice a week. He called on Mondays and I called on Fridays. Fridays became difficult because there were too many things going on—sporting events, frat parties, regular parties…. So, I called on Thursday and then sat through the weekend imaging the fun he was having until I heard from him on Monday. He always downplayed the weekend. "Same old boring things. I'm always glad to get back to class on Monday." They weren't so boring that he skipped them and came home.

First semester of school, he came home once a month. I had a standing invitation for Saturday dinner at his parent's house, where I endured his phony bubbly mother and his smug-ass father. These were not the kind of people I had hoped to have for my future in-laws. I was hoping for a big happy family, but I rationalized they'd be friendlier once David finished school.

Occasionally, David and I managed to get away and go to a movie or hang out with his old friends, but his parents always had plans to keep him busy and away from me. Strangely, he didn't appear to be interested in being alone with me or having sex. He said school was too stressful.

He came home for Thanksgiving and Christmas breaks, and we managed to slip off a few times and make love, but something was missing.

I took the bus to visit him twice. The ride was long and boring. I stayed in the girl's dorm with a girlfriend of one of his buddies. I enjoyed going to events on campus. Made me sad that I wasn't at school and part of the college scene. There weren't many activities at community college.

Like the bus rides, my life back home without David was also long and boring. My community college classes were dull though practical. I took typing, bookkeeping, shorthand, and office-related courses. I remembered when I was much younger, I had thought about being an archeologist. Mamere read me a book about archeologists in Egypt and I thought that digging up ancient ruins and mummies would be an amazing job.

David laughed at me when I told him that. "You in Egypt? It's hot and dusty there and there are spiders and other big bugs. You wouldn't last a week before you caught a plane home!"

He was right. I really had no idea what being an archeologist entailed. Still, I was angry at him for laughing at me.

I got a job as a sales clerk. My mother, who never worked a day in her life, other than as a part-time hat-check girl at her father's club and as a receptionist during the war, was simply astounded that I didn't find this to be the most fascinating and exciting way to spend my life. I worked four days a week and took classes three days a week. My paycheck covered my college fees. My father occasionally said how proud he was of me, pulling my weight. Getting out in the world. I didn't respond that I was just biding my time until David graduated and we could get married.

That first summer when David came home, things were like the old days. We still had the obligatory Saturday dinner, though occasionally we went to the movies or a restaurant or for a drive in the car. We made love every chance we got and talked about our future after we were married, when he was a rich successful lawyer and I was a stay-at-home mom with at least five kids, maybe more. We both regretted not having siblings and wanted to fill our home with lots of children.

David invited me over for the last supper before he left for his second year. His parents barely acknowledged me. Icy waves emanated from both his father and mother. David's father was worried and was once again willing to do battle with me.

We survived another year. There were fewer weekend visits. I had become busier with school and work, so I had less time to travel. Phone calls were reduced to once a week, and usually I was the one calling. I still sent two letters a week and little packages, but I only got one letter back twice a month. More scribbled notes than actual letters.

Before the end of his second year, David called to tell me that his dad had arranged an internship for him with a law firm in another town for the summer. He said he was lucky to have this opportunity. It didn't pay anything, David explained, but these were the kinds of things that looked good on a resume. I asked him why he needed a resume since he was going to work for his dad. That made him angry, and he told me in a huff that he needed these kinds of things to get into law school. The call ended on an awkward note.

That was the beginning of the end, though it had really been ending since that graduation party two years earlier.

Things limped along while he was involved in his internship. In our phone conversations, he kept mentioning a new friend who also interned at the firm. They had so much in common. Both went to Wake Forest. Both were pre-law. Both had fathers who were lawyers. He told me, "It's sooooo nice to have someone who I can really share things with."

Unlike me, who didn't understand what it was like to go to school full-time and spend your summer at a fancy, big-city law firm. I could have told him all about working in a shop and all the crazy, rude, hateful customers who complained about everything while I was supposed to simply smile and agree with whatever they said. It was obvious David wasn't interested in what was going on in my life.

I finally asked if this new friend had a name. "Yeah," he replied. "Melissa."

"So, this is a girlfriend as opposed to a boyfriend?" I asked, trying to sound innocent.

"Yeah. But she's just a friend. Like I said, it's nice to have someone out here my own age to talk to."

You could talk to me.

I finished my courses and got a new job that fall at a big financial firm. I was just a clerk, though I knew with my amazing skills learned at the best community college in the world, I'd be moving up the corporate ladder in no time. Maybe David would be impressed then.

When I called to tell him about my new "position," he said, "That's great. Love to hear more but I'm late for a lecture. Talk later."

Letters and phone calls dribbled down to nothing until finally a letter arrived in which David pointed out that we were drifting apart. He wrote that we were heading in different directions and were at different places in our lives. He thought it best for both of us to move on. Part of me was shocked but another part knew that this had been coming for a while. I called right away, but he didn't want to talk about it.

"Jane, I'm sorry. I've said everything I have to say in the letter. We aren't in high school anymore. People change. I don't want to hurt you. You'll always have a place in my heart. You were my first love."

"I thought I was your forever love?" I sobbed.

"Don't make this harder. I have to hang up now. I will always love you but it's time to let go and say goodbye."

I couldn't believe he broke up with me. I was sure I could convince him that he was wrong and we belonged together. It was fate. Just like when my father walked into that nightclub and met my mother. We were fated to be together forever and always. I had given myself to him. We had merged into one soul and one being.

I wrote letters to him almost every day. I was afraid to call again and thought I could be more rational in a letter, explaining how much I loved him and how much I knew he still really loved me.

One day, the phone rang. It was David. I almost died from happiness. He finally understood we were meant to be.

"David… I knew you'd call…"

"I'm calling to tell you to stop. You can't keep bombarding me with letters and little gifts. Melissa told me I needed to be more direct, that I was being too nice. I thought you understood when I told you we're finished." His voice was cold. "Why can't you face the facts?"

His voice continued, but after he said her name, my face began to burn. A roaring noise in my ears drowned out his words. He had discussed me with Melissa? How dare they speak together about me? She was a nobody. "A friend," he had claimed. Another lie. She stole him away when he was lonely and vulnerable.

The roar lessened. "Jane, are you there? Are you listening?"

I managed to squeak out a yes and when he said, "What?" I said in a small voice, "I am sorry. I won't bother you again."

As I carefully set the phone down in the cradle, the click proclaimed the end of our relationship.

9
A.D.: After David

*M*Y PARENTS NEVER ASKED ME what happened to David. I'm sure it was obvious we had broken up. I don't know if they didn't talk about it because they thought it was too painful or maybe they just assumed we had drifted apart and moved on. David had. I hadn't.

The break-up shattered me. Every night, when I went to bed, I reexamined our relationship. Dissecting every moment. David found someone who shared his interests, his life, his future. I was just the girl he used to love. I cried myself to sleep most nights.

Every morning, I pressed hot and cold washcloths on my eyes and face to reduce the swelling. I'd apply makeup to carefully cover the redness, look in the mirror, and paste a smile on. Slightly curved up lips. No downward mouth or sad smile. The mask worked. No one at work knew that I was brokenhearted. That slight smile kept people from seeing what was really going on inside. It was nice at the end of the day to let it slip.

Six months after the final David phone call, I was having dinner with my parents. They were more animated than usual and told me they had an announcement. I was immediately worried. They rarely had anything to tell me other than they were going out for dinner or away for the weekend.

"What's up? Nothing's wrong, I hope."

Dad looked at Mom with a grin before turning back to me. "Your mother and I have decided to sell this big house. Now that I'm retired and you're starting your own life, we don't need all this space. We've been looking at condominiums, and they're all so nice. They have clubhouses, swimming pools, and activities for the residents. These places are for seniors, so you couldn't live there with us. Not that you'd want to," he added. "It's the perfect time for you to move on. Leave the nest. Get an apartment with friends. Enjoy being young."

I slumped. It wasn't that I enjoyed living with my parents as much as I dreaded moving. How was I going to find an affordable apartment? Who would I live with since these mythical friends my father spoke of did not exist? And how would I feed myself? I didn't know how to cook since my mother had never allowed me in the kitchen. She was a neat freak who had always worried I might make a mess.

"I guess I never thought about you selling the house. All those years of moving around, owning a home was your dream."

"True." Mother folded her napkin neatly in half before setting it beside her plate. "It's too much for us now. We want to downsize and save our money for fun things like traveling."

"When should I start looking for an apartment?" Hoping they'd say a year or so down the road.

"We've found the place we want and hope to sign a contract soon. But of course, we have to sell this house first. We're meeting with a realtor this week. We'll have to fix it up and make sure it's perfect."

I looked around the perfect house that was clean and devoid of personal items, such as photos of me, their only child. It was probably ready to be shown tomorrow.

"I guess I better get busy finding a place as well." I flashed my biggest and phoniest smile.

I went upstairs after dinner and fell backwards onto my bed, staring up at the ceiling. It had never occurred to me that my parents were waiting for me to get set up in life, with a job and an income.

In the lunchroom at work the next day, I asked some co-workers about getting an apartment. They all agreed I wouldn't be able to get a place on my own based on my salary and suggested looking in the paper for "roommate wanted" ads. They were also full of cautionary tales and horror stories of roommates from hell, apartments from hell, and landlords from hell.

Encouraged by their tales of woe, I bought a paper on my way home. I threw it on my bed, thinking I'd look at it later.

At dinner, my mother and father told me they had signed the contract for a condo at a senior community. My mother is actually admitting to being a senior, I thought with surprise. The glossy brochure showed three different floor plans and, as promised, a clubhouse filled with smiling gray-haired people, standing in front of a swimming pool. My father loved to swim, and my mother liked sitting around the pool under an umbrella looking fabulous.

"Which floor plan did you pick?" I asked, figuring they got the studio apartment or the one bedroom so there was no way I could sneak in and live with them.

"We considered the one bedroom," my mother began, "but it was too small, so we decided on the two bedroom. Your father can use the second bedroom for his office. He plans to do consulting work."

"It looks lovely. Guess I'd better start going through the paper and see about roommate wanted ads. There's no way I can afford a place on my own." I waited, hoping for my mother to respond, but she didn't. "I just hate the thought of living with complete strangers."

My mother ignored that comment as well.

Back in my room, I picked up the newspaper and read the ads. I circled ones that sounded remotely possible.

There weren't many. Perhaps there'd be more listings in the Friday or Saturday paper. I circled one ad that didn't sound too bad. At least I'd have my own bedroom, though I would have to share the one bathroom with the other renters. It wasn't clear how many people that might be. Out of curiosity, I looked at apartments for one person and they were either completely out of my budget or so far from work I'd end up with a two-hour commute.

During lunch the next day, I called the number listed and made an appointment to see the place that weekend.

Over the next few weeks, I looked at dozens of places. Some had way too many people living in the apartment. Some were so filthy I wanted to take a shower the minute I stepped out the door. Some of the occupants were creepy. One place didn't have a room, just an alcove at the top of the stairs.

I was plunging into a deep depression when a co-worker asked how the hunt was going.

"Worse than I ever imagined."

She laughed and said renting a room in an apartment was an awful thing to endure. "One of those terrible rites of passage that must be experienced on our way to adulthood. A lot of women probably get married just so they don't have to live with roommates anymore," she said. "I might have good news for you. My sister just moved out of her apartment and the others are looking for a fourth girl. If my sister can find someone to take her spot, it would help her out since she's stuck on the lease for six more months."

She illuminated all the positives of her sister's former place. Centrally located, and I would have my own room and only share the bath with one other person since there were two bathrooms in the apartment. Her sister claimed none of the others was certifiably insane and enjoyed living there. It sounded perfect. What could go wrong?

I made an appointment to see it that day. I didn't want this chance to slip away. I met with the three girls and was offered the room.

It wasn't bad. Everyone had regular jobs and fairly normal standards of cleanliness. It wouldn't have met my mother's strict criteria, but I was tired of living in a sterile world. A little mess and dust were fine with me. As much as I hated to admit it, my parents were right. It had been time for me to leave the nest and strike out on my own.

Unfortunately, roommates come and go. They get boyfriends, new jobs, lose jobs, move back home, move to another city, state, country. My initial three roomies were succeeded by a series of roommates that ran the gamut from normal to super weird.

Beth had appeared quite ordinary but apparently was a bubbling cauldron of rage because we didn't keep the place as clean as she wanted. Instead of having a civilized conversation about it, she secretly cleaned the apartment from top to bottom while everyone was out. No one knew who was cleaning it, we all just assumed everyone was pitching in and thought it was great. Meanwhile, she became more and more enraged that no one was thanking her for her efforts. One evening, we were watching TV together in the living room, and someone set their glass down on the end table without using a coaster. Beth reached over and swept the glass off the table, shattering it against the wall. We stared at her, dumbfounded. Our mild-mannered roommate jumped up and began to rant about what pigs we were and that she couldn't take it anymore and that all her efforts to keep the place clean were constantly thwarted by our equal efforts to trash it. She stormed off to her room, packed a suitcase, and left. We didn't miss her, but we did miss the house being cleaned.

Poor Tina never ate a meal in front of anyone. If we made a community dinner, she always had an excuse: already ate, eating later, not feeling well, allergic to what we cooked. No one cared, but we began to notice food disappearing. I'd check at night to see if I had milk and cereal for breakfast, but when I got up the cereal box was empty, and the milk container was still in the fridge with only a drop of milk left in it. Another girl mentioned to me that she kept running out of food items as well. We didn't suspect Tina, since we had all decided she had an eating disorder, but our food hadn't disappeared before she moved in. I started putting my initials on my food but that didn't help either. One night, I got up to use the bathroom and found Tina on the couch surrounded by bags and boxes and bowls of food, stuffing her face as fast as she could. She was even drinking right out of my milk carton, which grossed me out. Turns out she'd lost her job and was barely making the rent each month. She couldn't afford food and binged nightly. At least that's what she told us. She left to no one's regret.

A few months after Lorna moved in, I noticed small amounts of money disappearing out of my wallet. Usually it was only five dollars, and I couldn't be sure that I had two fives in my purse instead of just one, so I convinced myself I must have spent the other five. But it continued, and I began to suspect Lorna. I didn't have evidence, so I didn't say anything. We were all in the habit of borrowing from each other occasionally, but she was adamant that she didn't borrow money. She didn't want to be in anyone's debt. It appeared she didn't need to borrow because she always had cash. Other things began to disappear. A pair of earrings, a bracelet, and finally an expensive ring. We all searched and searched. Even Lorna joined in the search. I finally decided to lay a trap. I casually mentioned I had just cashed my work check because I was making a major purchase that weekend. When I went to bed, I left my purse and wallet in the living room with a small mouse trap on top of the wallet at the bottom of the purse. Around midnight, I heard a scream and ran out to find her trying to get the trap off her finger. She was mad, claiming I had no business putting a mouse trap in my own purse. She left the next day.

Then there was the serial sex addict who brought random men back to the apartment. That was not acceptable on many levels, first the noise but also the fear that she was inviting a potential killer into our midst. She got booted out.

In the four years I lived in that apartment, I learned a lot about people and enjoyed it for the most part. It was fun to come home after work to a house full of people. We cooked together, drank together, and shared tales of our lives. Most of the girls had boyfriends and they shared stories about how their relationships were going. I didn't have a relationship to share with the others, but it didn't stop me from offering advice.

I also had a group of work friends that I went out with sometimes. Work kept me busy. Once a month, I went to my parents' place for dinner at their new condo, unless they were out of the country on one of their trips.

My job gave me something to talk about with my dad at our monthly dinners. He had never been comfortable with me when I was a child. We had nothing in common. Now he could help me strategize and make suggestions on how I could make my *impact* on the business world. I played along because it made him feel good. My mother just wanted to know if I had "met someone" yet. She thought being single was an excuse to sow wild oats and have unbridled sex with inappropriate men. No sex, Mom, I wanted to say. No sex, no men, no relationships.

One day at the grocery store, I ran into someone I had known back in high school. She acted so happy to see me, as if we had been best friends. She rushed over, giving me a big hug and a kiss on the cheek. I responded with a smile.

"Jane! How are you?" she exclaimed in an unnatural, high-pitched voice. I didn't remember her having a voice like that. "What have you been up to?" she squealed.

"I'm doing well. I work at Tobert and Jones, the financial firm. I'm an office manager there. Worked up from clerk. How about you?" I asked.

She waved a finger in front of my face. I assumed she was trying to get me to notice the diamond ring. "I'm engaged! So excited! Getting married in the spring."

"How wonderful." What else could I say?

"I'm engaged to Peter Smithers," she gushed. "I'm sure you remember him from high school. We've been together since senior year. We wanted to finish college and get our careers going first. I'm the HR director for the city, and Peter is an accountant with the Welfox Group."

"Wow. Still with Peter. That's great!" I tried to match her enthusiasm.

"Yeah. True love." Her bright smile dimmed for a moment. "I was surprised to hear that you and David split up. I would have bet money on you two. You were so cute together and so in love."

I was stunned to realize how much it still hurt to hear his name. My stomach knotted up and I felt physically ill.

"That's probably more the norm with high school romances," I managed to respond without throwing up on her.

"Did you hear he got married?" she asked, unintentionally digging the knife in deeper. "He was dating a girl at Wake Forest, and they got married before they went to law school together."

"Melissa." I don't know why I said the name.

"Yeah. Melissa. I'm pretty sure that was her name. Did you know her?"

"No. Didn't know her. I guess someone along the line told me he was dating someone by that name."

We exchanged a few other reminiscences of old high school acquaintances. Both of us said something about, "Oh we must get together and talk and catch up," but we managed to leave without giving out phone numbers or addresses.

10

A Place of My Own

AFTER SIX YEARS OF SHARING an apartment, I finally got a place of my own. It was a bedroom/living room combo, with a small kitchenette and bathroom. Still, it was all I needed and wanted, and it was mine to keep clean or leave messy. I could eat my food without fear of others drinking out of my milk carton or fondling my cereal and chips or stealing my money or bringing serial sex killers into my living quarters. It was so wonderful at the end of the day to get home, kick my shoes off, put on a pair of pajamas and watch whatever I wanted on TV. I thought being a partial hermit was going to be my life.

Around this time, I started dating the brother of one of my former roommates. Our relationship moved along at a snail's pace, which suited me, and he seemed to be okay with it. We'd meet after work and go to dinner or a movie. We hadn't moved much beyond hand holding and kissing. He could tell I was wary of a deeper physical relationship.

Just when I thought maybe we should move our relationship into a higher gear, he took a job in another town, a huge promotion. I was excited for him. I was waiting for him to discuss "us" and what this might mean for "our" future, but I guess there wasn't an "us" in his mind. He told me that he'd be packing and moving the next week. He took me out for a goodbye dinner, kissed me on the cheek, and walked out the door and out of my life.

I wasn't brokenhearted but I was disappointed. And hurt that he didn't consider my feelings. Though, to be honest, I wasn't invested in him. Did I put off some kind of vibe that signaled no long-term relationships?

I decided to have a housewarming party at my new apartment. I planned to invite my work friends and all my old roommates from the past four years, leaving out the psychos. There was this guy Ben from work that I particularly hoped would come. He worked in another department, but we sometimes ended up in the lunchroom together. He had a great sense of humor, which I like. Learning from my mistakes with my former "boyfriend," I thought this could be my chance to kick things up a notch, to let him know I was interested.

I was excited. I hadn't hosted a party before. I hadn't even been to many parties. For my birthday, my parents would let me have one friend over for dinner and cake. The thought of having hordes of children in the house dripping food and drink on the carpets horrified my mother. And if you don't have parties, you don't get invited to parties.

I got all the food and drinks and invited people. The night of the party, I had a moment of panic, thinking no one would come. Then the doorbell rang and people started arriving. With free food and alcohol, younger people always showed up. Ben, my crush, arrived with a girl. He explained that she was a new employee at our firm and thought it would be a nice way for her to get to know people from work. I said, "Fine."

But it wasn't fine. First, she was beautiful. She had skin like porcelain and almond-shaped eyes and a lush mouth that even I wanted to kiss. And to make it all the worse, she was tiny with an amazing figure. I handed them both a drink, smiled, and said, "Must take care of hostess duties," and walked off. Alarms sounded in the back of my skull but I turned them off.

Later in the evening, we all sat on the floor. Since there weren't enough chairs for everyone, I had tossed large pillows around. It was cozy, and I was happy that the party had gone so well. People talked in small groups. Ben and Lush Lips sat across from me, talking to each other. He looked at me and smiled before turning back and kissing her. It was obvious this was not their first kiss.

My plans for kicking our relationship up a notch went off the rails. He had already kicked it into high gear with someone else. I wondered how long she had worked at the firm.

I stood and started clearing glasses and plates. People got the message and began to get up as well. As they left, everyone thanked me for a great time. Ben squeezed my hand on the way out and thanked me. "See you Monday," he said brightly as he walked out with his arm around Lush Lips.

Later, as I brushed my teeth, I stopped and really looked at my reflection. I turned my face this way and that. I had become a drudge again. My hair hung lankly down to my shoulders. No style. My pale face displayed lips that were far from lush. It was a wake-up call. I needed to start looking like I cared. Stop hiding behind plainness. I was never going to be tiny and beautiful, but I could do better.

In my weekly talks with my dad about work, I'd ask how to get the top people to notice me. How could I better advance my career? He loved these talks. He liked to think of himself as a master of the work world. He had worked his way up from private to colonel, so he had done quite well. My mother usually didn't have that much to contribute, but at the next dinner after my party, I told her I needed a make-over.

She got very excited. Makeovers were her thing. She had transformed me once, and she could do it again. She looked at me again with a critical eye. "You're right. I don't know how I haven't noticed. You need a re-fresh, especially that hair. And it will make a big difference at work. You need to look the part if you want people to believe in you."

That weekend we did the rounds: hair, nails, skin, and new clothes. This time she told the clerks we needed suits that screamed success.

I got the same reaction when I went back to work on Monday that I'd gotten all those years ago at high school. People stopped and stared. Some smiled and said, "Wow, Jane! You look great. Love what you're wearing." Even Ben noticed. Not that it changed our relationship, even though I couldn't stop myself from fantasizing that he'd take one look at the new me and fall madly in love. My new look made a difference in my working relationships.

I had worked at the same place my entire career. Eight years. I started out as an hourly employee, moved up to clerk typist, working in a huge room of cubicles with the sound of a hundred typewriters and phones ringing. It was a wonder anyone could get anything done.

Little by little, I moved up from clerk to secretary to administrative assistant to office manager. I was good at my job. It was like the old turtle and the hare story. There were others who were perkier, had degrees, were better speakers, but I just plugged away year after year and slowly advanced up the work chain.

Even though I was good at my job and had some friends, I never could completely escape my ingrown feelings of inadequacy. Some of my promotions happened because of someone leaving unexpectedly and they needed to fill the spot immediately.

I was my own worst enemy at work. My shyness prevented me from representing myself in a positive way. Earlier on, if I was asked to make a presentation to a group, I'd practically black out from fear. I turned bright red, and my throat closed up so my words sounded high pitched and garbled. After a few attempts, my boss finally concluded that I wasn't good at public speaking. My reports were always given to co-workers and so I never was the shining star, even if all the work was mine. My co-workers were often nice enough to mention me as the main contributor of the report, but that still didn't get me the recognition I needed to move ahead more quickly.

So, I was never singled out for praise or reward. My year end evaluations were always "Meets expectations" never an "exceeds" or "excels". The comments were always something that you could basically say about anyone: "works hard, dependable, reliable, competent…" All from the thesaurus of praise to give to acceptable but unexciting employees. My immediate supervisor used to write a plus sign next to my rating. Sometimes she'd even draw a little happy face by something she had written, as if to let me know that I had done that task particularly well. She'd smile and say, "You know how much I appreciate all your hard work."

I was always the one who worked late or came in early or gave up my weekend to finish a project or help a co-worker but that was never enough to get me more than that little plus sign.

That year at the annual banquet, I was given two individual recognitions (more mugs!) and a group plaque. My boss even talked about what an asset I was to the company. On my annual review, I got an "Exceeds Expectations" for the first time. My boss gushed and told me that I had really stepped it up this last year and had finally become the employee she always knew that I could be. In truth, I had done nothing different in the last year. Funny that all the advice my dad had given me over the years hadn't made much of an impact on my work life. It all came down to a good haircut and a new suit. I thought about that ad: "You've come a long way baby!" celebrating women's liberation. What a joke.

Part
Two

11
My Marriage: 1981

I ENJOYED MY JOB. I was never going to get the corner office, but I had the satisfaction of knowing I was a good employee who worked hard and made a contribution. I had friends. We went out together. I kept up with some of my old roommates. I saw my parents occasionally. On weekends, I looked forward to hunkering down in my apartment, eating junk food, and watching TV. Life was good. After the Ben fiasco, I planned to become a nun. No more relationships, I vowed.

I wasn't surprised when there was an out-of-town work conference scheduled and I wasn't asked to go. My boss said I was needed to "hold down the fort." Everyone scheduled to attend was excited for the first-class accommodations, from the convention center to the hotel. At the last minute, one of the attendees got sick. Imagine my surprise when I was asked to go in their place. The firm didn't want to lose the registration fee, and I was the only one available to go since everyone else already had plans for the weekend.

When I walked into my huge, luxurious hotel room, I was thrilled. It was the same size as my apartment. And the bathroom was much nicer. I enjoyed the conference as well. The workshops were educational, the speakers were entertaining, and the sessions were full of useful information.

After the workshops, before people went to dinner, many of the attendees, including me, gathered at the bar. I listened while the others talked. People drifted in and out. One guy in particular caught my eye. He was nice looking with wavy dark hair, bluish-green eyes, and a strong nose and chin. That wasn't what really attracted me. It was his demeanor. He was quiet. He didn't try to dominate the conversation. He listened, sipping his drink. At one point, he glanced at me and smiled, scanning the group as if to say, "What can we do?"

The following evening, I was sitting with the group when he arrived. He sat down next to me, leaned over, and whispered in my ear, "Frank Jones."

I whispered back, "Jane Smith," and smiled.

"Alias Smith and Jones." He arched his eyebrows as if he wondered if I was kidding him about my name.

During the evening, he whispered sardonic comments in my ear in response to remarks people made. He was clever and had good insights. I told him that he should speak up and share with the group. He shook his head slightly and rolled his eyes. "They just want to hear themselves talk. They don't really care about ideas."

I laughed because it was true.

On the third night, he asked me if I'd like to come up to his room to "talk." I blushed down to my toes. I stammered something corny about "not being that kind of girl." He looked mortified, turning a deep scarlet. He apologized and said he really meant to talk without the others around. Nothing else. He said he knew I wasn't "that kind of girl" and that was one of the things he liked about me.

"Today there is so much blatant sexuality! Free love and women throwing themselves at men and thinking equality is having sex with as many people as possible. I like that you aren't like that. I can tell you respect yourself and want to have a relationship, not a one-night stand."

We went to his room and sat on the bed and talked. Then we lay on the bed and talked more. Surprisingly, that was all we did. Talk. He shared about himself. How he had come from nothing and worked his way up. The last ten years had been hard work and career building. He was now ready to get married and have a family. The "next phase" as he put it.

I loved lying next to him, with my eyes closed, listening to him talk about his past, his present, and his future. I could not believe that he had picked me out of all the women at the conference. It appeared that fate had arranged our meeting at a conference that I wasn't even supposed to be attending. My mother had made me believe in fate.

Monday morning, I woke with my old friend from childhood Nameless Dread firmly ensconced in my gut and the Greek Choir singing, *"It's over, it's over… the party's over…"*

In the lobby, I met up with my co-workers for our ride back home. Frank was nowhere to be seen. As I climbed into the company bus, Frank appeared, gasping as if he had run all the way from his room. "Thank goodness, I caught you. I overslept and panicked, thinking you were already gone. Here's my number. Please call. I mean, if you want to see me again, please call because I want to see you again." He looked so eager but at the same time afraid, as if I might laugh at him and throw his number back in his face.

"I'll call…" I managed to say as he stepped back and the door slammed. The bus pulled out of the parking lot. Waving goodbye to Frank, I clutched his phone number in my hand. My co-workers laughed and teased me about the conquest I had made. I was in a state of shock. This guy really liked me and wanted to see me again.

We lived in different cities so only saw each other on weekends. We talked on the phone several times a week between visits. It reminded me of my parent's courtship. They had only seen each other on weekends for six months before they married, and their marriage had been a huge success.

We crammed a lot into those weekends.

He quickly decided I should come to see him, rather than the other way around. He had already begun to control our relationship in subtle ways. He said that Denton was much more interesting than Bensonville. Plus, he had to be available for work if needed since he had an "important" job. He wasn't interested in becoming part of my world—meeting my family and friends.

Luckily for me there was a direct train between Bensonville and Denton, so it was a quick two-hour trip. Every Friday morning, I'd pack a suitcase. At the end of the day, I'd grab the 6:00 p.m. train and arrive at 8:00. Frank was waiting for me at the station with a big grin on his face. He usually had flowers or some other little gift.

During those weekend visits, I slept in the bedroom and he slept on the couch. We never had sex. He was content just to hug and kiss. It occurred to me that he believed I was a virgin because he mentioned several times that he had been saving himself for the right girl and marriage. He believed I had done the same despite having told him I had a serious relationship in high school. Since it had been over eight years since I last had sex, I figured I was practically a virgin, so I never enlightened him.

I asked him if he'd had a girlfriend in high school or college. He said no, he didn't have time for such frivolity. Frivolity? What a strange word to use to describe a high school romance. If it didn't further his agenda to succeed, Frank didn't bother with it.

He always had our weekends planned. After he picked me up, we went to his apartment. We'd order in dinner and catch up on our week, though of course we had already discussed everything in our phone calls. While we ate dinner, he'd talk about his job, how awful his co-workers were, all their attempts to get ahead at his expense. He didn't like anyone he worked with. They were either stupid, lazy, or conniving. Somehow, we never got around to discussing my work. When I'd start, he'd jump up saying, "Hold on," because he had something he had to take care of, and we never got back around to me. I didn't mind. I loved listening to him talk. My stories were boring in comparison.

Saturdays, we went to his favorite café for breakfast and afterwards to a park or a museum. Or we might go to a movie or a concert if there was something he wanted to see.

Saturday nights, we'd go to whichever restaurant Frank picked out. He never bothered to ask what kinds of food I liked. He was interested in trying different places. Even though I had told him I was a picky eater, he never let that interfere with his choice. "Live a little. Try something new." I smiled, hoping to find something on the menu I wanted to eat. Thank goodness for salads and chicken.

Sundays we slept in late, and Frank often surprised me by bringing me breakfast in bed. It was usually coffee and a slice of toast with a piece of fruit, but I felt pampered. We'd read the paper while drinking our coffee and then walk around downtown Denton and window shop. He pointed out the furniture he liked for "our" future home. It was clean and modern, which was not my taste, but I didn't say so. He'd show me clothes he thought I should wear and books he recommended I read. He'd give me a gift of perfume he said I should use, instead of "that cheap junk" I currently used. He commented on things like my makeup and the color of my eyeshadow pointing out a "better" brand and color. He was molding me into his perfect woman.

Sunday evening, I'd catch the 6:00 p.m. train to Bensonville. At the train station, Frank hugged me, holding me for a long time, whispering in my ear, "I'll miss you. Can't wait until next weekend." He'd give me a quick kiss on the forehead, no public displays of affection for Frank, before helping me up the train steps. He stood on the platform, waving until I was out of sight.

He said he loved me and I was the one for him. He talked about marriage right away, saying "We aren't getting any younger." He was perfect. I was so starry-eyed in love, I only saw the picture he painted of our future.

When I found out Frank had two brothers and a sister, I was so excited. If and when we married, I'd finally have siblings. The big family I always wanted. Once I casually mentioned that it must have been nice to grow up with siblings. He laughed bitterly. "Not in my case. I'm lucky I survived those nut jobs."

One night, he told me the story of his childhood and family. At the time, I was touched that he loved and trusted me enough to share it. It didn't dawn on me until later that he had been a bit drunk and alcohol had loosened his tongue.

The youngest of four, he had an older sister and twin brothers. They were a working-class family. They lived in a small house in an old, run-down neighborhood. Frank said at the time he thought everyone lived that way.

When he was six years old, his mother called them all together to tell them that their father was dead. They were obviously mystified, since he hadn't been sick as far as they knew. His sister said, "I saw him packing his suitcase yesterday and he looked fine."

Their mother replied, "Yeah, he was going to the hospital and had to take some things with him. They called this morning and said he had died from the procedure."

A week later, she put an old vase on top of the TV and said it contained their dad's ashes. "We don't have no money for a funeral and all that stuff. This will do. If anyone asks, just tell them your dad died."

When a few of the neighborhood kids noticed their dad wasn't around, Frank's brother told them, "He's dead," which apparently satisfied any curiosity anyone had about the situation.

Not much changed. Money was tight, though there had never been much to start with. His mother, who had been a cold, hard person, was possibly colder and harder. He said her mouth formed into a grim, straight line. Frank said she never smiled or touched him except to strike him across the back of the head for a perceived fault or misbehavior. He never remembered her hugging or kissing any of them. What he found most amazing was one time she told him he was her favorite because he hadn't been tainted by his father since he was only six when his father "left." Being the favorite didn't really amount to much, as far as he could tell.

I was sad because one of my dreams had been to marry a man with a loving family. A family who would take me in and treat me like one of them. It didn't appear that Frank's family would be what I was hoping for. Still, people change, so I remained positive, believing Frank's mother might have mellowed. How could she not love the woman her son loved?

One day, my mother called to ask why I had been skipping our monthly dinners. I was shocked she'd even noticed. I apologized and asked if they were available the next Saturday. "I'll tell you what I've been up to." Frank was going to be away on a business trip, so it was perfect timing. Mom said fine. They looked forward to seeing me.

After I arrived, we sat in the living room with our drinks. My mother said, "So what's been going on that's keeping you so busy?"

I could hardly contain my excitement. "I'm seeing someone," I blurted out.

"It's about time," she responded. "You're practically an old maid. I started to think you'd never going to get over that David thing."

That David thing. "Happily, I'm not going to be a spinster." I forced myself to smile. "This guy is pretty serious. We're talking about marriage."

That got my mother's attention. "Marriage? And you haven't introduced this man to your parents? How long have you known him?" She seemed genuinely concerned.

"About five months. He lives in Denton. I usually see him every weekend, which is why I haven't been around."

"Five months?" my mother said disapprovingly. I could hear the unspoken reprimand. "And you're already talking marriage?"

"You and dad only knew each other for six months when you got married," I replied.

"Things were different then," my mother sniffed.

My father folded up his newspaper. "If you're seriously planning on marrying this guy, maybe you should bring him around?"

"Sure. I'll talk to him and let you know."

I spoke to Frank about it the next weekend. "My parents wondered why I haven't visited, and I told them about you and how we've been spending all our free time together." I smiled to show him how excited I'd been to share the news about him with my parents. "They really want to meet you."

"Seriously?" Frank grimaced. "From what you told me about your parents, I didn't think they cared."

That hurt. I was excited my parents wanted to meet Frank. I forced myself to laugh. "They're not as bad as I might have led you to believe. All parents want to meet the person who might become part of the family. You and my dad will really get along. You have similar backgrounds. He's also a self-made man. He came from very humble beginnings and made a success of himself."

Even though I could tell Frank wasn't thrilled at the prospect, we picked a weekend and confirmed the date with my parents.

Frank drove into town Saturday afternoon, picked me up, and we went to my parent's place. Frank brought flowers for my mother. He was the perfect gentleman. He complimented my parents on their condo, admired the view, said dinner was lovely, talked about his work. But he was not really engaged. All conversation had to be dragged out of him. There were numerous awkward silences, which I tried to fill by babbling about nothing. At the end of the visit, he and my dad shook hands, and my mother thanked him for the flowers. We left and went to my apartment.

On the drive over, I tried to get him to talk about my parents. He was not very forthcoming except to hint that he was captivated by their condo and furniture. He said something about my father having done well.

This was the first time he had been to my apartment. It was a sharp contrast to my parent's place. I could tell he wasn't impressed. He practically sneered as he looked around at my second-hand furniture.

"It's a starter place," I explained. "This is the best I could afford. I was tired of having roommates." He didn't reply, acting as if he was afraid to sit on anything because he might pick up something unsavory.

"I don't get anything until I save up and am able to buy the best." He grimaced, running his finger over the cushions of my beat-up old couch.

"I enjoyed getting old things at bargain prices and fixing them up. I didn't have much money for furniture after putting a deposit on this place."

He left early the next morning, as if he couldn't get out fast enough.

I didn't see Frank the next weekend because he had to finish a project for work and said he'd be too busy to entertain me. I went to my parents for dinner instead. I was eager to find out what they thought about Frank. Nothing was said during dinner. I was surprised. I had expected them to rave about Frank. I mean, what was not to like? He was nice looking, well mannered, had a good job, and wanted to marry *me*.

We went into the living room for coffee, and I couldn't wait any longer. "What did you think of Frank?"

Mother cocked her head as if to get all the thoughts into one side of her brain before she spoke. "He's nice."

"Nice?" I was incredulous.

"Yes, nice. But there is something about him. A cockiness, like he was evaluating everything—us, our condo, our bank accounts. It's hard to put a finger on."

"I agree," Dad said. "When we were talking about his past and his goals for the future, he's a little cold and calculating about it. It's like getting married is one more item on his checklist and you're available."

"I'm sorry you both feel that way," I said angrily. "I love him and more importantly, he loves me! It's not like I've had men beating down the door to marry me or even to take me to the movies. At least this way I won't shame you by being a spinster!"

I slammed my coffee cup down, splashing a bit on the table. My mother winced. I was too angry to even take my cup to the sink and rinse it and put it in the dishwasher—a major sin in my mother's eyes. I stormed out of the house. They were wrong about him. Why was I surprised? They never supported me in anything I did.

A month later on my weekend visit, Frank said, "Let's do it! Let's get married. We love each other. Why wait?"

I laughed, giddy with excitement. I was so happy to be asked I didn't notice a few things were missing—a bended knee, a ring, and some other of the traditions of a typical proposal.

I jumped up and hugged him. "Yes, yes, yes! Let's do it!"

He said he wanted to keep things simple. "All those supposed customs are just a scam by the wedding industry to get money out of people. It's much better to save the money you would waste on a wedding for a down payment on a house." He added engagement rings were another waste of money and another trick thought up by jewelers.

"That's fine. I agree. Waste of money." I'd have agreed with anything. I was getting married at last!

"We can get married at the courthouse, with a justice of the peace. We only need a couple of witnesses. We could hire some!" He laughed long and hard at his witticism. I laughed along with him, though in truth, it made me a little sad in the midst of my happiness. Between us, we couldn't come up with two people to witness our marriage? He continued, "Who'd we invite to our wedding anyway? Your parents? My family? Some co-workers? No reason to throw a big party for them."

"My parents might like to come," I said quietly. I could tell he wasn't thrilled at the idea, though he agreed it was fine if they wanted to attend.

The next month was a rush of plans. I had to put in my notice at work, since I was moving to Denton. When the time came to tell my boss, I was overcome with a sense of loss and sadness. I had worked there for over eight years and moved up from clerk to office manager. I had celebrated birthdays, weddings, and holidays with these people.

My boss was shocked. "I'm sorry to hear that. You won't be easy to replace. You're quiet, hardworking, and efficient. It's hard to find those qualities!"

While I blushed with pride, I wondered why it took her so long to say this to me. For years, all I had ever gotten was a little plus sign from her until the year I got my haircut and a power suit.

"However, I understand. Congratulations on your upcoming marriage," she beamed. "If I'd only known sending you to that conference would end up with you getting married and leaving me, I'd never have let you go." She grinned but I could tell she meant it.

Before I left, the office threw me a wedding shower. My co-workers hugged and congratulated me. I wondered why I had never noticed how great they all were and why I'd never become close to anyone there. A few people commented on how I had met Frank and how lucky it had been for me to attend the conference. They told the story about Frank chasing down the bus to give me his phone number. Everyone smiled and laughed.

But I also overheard people whispering, "She hasn't known him long. She's rushing in to things. What does she know about this guy?"

I put it down to jealousy, but in hindsight, they were right. What did I really know about Frank? We had spent less than seven months together, seeing each other on weekends and the occasional holiday or day off. A total of twenty-eight weekends. Fifty-six plus days. If they were stretched end to end, it might have added up to a month and a half. What can you really learn about anyone in a month and a half? Sadly, not much.

There were so many things we never discussed. That we should have discussed. We should have talked about our core values and what we wanted out of life, because as it turned out, we were completely different. I wanted a family. A husband who adored me and lots of children to love. And friends. A house—a home—filled with love and friendship. Frank wanted success. A house that was a showplace. He wanted people to envy him. I wanted people to like me.

I was overwhelmed by Frank and his plans for me fitting into his world. It wasn't until after we were married, it occurred to me we had skipped these important talks about our future. He only wanted one or two children. I wanted a dozen or at the very least two, anything but just one.

We never discussed God and religion. To this day, I have no clue what Frank believes or if he even believes. I wasn't even sure what I believed. While my parents never exhibited any deep religious beliefs, I know if I said I didn't believe in God, my parents would have been horrified. Mamere was deeply religious and some of that had rubbed off on me during my summer visits.

Frank was good at expressing his opinion on issues. Once he spoke, there was no more to be said on the subject as far as he was concerned. If I had a different opinion and tried to express it, he dismissed me with a wave of his hand. I quickly learned it was easier to remain silent.

Years later, much too late, I had to acknowledge my parents had been closer to the truth about Frank than I was. Sadly, after we married, I discovered the qualities that attracted me to Frank initially later turned into the very things I hated in him. His dismissal of others that I thought was confidence later became domineering arrogance. His quietness showed up as brooding sullenness. His wit, which first made me laugh, later was used to belittle and demean me.

But, in the beginning, we were happy.

12
The Visit

$\mathcal{B}$EFORE WE GOT MARRIED, I needed to meet Frank's family. He was not enthusiastic. His mother called at least once a month and when he finally told her he had met someone and was getting married, the pressure mounted.

I heard him talking on the phone with his mom several times, and I could tell from his end of the conversation she was harassing him about visiting.

"I know, Mom…

"Yes, we want to come…

"We've been planning a visit… things keep coming up at work…

"Of course, Jane wants to meet you…"

I could hear her practically yelling over the phone, "How can you even think of getting married before your own mother has met the girl?"

I was excited to meet Frank's family. No matter how much he tried to convince me it wasn't a good idea, and it wasn't going to turn out to be the fantastic experience I envisioned, I still wanted to go. I wanted a big family. A warm, welcoming family. I knew people who said they ended up loving their in-laws more than their own family because they were so wonderful.

That's what I wanted.

Frank finally broke down and told his mother we'd come for a weekend visit. She was excited and said the whole family couldn't wait to see him and meet me.

I took Friday off, and Frank left work early because we had a five-hour drive to get to the western part of the state. On the drive, I chatted happily about how excited I was to meet his family. Frank grunted in response, concentrating on driving. I even suggested we invite his mom and family to our wedding. He almost swerved off the road. "Absolutely not!" he responded emphatically, straightening the wheel of the car. "It's not like we're having a big ceremony; we're only going to the courthouse. Why ask them to come all the way for that? We can visit again after we're married."

Because traffic was bad, we arrived at the house around 10:00p.m. The door was locked, and no one answered our knock. *That's odd*, I thought. Frank's mother had been thrilled when he told her we were coming.

Frank, however, didn't think it was strange, so I guessed he had shown up before to a locked door. He dug in his pocket, found a key, and started to unlock the door.

"You still have a key to your mom's house?" I asked.

"Yes. I kept it to remind me of where I came from and where I never want to go back to."

Wow. That was intense. The house was tiny. There was a small, eat-in kitchen to the left inside the door. A few steps away was an equally small living room. A hallway led off to the right from the living room. The first thing I noticed was the overwhelming stink of cigarettes. An ashtray filled with cigarette butts sat on the kitchen table and another one in the living room. For a moment, I was transported back in time to Mamere's house, but where her house had an underlying scent of pine and lemon, this place had a sour, unclean smell.

His mother was asleep on the couch. I worried our arrival had kept her up too late. Frank walked over and shook her shoulder.

"Mom. Wake up. We're here."

She sat up, confused and groggy, an empty bottle of vodka on the table next to her.

"For God's sake Mom," Frank exclaimed. "Couldn't you give up drinking for one night?"

She stared at him with a muddled look on her face. "Frank?" she said. "What are you doing here?"

"Never mind, Mom. Go back to sleep. We'll see you in the morning."

Frank turned around, grabbed our bags, and stormed down the hallway. I followed. There were four closed doors at the end of the hall. He opened one and walked into a bedroom with a bunk and a twin bed. Even though there was hardly room for anything else, somehow a desk and chest of drawers had been crammed in.

"This was the room I shared with my brothers," he said. It looked like it hadn't changed a bit since three little boys had lived there. The beds had faded baseball-themed bedspreads and a shelf laden with trophies and memorabilia hung on the wall. He dropped my bag on the bed. "You can stay in this room. I'll stay in my sister's room."

I didn't know what to say, because Frank was obviously embarrassed and angry. I was miserable about our "welcome home" and didn't want to stay in this strange house all alone. But I could tell Frank was even more upset, so I said nothing. I reached over and gave him a hug and a kiss. He was rigid in my arms, but finally relented and hugged me back.

"Sorry," he murmured. "I told you we shouldn't have come." He walked out and shut the door behind him. I put on my nightgown and climbed into the twin bed. The sheets were cold, and I wondered when they were last washed and changed. I lay in bed for a long time, staring up at the ceiling. This visit was not starting out the way I had hoped. I finally drifted off to a restless sleep.

When I woke the next morning, I was momentarily disoriented. I had no idea where I was. Looking around, I saw old trophies and it came back to me. Nameless Dread went into high gear.

Frank had not come in to say good morning, so I didn't know if he was up. I wished I knew where Frank was so at least we could walk out together. The last thing I wanted to do was go into the house by myself and meet his mother on my own. Climbing out of bed, I put my robe on and listened at the door. The only sounds I heard were the TV. No conversation.

Finally, I couldn't wait any longer. I had to pee. I opened the door and stared down the hall but didn't see or hear anyone. I was confronted by three closed doors, and I luckily found the bathroom on my first try. Running in, I quickly shut the door behind me. I thought about hiding in there until Frank came for me, but quickly realized I couldn't stay there. It was tiny and uncomfortable. I wished I had brought my toothbrush in with me. Using a towel that seemed to be clean, I scrubbed my face as best as I could and rubbed toothpaste on my teeth. I poked my head outside the door, glancing down the hall. Someone was moving around in the kitchen. Two quick steps brought me back to the bedroom. I closed the door quietly, got dressed, and put on a little makeup.

Now or never, I thought. Putting a bright smile on my face, I walked out to the kitchen. Thank goodness I had spent a lifetime mastering the fake smile. Frank's mother was at the sink with her back to me. Frank was nowhere in sight. I looked out the window and noticed his car was gone. "*Oh my God. Oh my God,*" sang my Greek choir. "*He has gone and left you all alone.*"

As I stood there, the car drove back into the carport and relief flooded me. I told the choir to shut up. Frank walked in holding a box with three cups of coffee in it.

"Good morning!" he said brightly. "I thought I'd let you sleep in after our long drive." He handed me a cup of coffee. "Mom ran out of coffee so

I went out to get some for everyone."

For some reason, this really struck me. My mother never ran out of anything, much less coffee if company was coming. It's not like we showed up out of the blue. She had known we were coming for a couple of weeks. Who doesn't buy coffee for guests? On the other hand, who gets drunk and falls asleep while waiting for their supposedly favorite son to show up?

All these thoughts flew through my head as Frank's mom turned around. She was small. Wrinkled. No make-up. (Oh no! I'm my mother now—judging people because they aren't made up first thing in the morning!) Her hair was short and curly. It looked like a really bad perm. The ends of her hair appeared to be singed. She walked toward me, and I was horrified. Seriously. Horrified.

"So, this is Jane. I'm happy to finally get to meet you. I wondered why Frank was reluctant to bring you for a visit." She said all this while looking me up and down with a critical eye. She scrutinized my face and didn't appear to be pleased by what she saw. Was I too plain? Too made-up? Too fat? Too thin? Was my hair too curly? Too straight? Much to my surprise, she reached out and hugged me.

Raising my arms, I hugged her back. "I'm happy to finally meet you too." It was a lie. I wished we had never come.

Frank handed her a cup of coffee, and we all walked into the living room and sat down. There was an awkward silence. I looked around the room. I remembered how Frank had practically sneered at my small apartment and hand-me-down second-hand furniture. I could see now how it reminded him of his childhood home. At least my place was clean and neat. The empty vodka bottle and glass were gone.

"Everyone is coming over later for a cookout," Frank's mom announced.

I assumed that meant his two brothers and sister, along with their spouses and children. I hadn't quite figured out how many kids Frank's siblings had.

"Sounds great. We can get all the visiting done in one meal." Frank laughed. It was not a happy sound. I could tell he wasn't excited about having all his siblings descend upon us at once. "Do we need to make anything or get anything?"

"No. Everything is prepared. Your brothers are bringing hamburgers and hot dogs. Your sister is bringing the buns and drinks. Of course, I made your favorite potato salad and coleslaw."

There was no mention by Frank or his mother of breakfast, so I sipped my coffee, realizing this was probably the only thing I was going to get until the cookout.

"What time is everyone coming over?" I asked, hoping I sounded bright and cheery. "I can't wait to meet them."

"Around two o'clock," his mother replied.

I thought I might faint from hunger before two.

Frank and his mother talked while I sat nursing my coffee. I wasn't really paying any attention to them and their conversation. Frank got up and went and looked in the fridge. "Geez mom. You've got nothing in here. No milk or orange juice or eggs. What the hell do you eat?"

"I've got stuff," she replied a bit testily.

"Do you even have a loaf of bread?"

"Yeah, but it might be stale," she admitted.

Frank shut the door and turned around. "I'm going to run to the store and get some food so we can have breakfast. You two get to know each other. I'll be back soon."

He left and his mother turned to look at me again. Was it my general paranoia or did this woman really not like me?

"So, Jane. Tell me about yourself." She asked, though it was more like a command. Was that a tone of skepticism I heard in her voice? Did she think I was a fraud? What had Frank told her about me?

Trying to smile, I said, "There's not much to tell. My dad was in the army. We moved around a lot. He's retired now, and he and my mom have a condo in a senior village in Bensonville. I have an apartment there. I've worked for the same company as an office manager for almost ten years..." I quickly ran out of things to say under her withering look.

"How did you and Frank meet?"

"At a work conference we both attended. Love at first sight—almost!" I chuckled, trying to lighten the mood.

Her mouth was set in a tight line. "To be honest, I am disappointed Frank is considering getting married so early in his career."

I wrinkled my brow in confusion. Early? He was thirty.

"Frank worked hard for everything in his life. He didn't have the advantage of a daddy in the military and living all over the world. He needs to concentrate on his career and not get distracted by a wife and worries about mortgages and children and things like that."

My mouth literally dropped open. I snapped it shut and stared at her. *Oh my God. What the hell had I walked into?* The Greek chorus went into overdrive. Nameless Dread, who usually only showed up first thing in the morning, knotted up my stomach.

"Frank is an amazing, hard-working guy," I finally managed to say. "I know you must be proud of him, and I am too. I hope I'll be able to help him as he moves up in his career. I plan to quit my job after we get married and take care of the home front."

"So," she drew the word out, "are you two living together? I'm wondering if you 'have to get married' since this seems all rather sudden?"

My mind went blank. I couldn't think of anything to say in response. I must have looked like the deer in the headlights because when Frank walked back in and looked at us, he said, "What's going on?"

"Oh nothing. Jane and I have been chatting and getting to know each other." His mother turned and smiled at him.

"Can I help with breakfast, Frank?" I asked desperately. His mother jumped up and said sweetly, "No dear. You're a guest in my house. You sit while Frank and I whip something up."

I sat and stared at the TV, watching the news, not comprehending a word. I was devastated. Not only was it unlikely Frank's mother was going to love me, it was apparent she already hated me.

I got through breakfast by smiling and muttering the occasional yes or no while Frank and his mother talked. I stared at my food as if it was the most fascinating thing I'd ever seen. She told him about friends and neighbors from the old days.

After breakfast, she asked if he could run to the store and pick up the cake she'd had ordered. Jumping up quickly, I said, "Can I come along for the ride? I have a bit of a headache and some fresh air might help."

His mother gave me a look like a lion whose prey has escaped. She was obviously unhappy at being denied the opportunity to interrogate me further. I grabbed my purse and got out the door before Frank did.

In the car, Frank asked me if everything was all right. What could I say?

Choosing my words carefully, I finally said, "I don't think your mother wants us to get married. It's not me… she worries getting married is a bad career move for you. She said you need to concentrate on your career. She's quite proud of you and how far you have come."

"Yeah, no thanks to her or anyone else in the family," he replied bitterly. "Getting away from here was like climbing out of quicksand. She didn't want me to go to college or move to the city to get a good job. If it had been up to her, I'd be driving a truck or working at a garage like my brothers. And now she has the nerve to say getting married could be bad for my career! I don't know whether to laugh or cry.

"This is why I didn't want to bring you here. I knew you had built this up in your mind as a warm fuzzy weekend of family fun. I warned you. My family is not fun. We only have to make it through the family gathering today, and we'll get out of here early tomorrow."

Frank reached over, squeezed my hand, and smiled at me. In that moment, I didn't care about his family. I was lucky to have found Frank even if it would only be the two of us.

At the store bakery, Frank asked the clerk if there was a cake there for Mrs. Jones. They brought it out and Frank had to pay for it. It was decorated with flowers and the words "Welcome home Frank and Jane." The cake was more welcoming than the woman who ordered it.

We got back to the house and managed to stay busy. Frank had to go to the store a couple of more times for things his mother had forgotten, like charcoal. About 1:30, I went into the back and changed into a simple blue sweater, with a matching cardigan and a plain khaki skirt. I had planned to wear a dress but had a feeling I'd be overdressed.

When I came out to the living room, Frank's mother stared at me like I was wearing an evening gown.

"No reason to get all dressed up. It's just family."

"Oh, these old things. They're comfortable," I replied.

"You look great," Frank said.

His mother appeared skeptical. I decided to ignore her. I couldn't wait for the rest of the family to get there. At least their arrival might take her focus off me. I hoped.

Frank's sister, Carla, arrived first with her husband Carl. This was apparently the big joke in the family that they were Carla and Carl. She had two children, Carl Jr. and Tiffany. Everyone was in jeans and t-shirts so maybe I was a little overdressed; still, I was the one trying to make a good impression. The kids barely acknowledged Frank or me or even their grandmother, as they ran past everyone into the living room and changed the TV channel to a cartoon.

"Thank God. That should keep them out of our hair for a while!" Carla exclaimed as she walked in, dropping bags of food on the kitchen table. She gave Frank a big hug and turned to me, but we didn't get a chance to even say hello because at that moment Frank's twin brothers Joe and Jim showed up with their wives Marty and Susie and several more children who also went into the living room to watch television. A squabble soon erupted among the kids about what to watch and Joe, or Jim, went in there roaring if he heard another word, he'd spank them all and put them in different rooms. Things quickly quieted down.

Everyone expressed great interest in meeting the woman who finally nabbed Frank. "He never had time for a girlfriend in high school or college. And he never mentioned a single girlfriend from the big city. We were starting to wonder about him," Joe (or Jim) laughed and winked at me. I didn't know how to respond.

We managed to get the food cooked and eaten. Joe and Jim and Marty and Susie all had way too much to drink. In fact, I was amazed by the amount of beer they consumed. Frank's mother appeared to be drinking water, but I remembered Mamere and how easily she switched water for gin without anyone being the wiser. Frank's mother appeared sober, though. The conversation centered around things that had happened when they were young. There weren't many questions about Frank's work, me, or life in the big city.

I sat quietly. I was not the best in crowds, and they were so loud and raucous I couldn't have gotten a word in if I tried. I laughed at the right moments and smiled and thought things were going quite well. Frank tried to tolerate the constant ribbing and stories about their childhood and school.

"Frank, do you remember when…?"

"Frank, whatever happened to Charley? Remember when you two…"

"Frank, remember Mrs. Lawrence our English teacher? You're never going to believe…"

Frank's mother filled them in on me from the few things I had managed to say during my interrogation. Apparently, I was not needed to tell my own story.

"Jane has lived *all* over the world…" (not true.)

"Jane's father was a *colonel* in the army…." (started as a private, I wanted to add.)

"Jane went to college too, like Frank…" (community college, I tried to clarify.)

All these things were said in a kind of sneering tone, as if they were bad. I tried to laugh it off and smiled as she went on.

As the day dragged into the late afternoon, I went into the house to change my sweater for a jacket since the temperature was dropping. In the bedroom, I grabbed my jacket and as I turned to go, I noticed the windows were open. I went over to slide them shut since I didn't want the room to get too cold. The windows were high up on the walls. As I stepped up, I heard voices outside. Something about the tone of the voices made me stop. Peeking out, I saw Carla, Susie, and Marty.

"Oh my God! Can you believe this girl?"

"What a rich, spoiled bitch. Lording it over us with her fancy clothes and hoity-toity talk. 'My father's a colonel. I lived all over.' Who the hell does she think she is?"

"I can't believe Frank has fallen for this snooty bitch."

"What a fucking phony. Did you see that look on her face as if she is looking down her nose at all of us? Like she's so much better."

"Yeah. She sits there like a spider in a web, a smug look on her face. Can't even be bothered to talk to us, cause we're so beneath her."

"Frank is becoming just like her. With his polo shirt and khaki pants. Like he's never worn jeans in his life!"

I looked down at my clothes. I was wearing a five-year-old sweater from Penney's and a skirt that was probably just as old. Fancy clothes? I had tried to dress nicely and be presentable, but since everyone wore wrinkled t-shirts and torn dirty jeans, I guess I was over-dressed.

I didn't look down on them. They looked down on me because I supposedly lived some exotic life. Tears sprang to my eyes. I was already upset because Frank's mother didn't like me and now it was obvious none of them liked me. They took my shyness for snootiness. My awkwardness for snobbery.

Moving back from the window before they saw me, I banged into the chest of drawers, knocking over a trophy. Carla, Marty, and Susie immediately got quiet. I didn't think they could see me, but I crouched down and slipped out of the room. I went to the bathroom and splashed water on my face, pasted on my best phony smile, and went outside. When I got there, they were all in the carport talking to their husbands.

Not too long after, everyone started to leave. There were hugs all around.

The kids stormed outside and climbed noisily into the cars. They had not spoken a word to Frank or me.

On the drive home the next day, I sat quietly for the first hour. Finally, I asked, "Why doesn't your family like me? It's like they already made up their minds before they met me."

Frank sighed. "They are sad, jealous, and angry people. They've done nothing with their lives, and they can't stand people who have. They kind of cut me off when I went to college. In their minds, I wasn't trying to better myself, I was saying I was better than them. So, I stopped coming home for visits. I'm sorry Jane. I should never have taken you to meet them. I tried to warn you. They are not nice people."

The one positive that came out of that horrible weekend was that I began to feel more positive toward my parents. Compared to Frank's mother, they qualified as parents of the year!

13
Our Wedding

FRANK CALLED THE COURTHOUSE IN Denton to arrange our marriage. The earliest date we could get was five weeks away. The next time I went to my parent's house, I told them the day, time, and location, and asked if they wanted to come. My mother acted miffed she hadn't been consulted about our wedding plans, such as they were.

"From the day her daughter is born, a mother looks forward to planning her daughter's wedding day," she sniffed.

Seriously, I thought. *You've never given a thought to me or my future from the day I was born. A day you never hoped to endure. A child you never wanted.*

"I'm sorry. Frank and I decided a simple ceremony would be best. His family lives far away, and it would be a burden for them to travel to attend a big wedding, staying in a hotel and all. Neither of us has extended family to invite, and we don't have lots of close friends either. This way we can put the money we're saving toward a house."

"By the way," Mother continued, "is your engagement ring at the jewelers being sized? I haven't seen it yet."

"We agreed engagement rings were just another waste of money. Who really needs a big diamond ring? We're going to get simple gold bands.

We're simple people."

"Your father had no money when we got engaged, and he still managed to buy me a ring. I thought you said Frank had a good job. Though I'm not really surprised about this." She arched her eyebrows and that was the last word my mother uttered on the subject.

The Big Day arrived. I wore a simple white dress and Frank wore his best suit. We parked in the garage across the street and walked up the steps of the courthouse. My parents had arrived shortly before us and were waiting in the lobby. My mother looked lovely, as always. She should have been the bride. It never mattered what I wore, I always looked like an unfashionable blob next to my mother. She radiated. I didn't. On my best days, I might have worked up to a low-level glow.

My parents stood next to me, and Frank held my hand as the Justice of the Peace read the wedding vows. I don't remember a word of it. I only remember saying, "I do" and hearing Frank say, "I do." Knowing he loved me made me the happiest person on earth that day.

We signed the register and my parents signed as our witnesses. My mother pecked us both on the cheeks, air kisses. My father gave me an awkward hug and shook Frank's hand. Outside, I looked up, half expecting to hear music playing and to see balloons and flowers falling out of the sky in celebration. However, the world remained mute on my wedding day.

We headed down the steps of the courthouse and I was ready to say goodbye to my parents, when my father surprised us by announcing he had made lunch reservations at the Tavern Park restaurant. It was the finest restaurant in Denton.

We walked in and were escorted to a room in the back. The room was beautifully decorated with a small wedding cake in the center of the table. Frank was quite impressed. "I've been meaning to try this place out. I've heard a lot of good things about it." Conversation lagged while we checked out the menus. I was determined to enjoy this meal.

In addition to making the reservations, my father insisted on paying the entire bill, which included a nice bottle of champagne. "It's the least we can do for our little girl on her wedding day," my father said as he signed for the meal. Even my mother enjoyed herself. But she always enjoyed the finer things in life.

After the best meal of my life, we walked my parents outside. There were more hugs and air kisses. Giddy from the champagne, I suggested they stay a little longer, but my mother insisted they needed to get on the road back home. I don't know why I even asked them to stay. I guess I wanted the celebration to continue. The valet brought their car around and they drove off. I waved until they were out of sight. I had a strange feeling in the pit of my stomach. Sorrow? Loss? Emptiness?

"Well, Mrs. Jones, what would you like to do now?" Frank asked. Jane Jones—my new name. And while some might say it wasn't much of an improvement over "Jane Smith," I thought it sounded lyrical. I loved saying it and listening to the "J" sounds sing together.

Even though this was the happiest day of my life, I felt a momentary let down. If we'd had a traditional wedding, we wouldn't be standing on a street corner wondering what to do with the rest of our wedding day. We'd be at our reception, dancing and dining and drinking with our friends and family. Now, the celebration was over.

"I guess we should head back to the apartment?" I suggested.

Frank laughed. "The apartment? This is our wedding day and we're going to celebrate! I've booked the wedding suite at the Grand Hotel. It's only for one night but it will be a night to remember!"

I was surprised and excited that our wedding day hadn't ended yet. How wonderful of Frank to have planned this all by himself.

We walked the few blocks to the Grand. When we checked in, Frank signed our names with a flourish in the hotel registry—Mr. & Mrs. Frank Jones. For the second time that day, we used our new legal names. We took the elevator to the top floor, the bellhop showing us the way.

The room was beautiful with a view of the whole city. "I packed a few things for you," Frank pointed at a suitcase. "Probably not what you might have packed but I wanted to surprise you. At least you'll have your toothbrush!" He laughed.

"Trust me, this is a wonderful surprise. Spending my wedding night at the finest hotel in Denton." I turned and hugged him. "Don't worry about what you packed. I don't need anything but you. Though I'm glad to have my toothbrush," I chuckled, kissing him.

We removed our wedding attire and put on the plush robes the hotel provided. It was all so decadent. Frank called down and ordered appetizers and another bottle of champagne. In a little while, there was a knock on the door and the same bellhop rolled in a cart with the food and a bottle of champagne in an ice bucket. He asked Frank if he wanted the champagne opened and Frank said, "Yes, please."

Since it was doubtful Frank had ever opened a bottle of champagne, I was happy the bellhop popped the cork for us. He put it back in the ice and said, "Congratulations." As he exited, he slipped the "Do not Disturb" sign off the doorknob and placed it on the outside of the door.

Frank poured both of us a glass of champagne, and we toasted each other, looking out the window at an amazing view of the city skyline lit up by the setting sun. Frank made a sweeping gesture toward the outside. "The world is our oyster!"

"To happily ever after," I replied, feeling my heart sing.

Neither of us were big drinkers, so we were soon both tipsy. We started kissing on the couch. Frank stood and took my hand, leading me to the king-size bed. He dramatically threw the covers back and pushed a button on the wall, dimming the lights. Music started to play. We sat on the edge of the bed and started kissing again. We quickly fell back on to the plush mattress. Frank kissed me everywhere and pulled off our robes. We were completely entwined. This was the moment we had been waiting for all these months. Our wedding night. We were both so shy, me from a long abstinence, and Frank from a complete lack of experience. Instinct took over.

Afterwards, Frank lay on his back with an enormous grin. He appeared quite pleased with the entire event. Though it hadn't been the earth-shaking moment for me that he had apparently experienced, I was happy to see him smile.

The next morning, I woke up with a headache. Champagne does that to me. Frank was next to me, propped up on his elbow, staring at me with a huge grin. "Good morning, Mrs. Jones." He leaned over and kissed me. He loved saying "Mrs. Jones," and I loved hearing him say it because it sounded like he was proud to be married to me.

In the bright light of day, our shyness returned. We hadn't yet seen each other naked. I've always been a prude and years of covering my body did not evaporate overnight. Clutching the sheets to my chin and finding my robe on the floor, I quickly slipped into it and hopped out of bed.

"I'm going to take a quick shower," I said, padding off to the bathroom. I ended up taking a lovely hot bath in the huge tub. Frank's apartment only had a small shower, so I wanted to take advantage of a good soak for the last time. There were all kinds of lotions and potions, including bubble bath, which I used generously.

Frank knocked and opened the door a crack. "Are you almost done?" he asked. "Breakfast has arrived." All this and breakfast too! It just kept getting better and better.

"Yes. I'll be right out." Frank sat at the little table in our room, also wearing his robe. There was a wonderful breakfast spread with eggs, pastries, coffee, and juice. I was suddenly ravenous.

Frank poured us both a cup of coffee and we clinked cups just as we had clinked our champagne glasses. "To the rest of our lives together."

14

The Rest of our Life Begins

I QUIT MY JOB IN Bensonville and moved in with Frank in Denton, leaving everything familiar—my job, my co-workers, my friends, even my parents. Frank didn't ask what I thought about moving. At the time, it was the way things were and always had been. The woman followed her man. The man's job was the one that counted. Women only worked while they waited to get married or if they worked after marriage, it was only while they waited to have children.

When I mentioned my worries about giving up the life I knew, he replied, "You've moved around a lot as a military kid. It's the same thing, except you'll have me. You'll be fine."

He assumed since I had moved around a lot as a child, I was used to change. I'd never told him how much I hated moving. Hated giving up the familiar to move to a new town. To start over. Trying to fit in. Trying to make friends. And wondering why I should even bother since we'd soon be moving again anyway.

I was comfortable with my life in Bensonville. I had a job. Co-workers. Friends. A routine. My own apartment, however small and crummy (according to Frank). Now I had no job, no friends, no routine. I was on my own with only Frank. Foolishly, I thought love would be enough.

Our weekend honeymoon was over too soon. Monday morning ushered in the first day of the rest of our lives. Frank got up, showered, and dressed. He came into the tiny kitchen and ate the breakfast I prepared, grabbed the lunch I packed, and headed to the door. But first he hugged me and whispered, "I'll miss you, Mrs. Jones. Keep the home fires burning." Then he was out the door and gone.

I cleaned up the dishes and looked around, wondering what I was going to do with my day. Frank's one-bedroom apartment was slightly bigger than my apartment, since at least the bedroom was separate from the living room, but it was not going to require a lot of time to clean. I straightened up a few things. Frank was a bit of a neat freak, so it didn't need much attention.

I unpacked my things from my old place, organized a few items and found places for them—clothes in the closet, books on the shelf, dishes in the cupboards. I was reluctant to put out my knick-knacks, so I left them in their box, which I shoved into the back corner of the closet. This was still his apartment. I didn't feel like a full tenant yet.

I focused on the meals I'd prepare. When Frank got home after work, I wanted him to sit down to a hot, home-cooked meal. I was not a good cook mostly because I'd never bothered to learn. Whenever my roommates and I got tired of takeout or junk food, we'd make a big meal together. I was usually given the task of making the salad, since it didn't require any skill except chopping. When I lived alone, I usually ate cereal for dinner.

One of my co-workers gave me a copy of *The Joy of Cooking* as a wedding gift. She said it was a tradition in her family to always give a new bride a copy. It had an amazing amount of information and lots of good recipes. For a novice like me, the step-by-step directions helped. I was quite proud when Frank came home that I had the table set and a good hot meal ready and waiting.

While many women at the time were embroiled in the feminist fight for equality and freedom from a life of domestic drudgery, I'm embarrassed to admit I loved it. Building our little nest together made me happy. At one point, I asked Frank if I should start looking for a job. He didn't want me to. "I want to take care of you. I want my wife to take care of me. And very soon, I want you to be taking care of our children."

This was what I had always wanted. To be loved. To love. To share my life with another person.

Even though I wasn't working, I quickly developed a plan. Both Mamere and my mother had an established weekly schedule for each household task. My day revolved around taking care of Frank. First, I got up and made breakfast and packed a lunch for him. After he left, I cleaned the breakfast dishes. Each day, I set myself a task to complete. If I had any free time, I explored the neighborhood.

Mondays I did the grocery shopping for the week.

Tuesday was laundry day. Washing and ironing Frank's clothes.

Wednesday was devoted to house cleaning, not that it required much, but I dusted and vacuumed.

Thursdays were catch-up day for anything I hadn't gotten done Monday, Tuesday, or Wednesday.

Fridays, I prepared for the weekend.

I also developed the bad habit of watching TV during my lunch break. My mother never watched TV except in the evening with Dad. It all started one day when I had the TV on while I was folding laundry and I heard the familiar strains of the theme song from *The Sandtimer*. Mamere's favorite soap. The one we had watched together every day during my summer visits.

This became my hour of guilty pleasure each day. Frank did not need to know. I was surprised that many of the original cast members were still on the show. I discovered that I hadn't missed much in the last twenty years. I remember Mamere saying she could sleep through half the episodes because the story line moved along so slowly. How true that was.

A year after we got married, Frank came home all excited to tell me he had found a little house he thought we should buy. "It's small. Just a starter home. In a few years, we can get our dream home."

I was speechless with excitement. I didn't know much about our financial situation. "Frank, how wonderful," I squealed. "Can we afford a house?"

"We'll have to tighten the purse strings a bit, still, I think we can manage, and it's a good time to buy what with interest rates and mortgages and financing…"

I zoned out. I knew he was prudent and wouldn't suggest getting a house unless we could afford it.

That weekend, we met with the realtor to look at the house. The yard was surrounded by a white fence. We walked through the gate up to a little white wooden house with blue shutters. The small front porch had blue rails matching the blue shutters. The door was the same color blue. *It's precious*, I thought, *like a fairy cottage.*

The realtor told us the story of the house and the neighborhood as we walked around the yard, looking at the exterior of the house. The yard was filled with flower gardens. "It's only had one owner, an elderly couple who purchased it when it was first built. All the houses in this neighborhood were built at the same time and most have had only one owner. Now the houses are finally starting to turn over, since the owners are too old to keep them up. Young couples are moving in. It's a perfect starter home."

I was already in love with the house from the outside, and I worried the inside would be a letdown, but it was just as wonderful inside. It was spotless and had obviously been lovingly maintained. There were three bedrooms, one full and one half-bath, a kitchen, dining room, and living room. There was also a small basement and attic. I walked around each room thinking about what paint color I wanted and picking out wallpaper for the kitchen. I could easily fill my days with this project.

I thought of the old couple who had lived there since they got married.

They must have been happy. I knew this was a house that had been filled with love.

On the kitchen door jamb, I found pencil marks that looked like a kid's growth chart. I looked closely and could see two faint names… Tim and Susie? Something with a T and an S. Tom and Sally? I couldn't quite make it out.

"Looks like they had two children. I wonder why they didn't move in when their parents got old," I mused.

"Goodness. Their children are probably in their forties or fifties by now. I'm sure the kids left long ago and moved away," the realtor replied.

I was going to put roots down in this cottage. And one day, a realtor would be showing another young couple around and talking about us and how happy we were here.

15
Joy

IT WAS A WONDERFUL TIME. I wish we had stayed in our little house forever. When I think back on that house and our lives there, I always smile at the memories.

Frank and I wanted children. Immediately. It was what I always dreamed of. I'd be the best mother on earth. I'd show my mother it was possible to love your children and how love would turn them into wonderful, capable people who could go out in the world, strong and confident. Children who'd never know the loneliness I had experienced.

"In your face, Mother," was going to be my message to the world!

Unfortunately, as often happens, I couldn't get pregnant. We couldn't manage that simple feat people had been achieving for thousands of years. We finally ended up going to a doctor. The first one said, "Just relax. It will happen." Good advice, but the more you wait and the longer it takes, the more difficult it is to relax. And at thirty, I wasn't getting any younger. The dreaded biological clock was ticking, and my fertile years were diminishing.

The next doctor gave us a chart which had the most fertile times of the month marked on it. We were supposed to have sex on those days. Now this became Frank's problem. I couldn't relax and he couldn't perform on demand. As those days drew near, he became more remote and often failed to do the deed on the day prescribed.

After two years of trying to relax and have sex on the right days, we found a third doctor, Dr. Morningweg. I really liked him. He was encouraging and comforting, a kindly grandfatherly type. He gave us the same advice as the others, but he also added some fertility drugs to the situation. And damn if it didn't finally do the trick. I got pregnant with twins! I was relieved it was twins and not quintuplets. Twins were so exciting. I didn't have to worry about my little girls (the ultrasound revealed two girls) never having a friend. They would be born with their best friend. Life could not get any better. I had a wonderful husband, a sweet little house, and I was having two baby girls to love forever.

I lay on the couch, rubbing my ever-expanding stomach, feeling the babies kicking. "Who's kicking now? Is it my little Sophia or baby Olivia?"

Frank laughed. "I thought they were Ruby and Amber? Your precious gems."

I smiled up at him. "I can't decide between princesses or precious gems." My girls were going to have beautiful names. Names they could be proud of and were suitable whether they married a plumber or a prince. Names that would look good on a nameplate on the desk of a CEO or a teacher.

Of course, my mother tried to rain on my parade. When I told her we were expecting, she exhibited a lukewarm enthusiasm. When she found out I was having twins, she was horrified. "You don't know how demanding children are. Having one is exhausting. I don't know how you'll manage with two babies, playing tag team with each other. When you get one asleep, the other will start screaming. Sounds like a complete nightmare."

I bottled up all the things I wanted to say to her, including how on earth could she act like she knew anything about children and how demanding they were. She was strictly old school. Putting kids on a rigid schedule, never responding when they cried or changing their diaper when it was wet or feeding if the baby was hungry, unless it was on the schedule. The idea in those days was to "train" the baby to your life, not to respond to their needs. I had no plans to treat my babies like that.

Frank and I had a wonderful time building our babies' nest. We turned the smallest bedroom into a nursery, painting it pink and putting a teddy bear border around the wall. We managed to get two cribs into the room, along with a changing table and a rocking chair. We had a playpen and two wind-up swings set up in the living room and two highchairs in the dining room. I read every baby book I could get my hands on and spent many happy hours in baby stores shopping for the perfect quilts and accessories.

Once again, the only dark cloud on my happiness was my mother. Frank's co-workers were giving us a baby shower, and I asked my mother if she wanted to be invited. She replied she didn't think so since she wouldn't know anyone there. So, I asked her if she wanted to throw a separate shower for her prospective grandchildren and invite her friends and maybe some of my old co-workers. She informed me it wasn't proper for the grandmother to invite people to an event to solicit gifts from them. I was so confused by her retort, I didn't respond. Isn't that what happens at birthday parties? You invite people and expect gifts?

She never went shopping with me. When she and Dad came over for dinner one night and I was showing them around the nursery and everything we had done, she said, "Don't you think it's a bit much? They won't need highchairs for at least a year."

Frank started bragging about how I had painted and put the border up in the nursery. "Isn't it cute?" he said proudly. My mother's response was something along the lines of how I shouldn't be doing all that while I was pregnant, which was really more a dig at him than a concern for me.

I tried not to let her get me down. It would have been so nice to have someone close, a mother, a grandmother, a sister, or a good friend to share the excitement with, but Frank was over the moon so that was enough for me.

Two weeks before the babies were due, my water broke. I called Frank at work, and he panicked. "Take a cab to the hospital now! Don't wait for me. I'll meet you there." He hung up abruptly.

I called a cab and got to the hospital in fifteen minutes. They took me upstairs and about twenty minutes later, Frank arrived. He looked relieved to have made it on time. He grabbed my hand and kissed me on the forehead. "Soon our babies will be here, and our family will be complete."

Twenty hours later, everything changed; the babies were stressed, and they were going to have to perform an emergency C-section. So much for my dreams of natural childbirth and holding my children right after they were born.

They rushed me into surgery. The last view I had of Frank was him standing in the doorway right before the doors swung shut.

I woke up to Frank sitting in the chair next to my bed. He looked completely drained. There was no joy on his face. I panicked. Where were the babies? Why did he look so sad? "Frank…" I managed to croak out.

He reached over, took my hand, and looked in my eyes. I managed to say, "What? What? Where are our babies? What happened?"

A sob slipped from his lips. "We lost one."

It must have been the effects of the anesthesia because my mind was not comprehending his words. We lost a baby. Where? How? Did they misplace it on the way to the nursery?

"Please. Tell me what's going on."

"We have a beautiful baby daughter. But just one. Her twin… I don't know… I still don't understand… something happened… they waited too long for the C-section… something about the cord…"

"Where are my babies?" I shrieked.

A nurse came into the room and said, "You're awake. Let me get your baby."

Frank laid his forehead on the edge of the bed.

A moment later, the nurse rolled in a bassinet with a beautiful baby inside. One beautiful baby. She reached down and handed her to me. My baby… my baby… my baby….

Dr. Morningweg arrived shortly after. He said he was so sorry and tried to explain. "Sometimes these things happen in multiple births. The cord wraps around the baby's neck and…" He couldn't finish the sentence. She had strangled, waiting to be born. He wiped away a tear. "You have a beautiful, healthy daughter. Don't concentrate on your grief. Focus on the joy."

I could not focus on joy. I sat in bed nursing my baby with tears running off my face, splashing on hers. The nurses got impatient with me as if there was something wrong with my grief. Everyone kept reminding me I had a baby. A healthy baby. Some women leave without a baby at all. I guess I was supposed to forget all about my other child.

The nurses came with my discharge forms and said we had to name the baby before we left the hospital. I looked at Frank. We had picked out two sets of names. Olivia and Sophia, our precious princess CEOs. And Ruby and Amber, our precious gems. Which baby was this? Who died? I looked down at our daughter. She had dark brown hair like Frank. "Sophia or Ruby?" I asked Frank. He looked down, shaking his head. He couldn't even speak.

We finally decided not to use any of the names we had picked. I thought of Dr. Morningweg saying I needed to focus on the joy. We named her Joy. She was our only Joy.

When I got home, I was afraid of all the reminders I'd find of our plans to bring home two babies. While I was in the hospital, Frank had returned all the doubles; now there was just one crib, one bassinet, one swing, one highchair. Just ones. No twos. It was the most loving thing he ever had done. I hugged him and we cried.

Frank accepted the wisdom we should be grateful for the baby we had. I wanted to wear a sign that said, "My baby died." When people said, "What a pretty baby," I could barely respond. I wanted to scream, "There were supposed to be two!"

During the day, I sat on the couch with Joy, feeding her or watching her sleep with tears running down my face. When Frank got home, the house was a mess and there was no dinner waiting. I could tell he was trying to be supportive, but he was tired of my misery. He thought I was being indulgent. "Pull yourself together, Jane. Joy needs you. Stop grieving for what you lost and pay attention to the baby in front of you."

He got angrier and I got sadder. My parents, who had been on a cruise when Joy was born, came over. My mother looked around the house in horror. Her house was always impeccably clean and neat. I looked around through her eyes and was a little horrified too. "Let's open the windows and get some fresh air in here. Smells a bit too much like diapers and stale food," she said, picking up dirty dishes and carrying them to the sink.

My father was quite taken with Joy. However, the first time he spoke to her, for some reason he spoke in a deep voice, saying, "I am your grandfather." His voice scared Joy, and she wailed in terror. It was not a good first meeting.

My parents obviously didn't know what to say about the loss of Joy's twin. I sensed my mother felt awkward because she'd said having twins would be awful. My mother busied herself cleaning and cooking lunch. My father sat beside me, patting my leg. It was the closest moment I had ever shared with either of them.

Before they left, Mom gave me an awkward hug. She patted Joy on her head. "I guess we need to decide what she should call us."

I thought about Mamere saying she never wanted to be called Grandma, and I was sure Mom had the same opinion. "Any thoughts?" I asked. "Grannie?" Mom winced and curled her lip. "Grammie?" That elicited a more disgusted look.

"I'll think about it and let you know," she said as they left.

16
Despair

FRANK'S MOTHER HAD BEEN CALLING since we got home
from the hospital. I heard Frank talking to her on the phone, saying he'd
talk to me about the possibility of her visiting.

When he hung up, he turned to me. "My mom wants to come and see
Joy. I can't keep putting her off."

"Oh God no. I seriously can't take a visit from your mother right now."

"Why not?" he asked in a disgusted tone. "It appears you could use
some help. Either you start pulling yourself together or I'm going to send
her money for a plane ticket. I can't live in this mess anymore."

That was enough for me to straighten up. Or at least to give Frank the
impression I had "pulled myself together." I started getting up early. I'd
feed Joy before going to the kitchen and making coffee. While the coffee
brewed, I prepared breakfast and packed Frank's lunch. By the time he
came down, breakfast was ready and waiting. When he finished, he gave
me a kiss, grabbed his lunch, and headed out the door.

While Joy napped, I frantically cleaned the house, did the laundry, and
prepared dinner. When she woke, we'd sit on the couch. I cried as she watched
me with her dark, serious eyes. "Do you miss her?" I asked. "You spent nine

months sharing a tiny space. I didn't even get to say hello or goodbye."

They hadn't let me see my baby. They were horrified when I asked. They kept telling me it was a bad idea. Even Frank discouraged it. There was a brief ceremony at a cemetery in a place called the Garden of the Innocents where babies who had not survived were buried. A small plaque on the ground with the name "Baby Jones" was all that marked her memory. The day she was buried was bleak and cold with a driving rain. Frank and I huddled together under an umbrella, though we had never been further apart.

Joy was a good baby. She wasn't fussy. She slept a lot. If she woke before I got to her, she lay quietly. Looking back, she was probably depressed too, but I didn't see it at the time. I was simply grateful she was so easy.

Frank thought all was well. I averted a visit from his mother, which was a huge relief. We had only seen each other one time and in my opinion, that was more than enough. She never spoke to me, even if I answered the phone when she called, it was always just, "Oh, hi. Is Frank there?" She didn't even say my name. Never, "Hi, Jane. How are you?"

One time, shortly after we married, she called on my birthday. I thought she was calling to wish me a happy birthday, but she asked for Frank as usual without another word. She had no idea it was my birthday. What kind of mother-in-law doesn't know her daughter-in-law's birthday? Even my mother knew Frank's birthday and dutifully sent a card. Frank announced, while rolling his eyes, "Got my card from your parents."

Eventually, we'd either have to have Frank's mom visit or go see her. I debated which location would be better. If we went to her house, I'd have to see all of Frank's awful family. I finally decided to tell Frank his mother could come to our home for a visit. Being on my own turf would be better for Joy and me, and we'd be spared the rest of the family. I was not prepared for what happened next.

17
A Funeral

FRANK WAS ABOUT TO CALL his mother to tell her to pick a date for a visit when Frank's sister, Carla, called. I could hear her sobbing even with Frank pressing the phone to his ear. He was trying to get her to calm down enough to explain why she called. "Mom's dead," she choked out. Her health had never been great. She was a smoker and a drinker. That morning, Carla had found her stone-cold on the living room floor, dead from a massive heart attack.

Death is never convenient. Frank was upset, though I wasn't sure if it was because of his mother's passing away or because he was going to miss his big presentation at work. He'd been working on it for months and now he was going to have to let his co-worker handle it. "This could have been my big chance. Now I'm going to have to let Jeremy do it and get all the glory," he muttered angrily.

We packed our funeral clothes and all of Joy's accessories and headed back to Frank's childhood home. Luckily, Joy slept most of the way. The silence allowed the guilt to ricochet around my brain. Why hadn't I let Frank's mom visit her granddaughter? Now she was dead and would never meet her. Was Frank angry at me? He hadn't wanted her to come either, but he might be twisting it around and blaming me. No matter how hard I tried to convince myself it wasn't my fault, I still felt guilty.

We stayed at Frank's mother's house. That was a small blessing, since I couldn't imagine staying with Frank's brothers or sister knowing how much they disliked me. But it added to my guilt that I wanted nothing to do with any of them.

Shortly after we arrived, the family descended. Joy launched into a screaming fit, and I couldn't get her to settle. I envied her ability to vent and wished I could have screamed along with her. I didn't blame her. There was a lot to adjust to—a strange house smelling of stale cigarettes, uncontrolled kids running around yelling, and adults coming up, getting in her face, and passing her around like a football.

Carla apparently had been crying non-stop and kept hanging on Frank, who quite obviously did not want to be hugged by her. She sobbed, "Oh my God! What are we going to do? She was the rock of this family." The rest of the family appeared to be over her histrionics.

I tried various facial expressions hoping to find one that wouldn't upset or offend anyone. Smiling was not a good idea. Frowning might make them think I was looking down on them. I tried for a neutral sad, concerned face and hoped I was pulling it off. Of course, no one mentioned the death of our baby. Not one of them had sent a card or flowers.

Joe and Jim once again were trying to outdo each other in the consumption of alcohol. Marty and Susie sat in the corner whispering to each other, and while they could have been talking about anything, like they were glad their mother-in-law was dead, or they were sad their husbands were drunks, or they were tired of Carla's hysteria and drama, I was convinced they were talking about me.

When I couldn't take any of them anymore, I made an excuse to slip off. "I'm sorry, but Joy needs to be changed, fed, and put to bed."

No one said anything to me as I walked out. I hid in the back bedroom until the last person left. Frank came back and asked, "What are you doing? I could have used some support out there."

My mouth opened and closed a couple of times while I considered the best response. I wanted to say I could have used some support too, instead I apologized and said I was sorry, but I had a blinding headache and needed to lie down. Frank stared at me before abruptly turning around, slamming the door behind him, waking Joy, who started crying again. I picked her up and tried to rock her to sleep. Frank didn't return.

The next morning, everyone gathered at the house, and we drove in tandem to the funeral home. I hoped Joy was all cried out and would be her normal, quiet self. There were names already on the guest registry when we walked in. Frank's family members scribbled their names and walked to the front row. Frank walked past the registry, so I stopped to sign it for both of us. The minister waited but it was evident no one else was coming.

It was obvious the minister had never met Frank's mother. "Dorothy Jones was a wonderful mother. She had a kind and giving nature, and all her children worshipped her," he intoned. Frank muttered, "Dot, not Dorothy. No one ever called her Dorothy." And Carla broke into fresh sobs, letting everyone present know her grief was the worst.

At the end of the service, everyone drove to the cemetery. Frank was still not speaking to me. The minister, standing over the grave, intoned, *"Ashes to ashes, dust to dust…"* as he sprinkled dirt on the coffin.

I remembered Father Michael saying the same words over Mamere's coffin. I couldn't help thinking, "that's how we all end up." An image of my little baby, Joy's identical twin, lying in the cold earth, rose up before me, and I had to stifle a sob.

I reached over and took Frank's hand and squeezed it. He gave a quick squeeze back. Was I forgiven? I looked up to see him staring into the distance. I followed his gaze and saw a man in a khaki raincoat standing under a tree. Oddly, my first thought was he was a flasher who came to funerals to expose himself to the mourners before running off.

People began to get in their cars to drive to the house for a gathering. I headed to our car, but Frank wasn't with me. I turned around and saw him talking to the man in the raincoat. Frank appeared angry. The man in the raincoat looked like he was trying to explain something. Frank put his hand up as if to silence the other man, then he abruptly spun around and walked toward me.

"Get in the car." He grabbed my elbow and turned me around.

"Who is that?"

"Later," Frank said curtly, as he walked past me and got in the driver's seat. He sat there staring at the spot where the man had been, while I buckled Joy in her car seat before climbing into the passenger seat. Frank took off before I even fastened my seatbelt.

We were the last to arrive. Frank's mother's small house was full and noisy. People had brought dishes and the family had ordered food trays. As usual, there was more food than people could eat. People kept coming up and introducing themselves to me and complimenting Joy on how good and how pretty she was. The whole day was a blur, and I just wanted it to end.

Around 5:00, Frank said we should be leaving. "We aren't spending the night?" I asked. "It's late and it's a long drive."

"I don't want to spend another minute here. Get your things."

While I packed our bags, Frank said goodbye to his sister and brothers. Even though everyone tried to get us to stay, especially Carla, who continued to cling to him, it was to no avail. Once Frank decided something, there was no chance of changing his mind.

We walked out to the car, and everyone waved goodbye as we drove off. Without so much as a backward glance, Frank snapped, "Thank God that's over. Hopefully this will be the last time I ever have to come here."

My heart pounded. I was shocked by Frank's anger. I saw no evidence of grief or a sense of loss, just a bubbling cauldron of rage. This was a new Frank, and he scared me.

We drove in complete silence for an hour before I finally found the courage to ask Frank about the man at the funeral. "Who was that man in the trench coat? He looked like some kind of weirdo. I thought he might be a flasher."

"Yeah," Frank replied, "he is some kind of weirdo." He was quiet for a such a long time I began to think he wasn't going to say anything else. "That was my father," he finally added in a flat voice.

I was bewildered. Had I misheard Frank when he told me his father had died? I remembered him telling me the story about the ashes on the TV. I couldn't have imagined that. "I thought you told me your father was dead?"

"Yes. I did say that. I guess the truth is more like he was dead to us but not dead to the world."

"What do you mean?"

Frank let out a deep sigh. "When I was little, my father fell in love with someone else and wanted a divorce. My mother refused. It was too humiliating, she said. Instead, she agreed to tell everyone he had died. He moved to another town and started a new life with a new family. I'm not sure if my parents ever divorced or if he was a bigamist. Maybe he and the other woman never legally married. I don't know, and I don't care. My mom got the house. Maybe he sent money for child support, though if he did, it wasn't much.

"About ten years after he 'died,' I saw him at a store. I was shocked. I knew it had to be my father or his identical twin. I went up to him and asked if he was Joseph Jones. He got upset and said, 'No,' and left. I jumped in my car and followed him. He finally pulled into a driveway. I waited until he went in the house to check the mailbox. The name on the mailbox was 'Jones'.

"At home, I found a 'Joseph Jones' listed at that address in the phone book. So, I kind of started stalking him. I'd drive by the house trying to catch a glimpse of him or anyone who lived there. One day, I saw him in the driveway, and I confronted him again. He didn't deny it this time. He took me in the house and told me the whole story."

My mouth dropped open. My brain was not processing what Frank said. If I read this in a book or saw it in a movie, my first thought would have been, "This is ridiculous. No one is going to believe anything so absurd." Yet, my husband was telling me this happened. His father left his mom for another woman, (which is not the part that is hard to believe) and his mother lied to him and his siblings, telling them their father had died. Who does that? I thought of the hurt and anger Frank must have experienced when he discovered the truth.

"Did you ever tell your brothers and sister?"

"God no!" Frank shouted. "How could I tell them their father was alive and had another wife and family? I thought it would be less hurtful if they continued to believe he was dead. It was a blow to me to find out my father cared so little for us. It's not so much of a surprise he left my mother… but his own kids?"

Frank stared out the window, concentrating on the road ahead. He wouldn't look at me. I think he was ashamed.

I reached over and put my hand on his shoulder. "Why did he come today?"

"More unbelievable crap. Apparently, the woman he left my mom for up and took off with someone else. She'd been cheating on him for years and maybe the kids they had together weren't even his. So, he shows up today to ask me if he could be accepted 'back into the family!' Can you believe the nerve of this guy? He thought he could just show up and start over."

"What did you say to him?"

"I told him he'd gotten what he deserved and if he ever showed up again or got within fifty feet of any of us, I'd have him arrested. I threatened to tell the police he had molested and abused us. I said I never wanted to see him again. He's dead to us, and he should stay dead."

Dumbfounded, I stared out the window.

"You know," Frank finally said, "I almost felt sorry for him. He looked so pathetic, but he's just a self-centered jerk."

We drove the rest of the way in silence.

18
Hope

JOY'S BIRTH WAS SUPPOSED TO solidify us as a family. It didn't turn out that way. Frank and I responded so differently to the loss of our baby. I wanted to scream and yell, and Frank didn't say a word. I wanted people to acknowledge the loss of our child, and Frank wanted to forget. We should have talked about it. But we couldn't. I was too emotional. He was too logical. The double emotional blows of Frank's mother's death and the revelation about his father created a chasm between us, and there was no way back.

I was probably suffering from the double whammy of grief along with a case of postpartum depression, an almost unknown ailment back then.

Alone all day, I had nothing to do but think, and I came up with a plan to get us back on course. We were supposed to have had two daughters. I decided the solution to our problem was to have another child as quickly as possible. My plan would give Joy a sister and give us back the child we lost. I thought it was brilliant.

At dinner, I outlined my plan to Frank. I had given it careful thought and explained it, knowing he couldn't help but agree. He stared at me for several minutes as if I'd lost my mind before looking around the house, taking it all in. I looked too. It was a bit of a mess.

"Seriously? You want another child? You can't even manage the child you have, let alone the house and your other responsibilities."

His response hurt. "We're doing as well as we can. I'm sad and I think Joy is sad too."

"Joy is sad? Don't be ridiculous. She's a baby. She needs her mother to take care of her and stop wallowing in grief."

For the first time, I saw another side of Frank. He didn't understand my feelings or care about what I was going through. All he wanted was dinner on the table and a clean house. How can a person move on and forget so easily?

People make foolish decisions. One decision can change lives. A wrong decision can plunge a world into war, poverty, famine, death, and destruction. On a smaller scale, it can change or destroy a relationship.

I made the decision to have another baby. I convinced myself Frank would be happy. He'd appreciate it was the best thing for all of us. Joy would have her sister and I would have my other baby, and all would be right in the world.

I secretly started taking some of my leftover fertility drugs and got pregnant almost immediately. At least I thought I was pregnant. I had all the symptoms, so I called my OB/GYN to schedule an appointment. I told them I needed a pregnancy test. The receptionist was confused. "Mrs. Jones," she said, "are you sure? Didn't you just have a baby?"

After confirming that I had indeed had a baby recently, I reiterated I thought I might be pregnant. They scheduled me for an appointment the next morning. I walked in with Joy in her carrier. The nurse took us back to the exam room, drew a blood sample, and left me alone in the exam room. Fifteen minutes later, Dr. Morningweg came in, shaking his head.

"You're right. You're pregnant." He didn't look happy.

"Isn't it great?" I exclaimed. "Joy will have her sister back. Just like it was meant to be. They'll be less than two years apart." I was sure Dr. Morningweg would share my excitement. He had been there for us through the infertile years up to the moment when he wept by my bedside over the loss of our baby.

"You're happy about this?" Dr. Morningweg asked. "This is not a good idea, Jane. You can't replace a lost child by having another one. Grief doesn't work that way. You need to love and take care of Joy." He glanced down at Joy sleeping in her carrier. "Not to mention, your body needs time to recover."

This was not the reaction I expected. He had always been so supportive and caring. Why was everyone so negative? I wanted to scream. Keeping my voice steady, I said, "I think it's wonderful. And I'm happy. More than happy. I'm thrilled." I got angry. Where was the kind, gentle soul I remembered?

"What does your husband think?" he responded sternly.

"I'm sure he'll be as happy as I am. I haven't told him yet because I wanted to be sure." Nameless Dread curled around my insides.

"You're about two months pregnant. Good luck." I noticed he did not add congratulations. "Make your follow-up appointments when you check out."

Dr. Morningweg's reaction filled me with doubt. I thought he'd be my ally. Now I had to tell Frank. As I cooked dinner, I tried to convince myself Frank would change his mind once he found out I was pregnant. Deep in my gut, Nameless Dread churned.

When Frank got home, I was anxious but also elated. I wanted to burst out with the good news the minute he walked in the door, but I had to wait because Frank always needed time to unwind after work. To take off his shoes, loosen his tie, and have a cocktail.

I decided to tell him during dinner. Momentarily, my resolve failed me. I remembered Frank saying he didn't want any more children. Courage,

I told myself, shaking my head to banish negative thoughts. Sitting up straighter, I told myself Frank might be a little surprised but once he heard the news, he'd be thrilled.

I took a deep breath. "I went to see Dr. Morningweg for my check-up today, and he told me the most fantastic news."

Frank looked up at me from his plate. He was obviously confused, wondering what the doctor's news could have been. He stared expectantly and nodded to encourage me to continue.

"I'm pregnant! About two months! Isn't that great?"

Frank's face hardened into a dark mask. When he spoke, his voice was tight with anger. "Are you kidding me? We talked about this. I said no. I was quite clear. I don't want any more children. Look around—one child is probably as much as you can handle, maybe more than you can handle." He pushed back his chair, threw his napkin down, and stormed off.

I sat at the table, tears running down my cheeks. "He'll come around," I told myself.

He didn't. Not through the next seven months. Not through the birth. Though he came to the hospital when I went into labor, he barely looked at our baby when she was born. He was obviously not interested.

"What do you think of the name Hope?" I asked. "She is my Hope for healing for all of us. Joy and Hope are such positive names."

"Whatever. I don't care. She's yours. Name her what you want," he said and walked out of the room.

What had I done?

Our marriage was ruined. The choice I made caused an irrevocable crack. I crossed the line. Ignoring Frank's feelings completely, I decided to have a baby, which he had quite adamantly told me he did not want.

We might have still ended up divorced. Frank and I were both damaged individuals who probably never should have gotten married in the first place. When we met, it was like survivors from a tragedy who saw a kinship in the other person. But just because you end up in the same lifeboat, it doesn't mean you're destined for a happily-ever-after.

We never recovered from that moment. We drifted further and further apart until we really only shared a house together. The only emotional connection was one of verbal and mental abuse.

I was right about one thing. Hope made a huge difference to Joy. She blossomed overnight. My quiet, serious baby was in love with her baby sister. She insisted on being as close to her as possible. One night, Joy climbed out of her toddler bed and managed to get into Hope's crib. In the morning, I found them in there asleep together.

Of course, Frank went ballistic, claiming Joy would suffocate Hope. I asked him why he was concerned since he didn't even care about Hope. He was obviously disinterested in Hope's existence, so what possible difference could it make to him if she vanished from our lives.

"Do you want to bury another baby?" he replied. "I would have thought one was enough." Before I could answer, he turned and stormed out of the room.

I was shocked and speechless. This was the first time he had mentioned the baby we lost since we had buried her. I decided to build Joy a little cot next to Hope's crib and told her she couldn't sleep in the crib with Hope, but she could sleep next to her. That night, I set her up and showed her how she could put her hand through the bars of the crib and touch Hope. She seemed to understand, and I found her on the cot the next morning with her hand in the crib. This went on for about a week before Joy went back to her own bed.

When Frank saw the cot I made for Joy, he sneered. "That looks like shit. Hopefully it doesn't fall over and injure her."

I had come up with a solution I thought worked for everyone but of course it didn't make him happy. He looked for any excuse to berate me. This became our new pattern. I messed up (in his mind) and he yelled. I quickly learned there was no point in trying to defend myself or explain, because it made him more belligerent. It was easier to bite my tongue. I kept my face blank while I clenched my jaw.

As soon as Hope was old enough to get out of the crib, I put her in the bedroom with Joy. Despite having separate twin beds, they slept together every night. I'd tuck them in to their own beds each night but in the morning, I'd find them together, snuggled up in each other's arms.

Joy was happier but now Hope appeared sad and depressed. Only Joy could make her smile or giggle. Perhaps she sensed her father didn't love her. Sensed her arrival had broken our marriage. It was a lot for a baby to handle.

The pediatrician was concerned about Hope. She worried Hope might be having issues with bonding. I'm having issues bonding too, I wanted to say. My husband has unbonded from all of us and we are free floating without an anchor. I am doing my best. Of course, I merely muttered words of concern and bounced Hope on my knee and spoke to her in a loving tone while she turned away, looking for Joy. I thought having children might finally give me someone to love and someone who'd love me above all others. My children loved each other, and my husband loved his job. I was out in the cold again.

My parents were not supportive. My mother made no secret of the fact she was "disappointed" by Hope's arrival. "I'm sure Joy must feel pushed aside, with a new baby coming so quickly," my mother said.

"Joy is fine. She loves Hope," I said. I was the odd man out, though of course I didn't say it to my mother.

19

Joyless and Hopeless

WHEN FRANK FROZE ME OUT, I tried to make positive changes. I was responsible for the lives of two little girls, and I wanted to make things better for them. Better than my childhood. Better than Frank's crazy childhood. I loved them. Hugged them. Kissed them. In those moments when they were little and depended on me, it was a perfect world. I could almost shut Frank and his negativity out. When he came home at night, I'd paste my fake face on and nod during dinner as he ranted about his job, his boss, bad drivers, stupid people, the world, politics, the weather… anything and everything. The girls and I sat quietly and ate while his words and anger washed over us.

As soon as dinner ended, he went to the den to read the paper. This was the moment the girls and I escaped upstairs. I'd let them play in the bathtub, dry them off, and put them in their pajamas. Then I'd grab a stack of books, and the three of us climbed into bed together. I'd read to them until bedtime. Frank never participated in these bedtime rituals. When I was done with the girls, the dinner dishes would still be piled up in the sink waiting for me. When I finished, I sat with Frank in the living room watching TV until he decided it was time for bed.

My favorite times were when Frank went out of town on a business trip. That was when the girls and I had fun, doing all the things he'd never normally let us do. We didn't clean every day. We built blanket forts in the living room, climbing in there to sleep at night, and read books by flashlight. We had pillow fights and jumped on the beds, falling into a heap, hugging and laughing.

One time he came home earlier than expected and the beds weren't made, several days of dishes were in the sink, and the remnants of our fort were still in the living room. He was furious, barely able to contain his anger as he stormed around, kicking pillows and tossing sheets around. "I come home to unwind after a week of hell at a damned conference, and this is what I find? A mess? A disaster? What do you do while I'm gone?"

I quickly dismantled the fort and handed the blankets to the girls, who ran up to their room to hide. I started washing the dishes and getting dinner ready while Frank stomped upstairs to unpack. As young as they were, Joy and Hope quickly learned when their father was around, they had to behave differently. Their fake masks were already being developed. Sadly, we all needed them to survive.

As the girls got older, they began to draw away from me. They had always been more bonded with each other, and I was often on the outside looking in. Our games stopped. They were too old for blanket forts and stories. They tried to win their father's attention. They figured out fairly quickly where the power in the family was, and it wasn't with me. Their father could grant their dreams—a party, a movie, a new dress. I was kept on a strict budget, so I had no ability to give them anything except things that were free, like love.

I fell into a deep depression. Every day after the girls left for school, I'd crawl under a blanket on the couch. I had finally given up on *The Sandtimer*, since seriously nothing ever happened and turned to reruns of *I Love Lucy*,

Leave it to Beaver, The Andy Griffith Show… the show didn't matter. I sat in my pajamas, unwashed, stuffing my face with Doritos. Mindless eating and mindless watching. I stayed on the couch for hours, not moving or doing anything.

I often thought I should get a hobby. Take up an activity or a craft. Start jogging or throwing pottery. But it was so much easier to tell myself I'd do it the next day. So much easier to watch old TV shows about fictional happy families whose every issue would be solved in the space of thirty minutes.

About two in the afternoon, I'd force myself off the couch and head to the kitchen to bury the chip bag at the bottom of the garbage can. I'd frantically run around cleaning and straightening. A quick trip to the bathroom to brush my hair and teeth and put on a little mascara, blush, and lip gloss, and I was ready to face the world. Looking somewhat normal, I'd walk to the girl's school and stand with the other mothers waiting for the kids.

When we got home, the girls sat at the kitchen table while I prepared a snack for them. When I heard the key in the lock, I put my face on and Frank would find me at the stove finishing dinner preparations and the girls at the table doing their homework.

A perfect Norman Rockwell family.

20

From Bad to Worse

OUR MARRIAGE CONTINUED TO WORSEN. My only hope had been to reach a plateau of indifference where we could manage to live like roommates in the same house, eat meals together, and share mindless tidbits, with no deep emotional connection. Unfortunately, it was not to be. Frank's anger at me grew. I was his whipping post, and he never missed any opportunity, public or private, to humiliate me.

Frank's criticisms were constant. *How can you be so stupid? Are you retarded? Does your mind not work?* He told me repeatedly I didn't know anything. I didn't understand math or science or politics or medicine. I didn't understand anything about psychology, physiology, anthropology, numerology, scientology, or any other "ology."

It was tempting to ask him if he was embarrassed to be married to someone who was so stupid. He had chosen to marry me. Someone so dumb they needed an instruction manual to breathe. Wasn't that more of a reflection on him than me? Apparently, I was born stupid, but he picked stupid.

This constant criticism affected my ability to communicate. I was tongue-tied around the women he worked with and the wives of his colleagues. At a work function, if someone innocently asked, "Jane, what do you think?" Before I could form a response, Frank would sneer, saying, "Jane doesn't have opinions. Her worries are about what to make me for dinner or the best furniture polish to use." Even though everyone laughed along, I could tell they were as embarrassed as I was.

Any time someone asked me what I thought, I'd almost have a panic attack. My throat closed up, the words got stuck, and I felt like I was choking. I might finally get out something like, "Whatever everyone else thinks is fine with me." People stopped asking my opinion. They thought there was nothing going on behind my face. In truth, there was so much going on, so many thoughts and opinions screaming to get out, but I could not give voice to them.

Worse than Frank's meanness was his indifference. Once I fell down the stairs—only the bottom two steps—but it made quite a racket as I tumbled and fell. The kids yelled from the living room, "Mom! Are you okay? What happened?" A moment later, they were beside me, helping me up and assisting me into a chair.

"Dad," Joy said, "Mom fell down the stairs. She's hurt."

Frank barely looked up from the paper. "I assume nothing's broken since she can still walk."

I sat on the chair, rubbing my ankle. "No, nothing broken."

"Your mom should be more careful," Frank said, returning to his paper.

I suspected Frank hated women, which was not a surprise, given his mother and sister. Most of his negative comments about work or the news pertained to women. Women getting uppity, women thinking they could do just as good a job as a man, women who got promotions only because they were women, not because they were smarter than men. And on and on.

It was a cosmic joke, since he was surrounded by women at home. I had hoped having daughters might turn him into a supporter of women's rights, but it didn't. Women were second-class citizens, in Frank's opinion.

Frank made all the decisions about everything in our lives. When he got the big promotion at work he had been hoping for, he immediately decided we should move. I didn't want to move. I loved our little house and my little yard. It was about all I could handle. He had to have a showcase. A place that screamed, "I have arrived. I am successful."

Of course, I wasn't part of the decision. He informed me that he'd already contacted a realtor and told her everything he wanted in a new house. We had an appointment on the weekend to see several houses.

Our realtor drove us from neighborhood to neighborhood, describing in excruciating detail all the positive features of each one. I hated every house we looked at. Our little house was old and charming and had been loved. These places were shiny and new, with no personality. But they had hardwood floors and granite countertops, huge rooms, and a home office for Frank. They were all located in miles and miles of curvy roads and cul-de-sacs with dumb English sounding names like *Oakdale Forest, Dales of Devon, Nottingham Knoll.* No one walked here except to exercise.

Frank finally found the "house of his dreams" which was identical to every house we'd looked at. Since I hated them all, it made no difference to me. We signed a contract on the new house, and I got our old house ready for sale. I looked at the door jamb in the kitchen with Joy's and Hope's height marked on it and burst into tears. Frank found me standing there sobbing and became irritated at "my nonsense," as he put it.

"You amaze me, Jane," he sneered, barely able to conceal his anger. "I buy you a beautiful new house, a house most women would dream of living in, and you stand here in this decrepit cottage crying over nothing."

It wasn't nothing to me.

Before we sold our house and moved, we needed new furniture. It was a repeat of looking at houses. We dropped the kids at their friends, and I followed him while we walked around the store. He told the furniture salesmen exactly what *he* was looking for.

The dining room and living room furniture he picked out was completely unsuitable for a family with children. I finally convinced him to keep the old living room furniture for the family room down in the basement. "You don't want the kids playing out in the living room on the new furniture or doing homework on that gorgeous solid cherry wood dining room table, do you?" He readily agreed he didn't want the children in the living room. They'd be relegated to the family room and their bedrooms.

Joy and Hope cried at first when we told them we were moving. They had lived in our old neighborhood their entire lives. They could walk to their friends' houses. Joy was about to start middle school, which was a difficult time to move and try to make new friends. They also had to give up their clubs and activities. Their whole lives were being upended.

However, when they saw the new house for the first time, they were a bit more enthusiastic. They came running down the stairs, almost colliding into me, excited. "Mommy, did you know we'll each have our own bedroom? And they're so big! Twice the size of the old one we had to share."

"I know." I smiled, trying to be positive for them. "This house is much bigger than our old house."

"Dad says the basement can be our playroom." They took off breathlessly, running into the backyard. They were also thrilled about the neighborhood clubhouse and the pool. "We can spend the whole summer at the pool. This place is so cool." The tears from waving goodbye to their old friends were soon forgotten with the excitement of a pool and having their own bedrooms.

Frank smugly smiled at me.

At dinner, he said to the girls, "You're going to be living in a gorgeous home in a better neighborhood. And you'll be going to a much better school with, I might add, a much better class of people. Of course, it will take a while to make friends, but it will all be worth it in the long run."

On our first night in the new house, I had to go to two different rooms to tuck the girls in. Sadly, they were already getting too big for those childhood rituals. Before going to their separate rooms, I told them the story of when I turned eleven and I had to move and switch schools. I tried to make it sound positive. "I moved a lot when I was a kid. Sometimes every year. It wasn't easy," I said, hugging them each a little tighter, "though it always ended up working out." That wasn't true, but they didn't need to know that.

The girls quickly made friends and settled into their new school. They were far more adaptable than I had been, but they also had each other. I spent my days driving them to school and to their after-school activities. I was the only one who missed our old house and neighborhood.

The women in Oakdale Forest frightened me with their toned flesh, designer clothes, polished nails, and chic haircuts. I could never imagine fitting in here. At soccer practice, the other mothers ignored me. They weren't mean. They smiled and said "Hi" when I showed up before turning back to each other to continue their conversation without including me. I'd sit with a frozen smile on my face and watch the girls play.

When I look back, I see how my failure to make friends was ninety percent my fault. Okay, maybe 100 percent. I could have made attempts to get to know people, to join the group and initiate a conversation. I didn't.

Mom turned sixty when Joy was born and appeared to be in a frenzy to see and do more before she was too old to enjoy life. A "squirrel in a wheel" was how Mamere used to describe her. How would Mamere describe me, I wondered? A "slug on a sidewalk" came to mind. What would she think about how my life had turned out? Less than pleased, I assumed. She had high hopes for me.

"I still go to the library and church," I said to her, looking up to heaven. At least she'd be happy to hear that, I hoped. I loved going to the library and picking out books. During the day, other than cleaning the house and polishing Frank's solid cherry wood dining room table, I read. I had finally weaned myself from my television addiction.

Though we attended church, it did not provide the solace Mamere's church had. Her church had been dark and filled with ancient organ music and mysterious rituals. Frank picked out a church because it was the one most of his colleagues attended. I doubt he believed in God or cared about the service. For him, everything was about appearance.

This church was brightly lit and modern. There wasn't even a cross over the altar. There wasn't even an altar. The minister wore khakis and a polo shirt and walked around the church with a microphone clipped to his collar. He'd sway and dance, jumping around, laughing and joking with people. The prayers and hymns were projected onto a screen so everyone could follow along without having to open an old musty book and try to find the right page. Instead of organ music, there were guitars and sometimes drums. I could see Mamere rolling her eyes, snorting *blasphemy*. I had to agree.

To me, it was another type of club rather than a church but it suited Frank. The girls enjoyed going since Sunday school focused on "fun"! They watched movies and went on camping trips. I was sure Jesus or God were rarely, if ever, mentioned.

We also joined the country club, and after church, Frank golfed with friends. I knew for a fact he thought golf was one of the most insipid games ever invented; however, when he found out his boss and other colleagues played, he professed to love the game. He immediately bought a set of clubs and took lessons, so he could pretend he'd played for years.

Once a month, the girls and I met my parents for brunch. With our recent move, we were only about an hour apart, so we met at a restaurant halfway between us.

The girls called my parents Opa and Mémé. Mom had never gotten around to picking names for the girls to call them. She was determined to ignore the fact she was a grandmother. I was afraid Joy might have to resort to saying, "Hey you," if we didn't settle on something. I knew Mom didn't want to be called grandma, so I suggested the girls call her Mémé since it was French and rather charming. I came up with Opa, for Dad, which I claimed was Norwegian but was really German. They both loved those nicknames.

My parents never warmed to Frank. I hadn't warmed to him either. In fact, we continued to grow further apart. My parents always dutifully asked, "How's Frank?"

Putting a fake smile on my face, I'd answer, "Fine." No doubt they sensed my unhappiness.

I enjoyed seeing them socially. They were more at ease around me now. It made me sad my girls did not have a regular grandmother, who baked cookies, read them stories, and doted on them. Even if Frank's mother had lived, she wouldn't have been that kind of grandmother. She had a heart like a stone. A horrible thing to say, but true.

21
Claire

THE FIRST FOUR YEARS IN Oakdale Forest were hectic as I attempted to navigate Joy and Hope through the dreaded middle school years. My sweet girls completely disappeared, replaced by raging, hormone-possessed monsters. They both became boy obsessed. They fought. They only cared about being popular and wearing the right clothes. Moodiness, meanness, and slamming doors became a daily ritual.

Of course, they saved all their worst behavior for me. They were still smart enough to not inflict their tempers on their father. When he came home, they effectively declared a truce and kept the peace through the evening, since they didn't want to incur his wrath.

Frank only cared about their grades because he wanted them to get into good colleges and have good careers. When report cards were issued, we gathered in the den and Joy and Hope stood in front of their father, like soldiers at attention, before handing him their report cards.

He looked over Joy's first. A smile and a nod meant an A. A short smile with no nod was a B. A C on the report caused a serious frown and a long look at the offender. Joy never had anything less than a B. Hope had the occasional C and got the most frowns. I was worried what might happen if one of her Cs slipped to a D.

It was the same with sports. Joy and Hope were on the same teams, but Joy was a starter and Hope mostly sat the bench. If Frank showed up for a game, he was always full of praise for Joy's performance and quite critical of Hope. On the ride home, he made endless suggestions on how she could improve so she'd get more playing time. Hope withered under his constant criticism. I always tried to make it up to Hope later with a special treat, but she was often too devastated to care.

When Hope was younger, I looked for an activity she could excel in. We tried dancing, gymnastics, karate, swimming—all to no avail. She never stood out in anything. Joy was always better at everything, and Hope wanted to do what Joy was doing. Finally, Joy settled on soccer and Hope followed along. It would've been fine if Frank hadn't been so critical.

When Joy and Hope were finally in high school, a freshman and a sophomore, the emotional rollercoaster of middle school life eased. They returned to their former selves.

Since the girls were more independent, I had time on my hands when I wasn't cleaning house or cooking. I spent what free time I had reading and since Frank considered purchasing books a waste of money, I got books from the library.

One day, as I walked in the main entrance of the library, the door crashed open and a woman fairly flew out. She had her head down, looking at the stack of books in her arms that were slipping, and she collided with me.

The books flew in all directions. "Oh my God, I'm sorry," she shouted as she bent to pick up the books she had dropped. "I should look where I'm going." She laughed loudly as she scrambled about.

I bent down to help. We both stood up at the same time and when our eyes met, we both stopped and stared and said at the same time, "Don't I know you?"

We both agreed the other one looked familiar and after exchanging a bit of information, quickly discovered we lived in the same neighborhood, only three blocks apart.

"Well, neighbor," she said with a huge grin, "how'd you like to grab a cup of coffee so we can chat some more?" I agreed, even though she was the kind of person I generally took an immediate dislike to. She was large and loud, which I usually found completely off-putting, but I was drawn to her. She made me smile.

At the coffee shop, we discovered we had many more things in common. We both attended the same awful church, though I didn't share my opinion about how horrible I thought it was. For all I knew she was friends with Happy the Mindless Minister. She had six children, three of them still at home, two in high school and one in middle school.

As I headed home, it occurred to me I might finally have made a friend. It had been so easy.

At dinner, I mentioned I met someone who lived in the neighborhood and also attended our church. Frank barely looked up from his paper and grunted an acknowledgment.

"What's her name?" Joy asked.

"Claire Fontaine." I loved saying her name. It was the most beautiful name I had ever heard. I blushed with embarrassment, like a teenager in the throes of first love.

"Fontaine?" Hope asked. "I know some Fontaines at school. Does she have any kids our age?"

"Yes," I replied eagerly, "She has about six kids. Two are in high school. One is in the same grade as you."

Frank looked up, rolling his eyes. "About six kids? Is she not certain how many she has? Did she loose count after five?"

"She and her husband Chuck have six kids. Sorry I was so unclear." I spoke slowly, holding in my anger. "One is married, two are away at college, two are in high school, and the youngest is in middle school."

"Sarah Fontaine is a freshman," Joy said. "Isn't she in your grade, Hope?" Hope nodded in agreement. "Her older brother Thomas is a junior," Joy added.

"Oh my God! That Thomas?" Hope chimed in. "Captain of the football team and debate team, president of the student council. He's so good looking."

"Sounds like a lovely family," Frank practically sneered. Then he hesitated. Maybe these people were important. Possibly someone we should cultivate. "What does he do?"

"He's the chief financial officer with the Zenith Group," I replied, knowing it was exactly the kind of thing that impressed Frank.

"We should have them over. Always nice to meet the neighbors," he said, and looked back down at his paper.

I called and made a date with Claire for her and her husband to come over for dinner. "Bring the kids," I said. "They can hang out in the family room. They all kind of know each other. Don't tell Thomas that Hope has a major crush on him." Claire laughed.

At dinner the next night, I informed everyone the Fontaine family was coming over Saturday for a cook-out. Frank nodded, indicating it was fine. I spent the rest of the week frantically cleaning and organizing to perfection. Not so much for Claire, but I didn't want Frank making any rude comments about my lack of housekeeping abilities.

I also was sick to my stomach thinking Frank would hate Claire. She was the kind of woman he claimed he didn't like. She was large. In the diet-obsessed world we lived in, she was probably considered overweight, though in my eyes she was absolutely perfect.

I hoped Frank would like Claire and Chuck. I wanted us to all be best friends.

Saturday arrived and the Fontaines came over at the appointed time, bearing gifts of flowers and a bottle of wine. I could tell Frank was already impressed. The kids acknowledged their connections at school and went down to the family room until dinner.

Claire had toned herself down a bit. She probably did that on meeting people for the first time in order not to completely overwhelm them. Chuck was tall and losing the middle-age battle to fat. He still had a full head of blond hair, and I could tell he had probably once been attractive. However, he was completely bland with none of Claire's magnetism.

I gave Claire a tour of the house while Frank tried to find something in common with Chuck to talk about.

At the end of the tour, she said, "Lovely home. You've really decorated it beautifully."

I rolled my eyes. "That's all Frank. He picked out every piece of furniture and hired an interior decorator to select the lamps and accent pieces."

She was surprised. "Chuck couldn't care less about that kind of thing. He's had the same old chair since our early days. He always says, 'If it ain't broke, don't fix it.' His chair is broke, and he still won't give it up!" She laughed. "He says the chair and I are both old and comfortable, and he isn't letting go of either of us. I guess it's meant as a compliment." We returned to the living room to find Frank and Chuck happily involved in a conversation about sports. Chuck was also a golfer, and they were making plans to get together the next weekend for a round at the country club.

From that moment on, Claire and I were inseparable. We did everything together. Shared everything. Once, I asked her, why me? She could have picked anyone to be her friend.

Of course, she laughed. "You don't give yourself enough credit, sweetie. You have many fine qualities."

"Name one," I joked, though I seriously wanted to know what my fine qualities were.

"To start, unlike most of these skinny rich bitches, you're genuine. Most of them won't give me the time of day cause I'm loud and brassy and 'fat' and have my own style. You don't care about those kinds of things."

True.

"And you're a good listener. Which you have to be 'cause I'm a good talker!" She threw her head back and brayed at her witticism. "No, seriously, you really listen. Most people are only half listening to other people cause they're thinking about what they're going to say next. You think before you speak."

Claire had an amazing zest for life and always suggested activities for us to try. Some of her enthusiasms were short lived, such as yoga ("I'm way too big for twisting myself in knots," Claire said), tennis ("too sweaty," Claire pronounced), and aerobics ("too athletic," Claire declared) but we both enjoyed laying around the pool at the country club, reading and talking.

Claire rarely said "no" to anything. She was always willing to give something a try before passing on it. I was a person who said "no" to almost everything. Even though she didn't end up doing some of the crazier things she suggested, she always thought of things we should do. It made me realize how much of life I had missed by not being open to new experiences.

At lunch, she'd show me brochures and suggest we try skydiving or bungee jumping or some other crazy activity. She'd hoot at my horrified facial expressions. When I made excuses why I didn't think risking life and limb was a good idea, she'd reply, "It's okay, honey. I thought it might be fun. We're not getting any younger. You've got to grab the gusto. You only live once. Don't forget that."

Once she managed to get us all, kids included, to try go-cart racing. At first, she presented it as something the kids would enjoy but when we got there, she got us all in carts. I was a little scared at first, but I began to relax and enjoy myself. I had to admit it was lots of fun. I hadn't laughed that much in years. Even Frank enjoyed the outing.

Another of Claire's passions was "junking," discovering great finds at flea markets and yard sales. When she told Frank about this hobby, I could tell he was flinching, thinking of all the germs.

"Once I got an entire service of sterling silver," Claire crowed. "Some young girl's parents left it to her, and she just thought it was a bunch of old junk. I asked her what she wanted for the whole lot, and she said ten bucks. I scooped it all into my bag. It was worth about five hundred dollars. Cleaned it up and sold it to an antique store. That was my best coup ever." I could tell Frank was intrigued at the possibility of finding a million-dollar painting or a rare gem so he encouraged me to go along, not that I could have spotted a Rembrandt or the Hope Diamond.

If Claire was larger than a perfect size seven, she didn't let it bother her. She wore wild colorful clothes, big jewelry, vibrant scarves with crazy patterns and other attention-grabbing accessories. Wherever we went, she turned heads, especially among men. Men were incredibly attracted to her. She was lush and exuded an air of sensuality. Sex appeal. The Germans have a word for it—*saftig*—which translates as juicy but means so much more.

Many women try to fade into the background when they gain weight. Claire didn't care and it worked for her. I never knew what color hair she might have when we met up. She was always experimenting with anything from blonde to dark purple. She also wore the craziest colors on her nails, sometimes different colors on different hands. She tried to talk me into a wild color once and I demurred, "Frank wouldn't like it."

"Fuck Frank," she said, while I blushed. "They're not his nails." She was loud and often coarse. Something else Frank didn't like in a woman. She had a big, raspy voice and a booming laugh that turned people's heads. She was full of life and joy. So different than me.

She inspired me to step outside my comfort zone. Once, I boldly had my nails done in a deep plum purple. Of course, I chickened out when I got home and immediately sat down and removed the color before Frank saw it.

Her vulgar language emboldened me to develop a bit of a potty mouth of my own—more of a potty mind than mouth since I never said the words I was thinking. When Frank went on and on about something, I'd repeat the mantra, "Fuck you, fuckyou, fuckyou" in my mind to blot him out.

When we drove, if it was raining, I chanted along to the speed of the windshield wipers –

Fuck… you

Fuck… you

And as they sped up:

Fuckyou… fuckyou… fuckyou

And finally:

Fuckity… fuckity… fuckity

Those words were strangely comforting. Once I slipped and spoke the actual word out loud. Suddenly Frank was in my face. "What did you say?"

I stammered. I hadn't thought I had said anything and said so.

"You did. You just said the F-word. You said, 'F-you." His face darkened in anger.

My mouth hung open as I tried to respond. I finally stammered out, "I didn't say that. Have you ever heard me use that word? I said 'thank you'. I hadn't realized I was speaking out loud. I was thinking of what I was going to say to Betty Fiddler. I was practicing my thank you speech for all she did for the girls' soccer team." I looked directly in Frank's face with a look of total innocence, hoping he believed me.

He stood there a minute longer. "Okay. It sure sounded like the F-word, though." I breathed a sigh of relief as he left the room. I decided no more potty mouth or mind. I went back to my old mantra of "shutup, shutup, shutupity uppity up."

Surprisingly, Frank never said anything negative about Claire. Occasionally, he'd grin and say something like, "That Claire is something.

Wonder how she puts up with Chuck. Nice guy, but a bit of a dullard."

He often brought up something she'd said or done and would smile at the memory. I was glad he liked her. He could have made things difficult for me if he didn't. But he was always agreeable when the subject of Claire came up, encouraging our friendship.

He often suggested we invite them over or go out together. We had dinners, went to movies, and played games together. If the game required partners, Claire would announce she wanted to play with Frank. "Husbands and wives playing together is an unfair advantage," she declared. And of course, she got her way.

One morning, I drove Joy downtown to a dentist appointment. I altered my route because of construction on Main Street. As we passed a little café, Joy piped up, "There's Daddy and Aunty Claire sitting at that restaurant."

Before I could turn and look, I had already driven too far. I glanced in my rearview mirror and saw someone who was dressed like Claire sitting at a table with a man. Claire had invited me to lunch, but I had told her I couldn't since I had to take Joy to the dentist. She asked what dentist we used, and I said Dr. Smithers on Main Street.

I didn't think any more about it since I couldn't imagine why Claire and Frank would be at a café together in downtown Denton.

At dinner, Joy said, "We were driving to the dentist today Dad and I saw you and Aunty Claire at a restaurant."

He appeared shocked for a moment before laughing and shaking his head, "You must have seen our identical twins, Joy, because I was in a business meeting all day. I can assure you I was not with Mrs. Fontaine having lunch." Frank glanced at me, shrugging as if to say he couldn't imagine what Joy was talking about. "Did you see these people Joy saw?"

"No. Not really. I was already past the restaurant when she said she saw you. I looked in the rear-view mirror and saw a woman who looked vaguely like Claire, or dressed like Claire, sitting with a man but I didn't really see them very well."

"Maybe Claire was having lunch with someone, but it wasn't me." Frank turned his attention back to his dinner.

Joy looked confused. I agreed with Frank. She must have been mistaken.

The next morning, I thought more about what Joy had seen and became concerned. Was Claire having an affair? Was she having lunch with another man? I believed Frank when he said it wasn't him, but I was sure it had been Claire. Should I ask her who she was having lunch with?

I decided it was none of my business. I knew Claire wasn't cheating on Chuck. She adored Chuck. She might tease him and roll her eyes at some of the things he did, but they had been through so much together. And shared so much, including six children. In the end, I decided if it had been Claire, it was probably completely innocent. She served on lots of committees. It was probably a business lunch.

Our friendship turned into a family friendship. Every weekend we were at the Fontaine's house or they were at ours for a cookout or drinks. The kids hung out together too. It was amusing to watch Hope who continued to have a crush on Thomas. She tried so hard to get him to notice her. Unfortunately for Hope it was unlikely the captain of the football team would be interested in a sophomore. He was always nice to her. He was probably used to the adoration of the female population. I also liked Sarah and the youngest child, Lucy. They were well-mannered children.

Between dinner parties, golfing, and shopping, our kids grew and graduated high school. Thomas played football at Duke, where Chuck had played. The next year, Joy graduated and went to Wake Forest, the same school that had stolen David from me so many years ago. Hope had one more year of high school. She was unsure of what she wanted to do after graduation. She reminded me a little of myself. A bit reluctant to step out into the world. To leave the safety of home.

This was the happiest time of my life. The best part was Frank seemed to have lost interest in being mean to me. The few times he began to criticize me in front of Claire, she'd raise her eyebrows and give him a look and he'd stop. All these clues she had more power and influence over him than I did went right over my head.

Claire and I turned fifty the same year. We celebrated with a big blow-out birthday party and invited all the neighbors, mutual friends, and some of Frank and Chuck's co-workers and their wives, as well as all our kids. Even my parents came. My mother always loved a party.

When Frank went out of town, Claire sometimes spent the night with me so we could have more girl time. Once during one of these sleepovers she asked me if Frank and I still "did the deed." I must have looked confused. "Sex! Are you guys still having sex? I'm wondering because Chuck has kind of slowed down in that department and you aren't that much in love with Frank... so I'm curious."

"If it was up to me, I'd happily skip that activity." I laughed bitterly. "Unfortunately, Frank likes routine so no matter what, we still have sex... I can't say 'make love,' every Friday night."

This news appeared to upset her, which baffled me. Why would she care if we still "did the deed" as she euphemistically referred to it? Was she upset because Chuck apparently couldn't get it up much anymore? Claire quickly changed the subject and we never talked about our sex lives again.

22

The End

WITH MOST OF THE KIDS gone, or old enough to take care of themselves, the four of us decided to go on a vacation to the beach. We'd taken numerous weekend trips together over the five years of our friendship, but this was the first week-long trip. Frank always said Chuck was too dull to spend much time with, so I was surprised when he agreed to go.

We were having a good time, though as the days progressed, Claire behaved rather oddly. She was in a strange, manic mood. Far too happy for a simple vacation at the beach. Smiling constantly and laughing at everything, even a request to pass the salt. Frank was unusually jolly as well.

One evening, Claire wanted to go for a walk. Frank immediately jumped up and offered to go with her. I asked them to hold on because I wanted to go too. I ran upstairs to grab a sweater. When I came back down, they were gone.

Chuck sat on the couch watching some sporting event on television which did not interest me. It didn't matter to Chuck what he watched as long as a ball was involved.

"Did they leave?" I asked, struggling to get my sweater on. "I better hurry and catch up."

Chuck turned. "Yeah, they told me to tell you not to bother, they'd be back soon."

Sitting down, I yanked my sweater off. I was pissed off at them for not waiting. Part of me wanted to run after them but another part decided if I wasn't wanted, I wouldn't go.

A half hour passed, and they didn't come back. An hour later, they still hadn't come back. A quick walk? I thought. Not really. I got up and started washing the dinner dishes to pass the time. I went back to the living room and sat looking at a magazine. Every five minutes, I stared at my watch. I tried to chat with Chuck, but he was too engrossed in his game and obviously did not want to talk.

With a resounding crash, the door flew open, and Frank and Claire came in like they were being blown in by the wind off the ocean. Claire's cheeks were bright red and her eyes were shining. She had an enormous smile on her face. Frank came in with a strange little grin on his face. *Why are they so happy? Must have been a great walk*, I thought angrily.

Before I could pipe up and tell them how upset I had been they'd left without me, Claire said, "Please sit down. Frank and I have something to tell you both."

I sat in a chair next to the couch. Chuck turned a bit to look at Claire though I could tell he really wanted to get back to his game. Claire and Frank stood very close together. He was slightly behind her, and she turned and looked at him and smiled again. He smiled back. I was seriously starting to get annoyed with them.

Claire turned to us, really me, since Chuck was half staring at the TV. She clasped her hands in front of her like she was praying. "This is not easy. We were going to wait until the end of the vacation, but we decided to tell you now." She stopped for a moment and sucked in a huge breath of air. Then she slowly exhaled. "There's no easy way to say this, so I'll just spit it out. Frank and I are in love. We have been in love for a while now. We were waiting for all the kids to get out of high school, but you know, life is short. We want to grab onto happiness now rather than later. Plus, it's not fair to the two of you for us to sneak around behind your backs. We wanted to come clean."

When she said, "we have been in love for a while," the blood drained out of my face. My stomach turned to rock and there was a roaring in my ears. As she kept talking, occasionally looking back at Frank to smile, I lost track of what she was saying. I noticed Chuck had turned back to the game on the television. Part of my brain thought, "Seriously! You can watch baseball at a time like this?"

Her words started coming through again as she explained, "We're going to leave, since obviously it would be awkward now. You two can stay the rest of the week since it's paid for. We'll meet and sort things out when you get home. We're sorry. It wasn't our intention to fall in love. We didn't mean to hurt anyone, but you can't help who you love."

Frank hadn't spoken a word at this point. He hadn't looked at me the whole time Claire talked. He hadn't taken his eyes off her. You could tell he was trying not to smile, that he was trying to look a bit sad and serious but he couldn't help himself. When she finally stopped speaking, he looked at me and said, "As Claire said, life is short and you have to reach out and grab all the happiness you can before the end. I found my soulmate. This is the person I am meant to spend the rest of my life with."

Claire smiled up at him. "Soulmates," she concurred with starry eyes. She looked back at me and Chuck, mostly at me since Chuck still had his back turned. We were obviously not Frank and Claire's soulmates.

They walked upstairs and I could hear them opening and shutting drawers. They came down a few minutes later, muttered some last incomprehensible words along the lines of "sorry," and were gone. After the door slammed shut behind them, I sat there thinking I should have said or done something. I was furious at Chuck for sitting there doing nothing but watching his damn game. I looked over at him and while he was still staring at the TV, tears streamed down his face. Moving over from the chair, I touched his shoulder. He broke into sobs, huge body-shaking sobs, as he said, "I love her. She is my life. What am I going to do?"

There was nothing I could do or say. Eventually, I went upstairs and tried to sleep. I was shocked and devastated, not by Frank's betrayal but by Claire's. She was my friend. I had told her everything. She was the shoulder I cried on when I was upset with Frank. I burned with shame and anger thinking of the two of them lying in bed together and her telling him what I had said to her and of them laughing at me. I winced at the thought. It was bad enough to be put down by Frank, but to know she had betrayed me was too much to bear.

Chuck stayed on the couch. The next morning, I found him still sitting in the same spot. Apparently, he hadn't moved the entire night. He'd stopped crying but looked terrible. I made coffee. We drank it in silence. After a cup, he said, "I want to go home." I nodded. We packed and left. Frank had taken our car, so we drove home in Chuck's.

23
What Happens Now

THE HOUSE WAS EMPTY. HOPE still lived at home but was off at the beach with a friend. Frank was not home, so I was spared the embarrassment of seeing or speaking to him.

Walking into our bedroom, I was struck with a terrible image of finding Frank and Claire in bed together, sheets pulled up over their naked bodies, with sheepish grins on their faces. I shook my head to clear that thought. I noticed an envelope with my name scrawled on it, propped up on the pillow.

I ripped it open to read what Frank had to say. It was typical Frank, presenting the facts and step-by-step plans. All very rational. No apologies.

Jane,

I know you are probably in a bit of a shock, but you have to admit we have not been happy for a long time. This is a chance for both of us to enjoy the rest of our lives.

For all our sakes, I hope we can end our marriage amicably. I have scheduled an appointment with a lawyer on Tuesday morning. I've already shared with him the list of our assets and he will draw up paperwork for a simple divorce with everything split down the middle.

I'm staying at a hotel. You can remain in the house until after the papers are signed. I want to keep the house and buy out your share. I hope that's agreeable with you.

I have asked the girls to meet with us Saturday at noon so we can tell them together what is going on. Once again, I hope we can do this with their best interests in mind.

I hope you can behave like an adult through this process.

Frank

A card with the lawyer's name and address and the date and time of our appointment was also included.

Staying at a hotel? No doubt with Claire, living high off the hog on room service. I should have called him and said, you can come back to the house and put me up in a fancy hotel.

The thought of them together at a hotel threw me into a rage. I stormed around the house screaming, "Fuck you, Frank! Fuck you, Claire! Fuck both of you, lying, cheating, back-stabbing, deceitful, dishonest, double-dealing, phony-ass fucks!" He wanted me to be an adult about it, not for his sake but for the girls? I wanted to break something. I wanted to destroy all his precious lamps and vases and crap he and his decorator had picked out together. I picked up various objects and considered throwing them but as angry as I was, I couldn't overcome years of being a submissive doormat.

Finally, I collapsed on the couch in frustration and sobbed. I bolted upright, struck with the sudden fear my tears might stain Frank's beloved sofa. And they had. Black streaks were smeared on the white fabric. Which brought on a new wave of "Fuck you, Frank! Fuck you and your couch and this house! Fuckfuckfuckfuckfuckfuck YOU!!"

Once again, old habits die hard, so I tried to clean the cushion. It wasn't possible so I just flipped it over. Picking up my suitcase from the bottom of the steps, I carried it up to the spare bedroom, thinking I'd be more comfortable staying in there for the time being. The anger and grief and shame overcame me again, and I fell on the bed and cried until I was too exhausted to cry anymore. I lay there a long time. I was in shock. Finally, I went to the bathroom and splashed cold water on my face. I was restless. Agitated.

I put my pajamas on and went downstairs for a dinner of cereal. When I got to the kitchen, I decided to look in the wine cabinet. I dug around and pulled out a very expensive bottle Frank had been saving for a special occasion. "Well, it don't get more special than this," I said, pouring myself a glass and raising it in a mock toast. "Those are the last damn tears I'm going to shed over you, Fucking Frank Jones and Fucking Claire Fontaine."

I took a sip of Frank's precious wine and began to assess my situation. It wasn't all bad. I no longer had to put up with Frank and his rules, opinions, and his way of doing things. This could be a good thing after all. I had freedom—my invisible chains were snapping off.

I'd only be staying in the house until the papers were signed. Frank wanted his beloved house to live in with his whore. "Oh, sorry. Did I call you a whore, Claire? Well, if the shoe fits." I didn't care about the house. I hated that house. Had hated it from the moment Frank picked it out. I was glad to be getting out.

I poured another enormous glass of wine before I called Chuck to check up on him. He had not recovered one bit from the shock and was still completely stunned and heartbroken. When he told Lucy, his youngest, what happened, she became furious at her mother. I wondered how Joy and Hope would react to our news.

Chuck kept asking, "What am I going to do…?" How could I answer that? I didn't even know what I was going to do. Instead of replying, I asked him if Claire had been in touch about a lawyer. He said yes. She had left a note telling him to be at the lawyer's office on Tuesday. Same law firm, different lawyer. He told me Claire was not at their house, which confirmed my suspicions of them being at a fancy hotel together.

Carrying the wine bottle upstairs with me, I climbed into bed, wondering where I might be sleeping after this week. I overslept and woke up feeling groggy. Opening one eye, I spotted the empty wine bottle on the bedside table. I groaned and rolled over. Was it possible I had drunk an entire bottle of wine by myself? That explained my pounding head and burning stomach.

It took me a moment to remember my husband was divorcing me. Smiling ruefully, I winced from the throbbing pain in my head. The memories flashed back of the plans I had made to get back at Frank. I had fantasied about tossing ketchup on all the paintings he had chosen and taking a bat to all his baubles and figurines. There had also been thoughts of burning Frank's clothes or at least cutting all his precious silk ties in half. Other memories floated back of plans to urinate all over the house and gouge holes in his precious cherry wood table with a butcher knife and slice all the cushions on the chairs.

I stood up. I was a bit wobbly and went to take a shower in the master bath. Walking through the master bedroom, I didn't see any piles of burned or cut up clothing on the floor. Heading downstairs, I happily discovered I hadn't carried out any of my plans for mischief and mayhem. I didn't want Frank to have the satisfaction of accusing me of not "behaving like an adult."

I made a pot of coffee and sat in the kitchen. First, I decided to call my parents. Other than the kids, I had no one else to call. Once again, I felt a stab of pain when I realized I couldn't call my supposed best friend because she was off somewhere fucking my husband. Bitch! Whore! I had to stop and focus.

I considered for a moment never telling my parents Frank and I got divorced. That made me chuckle. It was unlikely my parents would randomly drop by the house since Frank had never made them feel welcome. Years could go by, and they might never know. I could continue to meet them for brunch and say Frank was fine when they asked. However, I was afraid they might run into a mutual acquaintance and feel aggrieved I hadn't informed them my husband had left me. At fifty-some years old, I still worried about my parents judging me.

I wanted to talk to them together, so I didn't have to tell the story twice. It would be hard enough to swallow my pride and tell it once. During the day, my father might be out golfing or my mother might be at one of her clubs or lunches or whatever she did every day. I decided I'd better call immediately since it was still early.

Dad answered, and I asked if Mom was home. He said yes. "Can she get on the extension? I have something to tell you both." Dad called my mom and told her to pick up the phone. When she answered, I took a deep breath and said, "I wanted you both to know Frank and I are separated and in the process of getting a divorce. We're meeting at a lawyer's office on Tuesday."

There was silence on the other end of the phone. Finally my mother said, "I never liked him."

"That's certainly no surprise, Mom."

"He's a weasel. Shifty eyes. Always a giveaway of a weak character."

I sighed inwardly. Maybe I should have listened to her years ago.

"I wanted to let you both know before you heard it from someone else. Also, the girls don't know yet, so please don't say anything to them. We'll be telling them the news together Saturday, after we meet with the lawyer."

"How are you doing?" Dad asked. Before waiting for my response, he added, "Be sure you get him to pay. He has plenty of money. He was good at making money, at least. You'll get the house, I'm sure. The wife always gets the house."

I sighed again. This was not going well. "No, Dad. I'm not going to get the house. Which is completely fine with me. I always hated this house.

Can't wait to move out. Maybe we can get together after we see the lawyer?"

"So, what happened? Has he been cheating on you?" Mom asked, assuming that could be the only reason people our age might get divorced.

"Yes," I replied. "I'm embarrassed to have to admit he has been." I didn't say he had been cheating on me with Claire, my supposed best friend. I couldn't say it out loud. It was too humiliating.

Dad asked more questions which I didn't have the answers to. "I don't know anything yet until we meet with the lawyer. Frank said he wants to split everything down the middle. He wants to end the marriage amicably for the sake of the girls.

"Bullshit," my father said. He didn't curse often so I could tell he was angry. "Don't sign anything until you talk to me." He gave me some words of encouragement and we hung up.

That evening, I dug though the wine cabinet again and found another expensive bottle of wine. I only drank half of it. "See how adult I am acting, Frank?" I said, as I raised my glass in a toast to my absent husband. "You should be happy I haven't burned your damn house down."

Sunday, I went to my parent's. They were being so supportive it made me want to cry. Why hadn't they been like this my whole life? I told them I didn't want to talk about Frank or the divorce until after I saw the lawyer, since I had no answers to any of their questions.

Tuesday finally came and we all arrived at the lawyer's office about the same time. I almost bumped into Claire walking into the ladies' room. It was very awkward. When I came out, I saw Chuck standing outside a door down the hall. I gave him a little wave, and he nodded sorrowfully back.

Frank came around the corner as if he didn't want me thinking he and Claire had arrived together. How stupid was that? We stood in the hall looking at the pattern of the carpet on the floor. A door opened and Frank and I were ushered into a room by a young woman. A tall, distinguished looking man stood up from behind his desk. He had a mane of gray hair and wore an expensive suit. He approached me and shook my hand.

"Hello, Mrs. Jones," he smiled. "I'm Edward Wexstone. I will represent both you and your husband during these procedures. I'm here to ensure everything is done in such a fashion so both of you get your fair share. When your husband called to make the appointment, he implied this would be a no-contest divorce with all assets divided equally?" He said this last bit as a question, as if confirming I would not be making an undue fuss.

Turning to Frank, the lawyer shook his hand and introduced himself as if they had never met, but I had the feeling they knew each other quite well.

We sat down at a table in the office, and Mr. Wexstone began to slide papers in front of us while he explained what each one represented. Frank didn't speak, but I had the sense that he and the lawyer had already gone over everything and Frank had told him how he wanted the meeting to go. He sat there looking stoic and noble as the lawyer presented us with a list of our assets—cars, house, furniture, and money in the bank. As the lawyer talked and handed me papers, I could tell Frank wanted to jump in and take over the meeting, no doubt to get the papers signed quickly.

When this happened, Mr. Wexstone glanced Frank's way, lifting his hand slightly to remind Frank not to speak. He turned back toward me and explained Frank wanted to keep the house and buy me out. Frank also wanted all the furniture and would give me some recompense (depreciated value, of course) for it. He was also letting me keep my car. Wow. He was going to let me keep my car. What a guy.

The lawyer had all the papers already drawn up, showing the facts and figures with what I was being "given" and what Frank was keeping. Frank sat looking very serious while his lawyer explained how generous Frank was being since I had been a good wife and he wanted to be fair.

Pushing over yet another piece of paper, the lawyer explained it was the appraisal on the house. How had he managed to get that done so quickly? Looking down at the figures, I thought it was very low for a house in our neighborhood. He continued talking while I stared at the appraisal. The lawyer went on saying the money in the bank would also be split equally. I could tell by the way Frank curled his lip at that, he didn't think this was fair since he had "earned" it. He acted like he was being magnanimous by splitting it with me. I pushed aside the house papers and looked at the bank statement. I was taken aback by how little money was in the savings account.

"I thought we had more money," I muttered. Frank blurted out I didn't have any idea what it cost to run a household. The lawyer held up his hand again to stop Frank from speaking directly to me.

Looking back at that meeting, I saw what a joke the whole episode had been. Both Frank and Mr. Wexstone deserved academy awards for their performances as concerned decent husband and fair, honest lawyer.

Frank wanted me to sign right there and then. "I want to talk to my father first," I said. I thought Frank might have a stroke. He turned bright red and started blathering something about my father wasn't a lawyer and didn't need to be involved.

Mr. Wexstone held up his hands again. I could tell he was getting a little frustrated with Frank. He looked at me and said it would be perfectly fine if I took a day or two and talked to my dad. He was probably surprised because Frank had no doubt told him I was a pushover and I'd sign the papers without any fuss, but he was smart enough to know yelling at me wouldn't help.

As soon as I left, I went to Mom and Dad's. My dad looked over the papers the lawyer had given me while I helped Mom make dinner.

"Looks like he's been planning this for a while," he muttered as he shuffled through the paperwork. "Something seems off about the amount of money in the bank. There should be more. Wonder if he's hiding money."

"You could be right. I got the feeling he and the lawyer have been working on this for some time, though the lawyer pretended he'd never met Frank before. He made a big show of saying he was 'working for both of us' and had my best interests in mind.

"Frank wants the house and says he will buy me out, so I'll get half the value. Though he did mention he might have to pay me over time. I don't care about the house since I don't want to live there."

My dad looked up with an angry expression on his face. "My advice is to get your own lawyer and pin him to the wall. Make him squirm. Make sure you get a good settlement, alimony and all that. Make him show you all his bank accounts. He probably has the money hidden somewhere. We have a friend here who is a retired lawyer, and he could give you some advice."

"Thanks Dad. But frankly, I don't want to waste any money on a lawyer. I just want my fair half. I also don't want to drag out the process. Apparently, I can't get alimony since the kids are grown. The lawyer acts like Frank is being generous since he's splitting everything evenly. Also, for the kid's sake, I don't want this to turn into an ugly, drawn-out battle."

Dad snorted. "I don't trust that man. Never did. Your mom's right. He's a weasel. At least make sure you get fair market value on the house."

The next day, I called a realtor and asked what houses in the neighborhood were selling for. Frank's appraisal was off by about $75,000. I called his lawyer to say I'd sign the papers, but they needed a new appraisal on the house since the price they had come up with was way too low. That news probably sent Frank into a fresh rage, but I didn't care. I had to take care of myself. As a final blow, I threw in I wanted a clause added to ensure Frank would be responsible for the girls' college tuition.

Two days later, we were back at the lawyer's office. Now that we had reached an "amicable" agreement, I signed the papers. In the end, I settled for half the money from the bank, which was probably nowhere near how much money Frank had. I only had myself to blame since I hadn't paid attention to our finances. Mr. Wexstone also told me I also was entitled to half of Frank's pension when he died, though unfortunately I'd have to wait for that happy event for my payoff. Other than that, I'd get a check each month until I got all the money from my half of the house. I hoped it would cover rent or a house payment. And he let me keep my car.

"We" still had to tell the girls. We planned to meet at the house on Saturday. My occupancy there would end Sunday. I used my last days to pack all my possessions, which were pitifully few. All I had to show after over twenty years of marriage was my clothes, my books, and some personal items that had been boxed up since we had moved to Oakdale Forest. Frank hadn't wanted me to put out any of my "old junk" as he called it.

Frank told me he'd be there at noon, but he showed up early. I thought I had plenty of time and was surprised when I walked downstairs to find Frank already there, sitting with the girls around the kitchen table. Frank had obviously already shared the news with them we were getting a divorce. So, despite his "let's present a united front," he got to talk to them first and give his side of the story, which I'm sure was filled with how he had put up with a loveless marriage for their sake. As Mamere used to say, "God give me strength."

When I walked in, Joy and Hope looked like they'd been crying. Even though we'd never been a typical happy family, no child wants to hear their parents are getting divorced. I wondered if he had also shared the news about Claire. By the time I talked to my girls, I had no story to tell. Joy, after getting over the initial shock, thought it would be good for me. Hope bought into everything Frank said about me and she was happy her dad was going to be able to eke out some small joy in his golden years. Hope's reaction devastated me. It was almost as bad as Claire's betrayal.

Both girls went out to see friends Saturday night, so I spent my last night in the house by myself going through all the rooms. I thought I'd have some happy memories of that house, but none came to me. Early Sunday morning, I made a last pot of coffee and started piling my boxes by the door. Joy came downstairs and helped me carry it all out to the car. I had picked out a toaster oven, a small TV, an old set of everyday china, a set of flatware, various kitchen utensils, and my personal items. I also had helped myself to several bottles of Frank's wine. As I slammed the trunk shut, I thought how pitiful it was I could fit everything I owned into my car. It occurred to me I had nowhere to go and no one to ask for help. My one and only friend would soon be living in my former house with my former husband.

I thought for one crazy moment of going to Chuck's and staying there. Chuck ended up better off financially than me. He didn't have to pay alimony since Claire had walked out or child support since Lucy was staying with him. He also had the support of his children, since they were all furious with their mother for betraying their father. For destroying the family. I quickly rejected the idea of going to Chuck's. Seeing me always upset him.

Standing in the driveway, I tried to figure out where to go. When you haven't been "out in the world" you don't really know how it works anymore. I didn't want to rush out and rent or buy something. I needed time to think. Joy walked up to me with a look of concern. She could tell I was in a quandary. She gave me a hug and said, "Mom, this is a terrible shock, but it's not like you and Dad have been happy together. Ever."

I couldn't disagree. "Oh no. It's just that I'm homeless." Tears sprung to my eyes and I wiped at them furiously. I didn't want to cry in front of Joy. "I'm sorry. I know I'm being pathetic. I don't know where to go, other than a hotel, but that will get expensive."

"Poor Mom." She smiled and hugged me.

Hugging her back, I whispered into her neck, "Thank you." She stood back and looked at me.

"For what?'

"For your support. For your love. For your concern. In addition to everything else, it hurts me so much that Hope has taken her father's side in this and is acting like I'm the one to blame."

Joy shook her head. "Don't worry about that. She has to live here. She kind of has to take his side. And you know that Hope had always been obsessed with getting Dad to notice her."

I thought of that scene long ago in the hospital when he walked out on me and Hope, saying he didn't care about her. I never shared this story with either of the girls. "Poor kid. Maybe she thinks if she's loyal to him during this, he'll finally notice her."

Joy nodded.

"But your father cheated on me. I didn't do anything."

Joy made a face. "I know. And with Aunty Claire. How creepy is that? I wonder how their kids are taking the news. I always got the feeling they all really love their dad."

"It's a sad and terrible thing for you kids. Especially Lucy. Like Hope, she's still living at home." I turned to go.

Joy stopped me. "You need to check into one of those extended stay hotels. They're like mini apartments with kitchenettes and they're fully furnished and best of all, have maid service. You can rent for a week or a couple of months until you decide what to do. And they're more reasonably priced compared to a hotel."

It sounded like the perfect plan. I ended up staying at a Suites hotel for about two months. The first month, I mostly sat on the couch, ate Doritos, and watched TV. It was ridiculous, but I was afraid to go out, worried I'd run into Frank and Claire.

I spent a lot of time obsessing about Frank and Claire. I remembered her asking about our sex life and how she became upset when I admitted we still had sex once a week. She had no doubt been distressed because Frank had probably told her we were finished in that department.

How had they had managed their sex life? We were together almost all the time, either Claire and me or all four of us. Little memories began filtering through. Once a month, Frank had to attend an out-of-town conference. At first, I was happy about it because I thought Claire and I could have a girl's weekend while he was gone. Coincidentally, she had to go that same weekend each month to check up on her aged aunt. She couldn't change the weekend because she divided the care with a few other relatives and she'd been assigned that weekend.

Also, I remembered calling her on a Monday evening and Chuck answered the phone. When I asked for her, Chuck told me she had a library committee meeting every Monday. And Frank always worked late on Mondays. I'd been so dense. I'm sure they had other arrangements.

Other incidents came back to me like the time Joy said she saw Claire and Frank having lunch together and I'd dismissed it. There were so many hints about what was going on, and I ignored all of them. Mostly because I loved Claire and hated Frank and couldn't imagine them together. I laughed bitterly when I remembered how worried I'd been Frank wouldn't like Claire. Well, he liked her plenty. Obviously way too much.

Claire always said life was short and we had to grab all the gusto we could. I wanted to call her and say, "I thought grabbing the gusto meant being adventurous, not being adulterous." I imagined her and Frank grabbing their gusto. Disgusting.

If we all had twenty-twenty foresight, what decisions might we change? People talk about hindsight. What if we were able to see the future every time we were about to make a momentous decision? Would we make the leap? If I could see twenty years into the future when I met Frank, might I have turned around and run? If I could have seen my decision to have Hope would ruin my marriage, would I have still chosen to have her or settled on having only one child?

Yes. I'd do it all again. I would marry Frank. I would have Hope. I would live with a man I didn't love and who didn't love me because he gave me my two greatest treasures: Joy and Hope.

Part
Three

24
Just Me
2006

ONE MORNING, I LOOKED IN the mirror and saw my pale reflection and said, "Enough. Time to get on with your life. Make a plan. One that obviously doesn't include Frank, or that bitch, Claire."

A long time ago, before I was a wife and mother, I'd been a capable person, managing an office for a large firm. I knew about budgets and finances. Time to resurrect my forgotten talents. I bought a ledger and assessed my situation. In the plus column, I recorded the money I had in the bank and the check I received each month from Frank for my share of the house. If I got a new place to live, I had to factor in costs for utilities and a down payment as well. After completing my chart, I calculated how much money I could afford for rent or a mortgage.

First, I needed to decide where I wanted to live. I thought about seeing if the little house we had first lived in might be up for sale, but I quickly rejected that idea. Time to move forward not backward. And in my current situation, the little house would be too large for me. All I needed was a place with two bedrooms and maybe a small yard. The second bedroom was in case one of the girls visited or needed to move in for a while. It still hurt me that Hope had chosen her dad over me. Still, she might wake up one day and finally come to appreciate what a jerk he is.

It suddenly hit me that I didn't want to stay in Denton. Denton had always been Frank's town, not mine. I decided to move back to Bensonville. I'd been happy there long ago. Maybe some of my old roommates and co-workers still lived there.

The girls had bought me a laptop for my last birthday, saying it was time I joined the modern world. I didn't do much on it besides play games. I didn't even have an email account. I had to set up one of those. So much to do in this brave new world. Besides email, I had to get Wi-Fi and a cell phone. Another expense to add to the ledger.

Once I set up the internet, I looked at apartments, townhouses, and condos in my price range in and around Bensonville. I laughed, remembering the "old days" when I had to look in the newspaper to find an apartment. Life was easier in some ways now. I found a few places and noticed the photo of a realtor under one of the listings. She looked to be about my age, and I wondered if she had to work because her husband ran off with another woman. I slapped myself mentally.

I called her because I thought she'd understand my needs. I hoped for some solidarity—women against the male oppressor! We picked a date and time to meet at her office in downtown Bensonville. Driving over from Denton, I arrived at the appointed time, parked in the town parking garage, and walked up Main Street. Since I had been there last, the street had been closed to vehicular traffic, and cafes and restaurants lined either side of the former road. Trees and flowers had been planted. It looked charming. I was happy with my decision to return to Bensonville. Denton's downtown, like so many, had shut down and now all shopping was done at huge malls outside the city center.

The realtor's small office was a one-woman operation. My realtor was every inch the successful businesswoman in her navy three-piece suit.

Her dark brown hair, smoothed back into a tight chignon, had only a touch of gray. She reached out and shook my hand, introducing herself as Vicky Frost. She indicated a seat for me next to the desk and turned her computer screen to face both of us. "We have to decide two things. What are you looking for, and what can you afford?"

I handed her the figures I had worked up. I could tell she was impressed. "Something small," I said. "I'm tired of cleaning a big house. It's just me, and I don't need a lot of space. I want two bedrooms, in case my girls visit. And a porch or a deck or a balcony with a view. I want to be able to sit outside and watch the sun rise or set or whatever it's doing. I don't want a big yard, though I'd like a little bit of ground to putter around in. Plant flowers."

"I like working with a client who has a clear idea of what they want," she said as she typed on her computer. A few moments later, the printer hummed and out popped sheets of paper with possible places. We spent a week looking. When I saw it, I knew I'd found my home. A small townhouse that backed up to a marsh. Maybe it was a swamp and I romanticized it by calling it a marsh, but no one would be able to build behind me and ruin my view. It had a nice patio, and the second floor had a balcony off the master bedroom with a view of the marsh. It had two bedrooms with flowerbeds in the small backyard. There was a homeowner's association fee to take care of the grounds and shared maintenance items such as the heating and AC, but fortunately there wasn't a clubhouse with a swimming pool and tennis courts or other such things which would have added to the expense.

After signing the papers, I waited to hear back from Vicky. A few days later, she called and told me I could take ownership at the end of the month. When the day finally arrived, I packed up my few things and drove to my new place. Vicky met me there. It reminded me of moving into my first little apartment so many years ago. How proud and happy I'd been to have a place of my own. Life had come full circle, and I was ready for it. Whatever it might be.

25

Jane 2.0

TIME FOR JANE 2.0. TIME to own my mistakes. Time to banish Nameless Dread and the Greek choir forever. To accept I'm not perfect. To reach out and say, "Hey, would you like to go for a coffee?" I hoped to be a better daughter and a better mother. My parents didn't have a perfect life either. No one does.

My relationship with Joy had always been good, and thankfully, Hope had started to come around. She sadly realized her father really didn't care about her, he only wanted to turn her against me. I couldn't understand why he needed to stick the knife in deeper. Why couldn't he be satisfied with his new "love," his disgusting large house, and all the money he hid so he and Claire could live the high life?

After I moved into my new place, I kept busy fixing it up. I didn't want to spend a lot on furnishings, since I didn't have a lot to spend. My one extravagance was buying a new bed which I had delivered the day I moved in. It was exhilarating to decorate as I wanted and not worry about anyone else's opinion. I planned to go to yard sales and flea markets and find secondhand furniture. Every time I bought a piece of "junk," as Frank called it, I could see him wince. In your face, Frank! For the first time in a long time, I didn't answer to anyone.

The best thing was finding and opening a box filled with all the old family photographs from Mamere's house. I couldn't believe I had forgotten about those.

I also found a rather sad looking Bear, the beloved companion of my childhood years, a bit worse for wear having spent some twenty years shoved in a box. He got a special spot on my bed after I washed him and fluffed him out as best as possible. I looked at him with great love, and he appeared to smile back with his somewhat squashed up mouth.

I put Mamere's demitasse cups out on a small shelf. They made me smile. Each photo brought back so many memories. I hung those photos, along with the girls' baby and school pictures, in frames I found at yard sales and flea markets. I loved how they looked. It made my new place feel like home. My home.

I got a second-hand couch, which appeared to be brand new, from an online marketplace. Amazing what people got rid of. My first flea market purchase was a beat-up old wooden table, along with a variety of mismatched chairs. Once I got them cleaned and re-stained, I invited my parents and my girls for dinner.

I worried Hope wouldn't show, but she did. We hadn't spoken much. Joy kept me updated. Hope finally packed up and moved in with Joy, instead of living with Frank and Claire. Joy told me it had become awkward for Hope to live there since it became more and more obvious she wasn't welcome. It made me happy Hope and Joy were back together.

Joy had graduated from college with a teaching degree. Of course, Frank was not pleased. She laughed when she told me his reaction. He thought teaching was for those who weren't smart enough to get "real" jobs. Joy didn't let his opinion bother her. She was happy with her choice. Hope considered going back to school to get a degree and had signed up for some classes at community college. Luckily, I had demanded Frank pay for her college if and when she ever went.

Hope gave me a long hug when she and Joy arrived. "I'm sorry, Mom," she whispered in my ear.

"Don't be," I said, hugging her back, remembering her as a tiny child. "I'm happy to see you."

The girls arrived before my parents, and I gave them a quick tour. They lingered over the old family photos, asking about them. They were fascinated by the photos of their grandmother Mémé as a baby, a teenager, and a young bride. Just like me, their favorite was their grandmother as a fairy rose baby.

"These are so wonderful," they both said. Discovering they had a gangster great-grandfather was quite a revelation and I couldn't tell if they were shocked or secretly delighted. They had lots of questions about Mamere and Old Joe. It occurred to me I had never told my girls any stories about them. Why hadn't I shared the stories of my two favorite people with my daughters?

They were both taken aback by the almost hairless, misshapen creature on my bed. "That's Bear. Mamere gave him to me when I was born, so he is quite old and rather worn. And much loved."

"Nice." Joy smiled at Hope, and I could tell they were amused by me keeping my childhood lovie on my bed.

Back downstairs, I said, "This place is small, but it's everything I need. And if you ever need a vacation, there's a spare room upstairs."

"Thanks Mom," they said. It was so good to see them happy and smiling. We walked out onto the patio. "Lovely swamp," Joy commented.

"It's a marsh," I said, feigning haughtiness. "There are all kinds of birds and other animals out there and it's nice to sit and watch them. I put up a bird feeder and enjoy watching all the little birds come and go."

"Do you ever miss our huge house in Denton?" Hope asked.

"God no! I hated that house. Do you remember the house we lived in before that? The little cottage? I loved that place."

"Yes," Joy replied. "What a wonderful house. I have many happy memories of that house and neighborhood."

"Remember the forts we used to make when Dad went out of town?" Hope said, smiling at the memory. "And reading under the covers with a flashlight."

"And walking to school… and the bakery on the corner where they made the best pastries…"

The front door opened, and my dad's voice boomed out, "Hello… anyone home?" Followed by my mother's voice saying, "We're here."

I gave Mom and Dad the quick tour while the girls fixed drinks for everyone. Mom was genuinely surprised and touched by all the family photos I had hung. She paused in front of the one of Mamere and Old Joe I had taken. "I remember you getting this from Mamere's house the last time we were there."

Mom also loved the display of the demitasse cups. "These were one of the few things that your grandmother took from her parent's home when she left. They are probably over a hundred years old. Real family heirlooms."

"Thanks for taking me down to the funeral and back to Mamere's house for one last time." I squeezed my mom's hand.

My mother had the same reaction to my second-hand furniture that Frank would have had. She also liked the finer things in life. I told her I enjoyed my finds. She smiled tightly but said nothing. At least she was trying.

It turned into a lovely evening. After my parents left, I told the girls how I hoped to locate some of my old friends and colleagues. They said the quickest and best way was to search on Facebook. They sat down with my laptop and quickly set me up with a profile.

Joy asked me for the name of one of the people I wanted to find. I told her and she typed the name in under the search function. Luckily, since it wasn't a common name, only a few choices popped up. I looked at each one and said, "That's her." Joy sent a friend request.

"When you hear back from her, you can ask her about other people you both knew and soon you'll have a thousand friends on Facebook."

"I hope not!" I said in horror. "A dozen would be more than enough."

"I'm kidding, Mom."

Joy asked me if there was anyone else I wanted to find from my past. "Any friends from before you started working? Friends from high school? Or middle school? I know you moved around a lot but maybe you remember some names?"

I thought about it. "Truth be told," I finally admitted, "I really didn't have many friends. Actually, any." I sighed deeply. "Seems as soon as I started to make a friend, we up and moved again."

"No one?" Hope asked incredulously.

"In high school, I was kind of in the bottom rung socially. And the few friends I had dumped me when I started dating David."

"David?" both girls said simultaneously, curious about this name from my past.

"Yes. David. My first love. Who, I will add, broke my heart. Took me a long time to recover. In fact, the very next guy I was serious about was your father."

"Let's look him up!" Joy said, her fingers hovering over the keyboard. "Don't you want to know what happened to him? Maybe he's divorced and lonely and looking for love," she added gleefully.

"No, let's not," I laughed. "I don't want him to think I'm stalking him. I'm sure he's happy and healthy wherever he is." I admit it intrigued me to know I could just type in someone's name and they might just pop up on my screen.

"That's it?" Hope said. "No friends at all from when you were a kid?"

"Well…" I slowly said, wondering whether I should bring up her name, "there was someone when I was seven. We were best friends. We were going to grow up and open a stuffed animal store together. And make sock puppets." The girls hooted at that.

"Wow Mom! Didn't know you were so ambitious when you were seven. What happened?"

"What happened was what always happened. Your grandfather got orders and we moved away. We wrote to each other for a year, but it's hard for little kids to keep up writing letters. But… I always wondered what became of her."

"What's her name?" Hope practically shouted. "Let's find her. Your first best friend."

First and last, I thought bitterly. I no longer considered Claire a friend, just the bitch whore who betrayed me.

Hope was still talking. "I hope her name wasn't Susie Johnson or something else where a thousand names will pop up if we search for her."

"No, she had a unique name. Jeannie Gertz."

Joy's fingers were flying as she asked me how to spell Gertz. "And is it Jeannie with a G or a J? One or two n's?"

A half dozen names popped, and I looked them over carefully. "Too old. Too young. Oh! That must be her." I pointed at the fifth name down. "Click on that one."

A profile popped up. The age seemed right, and she still lived in the same town. She looked like an older version of the little girl I remembered.

"Send her a friend request," both girls shouted gleefully. "Right now."

I did. A few days later, she responded and confirmed she was indeed my best friend from way back. She had done a bit more with her life than I had. Married with three children, she was a veterinarian. "I turned my love for stuffed animals into a love for the real thing," she told me.

I told her about my many moves after we parted. I said I had often thought about her over the years. I didn't want to be like, "woe is me,

I did nothing with my life." So, I focused on the positives. My work, my marriage, and my two daughters. I told her unfortunately I just got divorced and was starting over.

She said she was so happy to be back in touch. "With a name like Jane Smith, there was no way to find you. Glad I had a unique name and you remembered it."

Besides reconnecting with Jeannie, I ended up finding a half-dozen people I used to know, and one or two still lived in Bensonville. We made dates for lunch to catch up. I wasn't going to wait for others to reach out first anymore. I remembered what Claire had said. I was a good person. I was "genuine." I cared. I was a person people would want for a friend.

My new resolution was to be the one who said the first hello. To introduce myself. To invite myself, instead of waiting to be included.

Each morning, a group of women walked in my new neighborhood. They wore old sweatpants and t-shirts, unlike the hoity-toity women from Oakdale Forest, who wore the latest workout fashions with designer sneakers and listened to music while they walked or jogged. These women talked and laughed while they walked along at a slow pace.

This was my first opportunity to test my resolve to reach out. One morning, I told myself it's now or never. I got ready before they arrived. Matching their attire—sweats and a t-shirt with a hoodie tied around my waist—I walked out to the sidewalk and stood there, pretending to check out the contents of my mailbox until they approached. I looked up with a big smile and said, "Hi. I'm Jane. I just moved in. I've seen you all walking each morning and wondered if I could join in?"

They smiled agreeably and stopped to introduce themselves while pointing up and down the block to indicate where they lived, and off we went. I joined them almost every morning, which led to invitations to coffee, a book club, and a game night. Half of the women were married, and the other half were widowed or divorced. I had made my first contacts.

Next, I found the local library and asked if they needed any volunteers. Everyone is eager for volunteers and so one day a week I went to the library to shelf and check out books. Made some more friends there. Amazing what you could manage just by smiling and talking to people.

Life was good, so I don't know why getting the final divorce papers affected me so much. All those memories and emotions bubbled up again. Frank's deceit. Claire's betrayal. My past failures. My failed marriage and my failed friendship. I looked at the papers again. "Who cares," I said, holding my head high, trying to "rise above." It worked. I didn't care. I was glad that part of my life was over.

I had learned some lessons about life. Learning about my parents' and grandparents' lives had been shocking. Their stories in many ways turned out to be a legacy of sorrow and unhappiness. Still, they had survived and, in my parents' case, had gone on to build a wonderful life together.

I also learned to deal with my demons and ghosts in more constructive ways. Taking responsibility was a big step. Starting with my daughters, I am owning the things I did wrong and trying to not blame everything on their father. I don't want them to repeat the mistakes of the past generations. At least I gave them lots of love, which I hope will sustain them.

My life had settled into a new pattern, and I could put that chapter officially and legally behind me. Now when filling out official forms, I'll click "divorced" under marital status. In some ways, it's an acknowledgment of failure, but I chose now to consider it a badge of honor. I wonder if I can add, *and happy about it*. Smiling, I threw the papers in the trash. A dramatic gesture.

A moment later, I reconsidered my rash impulse and dug the papers out of the trash, smoothing them out. I should file these official documents away in case I need them in the future.

26
Chuck

THE DAY THE DIVORCE PAPERS arrived in the mail, Chuck killed himself. He locked himself in the car in the garage and started the engine. Lucy found him when she got home from school. On the dining room table sat the opened envelope with the divorce papers.

Maybe I should have called Chuck the day I got my final notice. He had not been doing well. I had tried to keep in touch with him over the last year, calling and suggesting we get together for lunch or dinner. I invited him to my new place, but he always had an excuse not to come. Sometimes he didn't answer the phone or return my calls. Seeing me was just too painful. It reminded him of that moment when his world ended.

His children tried to visit often, and he still had his youngest at home. I'd hoped that would be enough to keep him going. No one really knew how much Chuck loved Claire and how totally devastated he had been by her betrayal. He seemed so unemotional, like nothing ever bothered him. Except when his favorite team lost a game.

He left a note next to the divorce papers that simply said, "I cannot live without her. She was the love of my life. Please forgive me." His children were inconsolable. They hadn't even adjusted to their mother walking out on them and now they had to plan their father's funeral.

His suicide divided the old neighborhood. Most people had been on Frank and Claire's side. After all, most people considered me the neighborhood drudge and probably wondered why Frank hadn't left me years earlier. Claire was so bubbly and lively no one could understand why she'd married Chuck in the first place. While the divorce might be hard on the kids, common thought held that two deserving people had found each other and could now spend the rest of their lives with someone just as wonderful as themselves.

But it's harder to take the side of a woman whose husband has killed himself. No one knew if the ink had completely dried on the divorce, leaving it in doubt whether Claire was a widow or just an ex-wife. Awkward!

The whole thing came to an appalling end at Chuck's funeral. It wasn't at a church, since Frank and Claire had kept membership at the Church of Eternal Happiness with the jumping cheerful minister, so Chuck lost that anchor as well. Even Lucy had stopped attending the youth group events since she didn't want to run into her mother. I was glad I'd never have to go to that church again and listen to the minister's mindless drivel.

Chuck's oldest daughter, Vanessa, was in charge of the memorial. She stood at the front of the room of the funeral parlor, behind a podium, inviting people to share stories about Chuck. Chuck's brother was in the middle of reminiscing about their childhood when Frank and Claire walked in. Chuck's brother stopped in mid-sentence, staring at them with his mouth open in shock. Everyone turned to see what he was looking at and gave a collective gasp.

Frank and Claire had what I guess they thought were sincere sorrowful expressions on their faces as they stood in the entrance. I wondered if they had practiced them in front of the mirror until they decided they were perfect. They were looking for a seat, but the room was packed full.

At the podium, Vanessa stood next to her uncle. A look of complete fury came over her face as she stared at her mother. "What are you doing here?" she demanded. "How dare you! How dare you!" she screamed. The funeral director tried to calm her, but she pushed him away. The other kids got up and they all started shouting, "Get out! You don't belong here. You two are the reason he's dead."

Claire looked stunned, as if it never occurred to her that her children blamed her for causing their father's death. She held up a hand and said, "I'm sorry. I loved your father. We had many good years together. I just wanted to come to—"

She didn't get to finish explaining because Lucy jumped up, ran to her mother, and slapped her across the face. For a moment, I thought Frank might punch Lucy, but he restrained himself. Thomas started down the aisle and hissed at Frank, "Get out. We don't want to see either of you again."

As the other kids advanced angrily toward Frank and Claire, it appeared a free-for-all was about to erupt, but fortunately a few men stood up and got between the two groups. The funeral director walked down the aisle toward Frank and Claire. Taking Claire's arm, he turned her around and led her to the door, saying, "It might be better if you go."

They left. The service never got back on track. None of the children could speak. A few friends got up and said some kind words. There were lots of tears. I had wanted to say something, but as the other half of the Frank dynamic, I decided it would cause more upset. Joy and Hope had come to the funeral with me, and I knew they were completely humiliated to be associated with their father at that moment. We left immediately after the service. I didn't want to go to the gravesite.

I felt guilty about Chuck. Guilty about feeling good about myself and my new life. Guilty I didn't see that Chuck would do this. I certainly never considered killing myself over Frank, but then I hadn't loved Frank the way Chuck had loved Claire. Poor guy.

I hoped to hell Frank and Claire were eaten up by guilt and tormented by what they had done to Chuck and to her children. Was she really happy about trading her life with Chuck and her kids for a life with Frank? How did she feel about her kids disowning her? She deserved it for walking out on them. I wouldn't give up my kids for anything.

27

Tom: My New Man

I WAS QUITE SURPRISED WHEN a new man walked into my life. It's not as if I'd been looking for a new relationship. I was happy living alone.

He had orange-colored matted hair and wasn't very well groomed. I imagined my mother describing him as scruffy. I couldn't figure out his age the first time I saw him. He could have been anywhere from middle-aged to ancient. He had obviously lived a hard life.

He showed up one morning while I was on the patio enjoying my morning coffee. Drinking coffee outside always made me think of Mamere and Old Joe and those wonderful mornings we had shared. It was hard to believe Mamere had been gone for forty-two years. I could hardly wrap my head around that. Sadly, I never knew what happened to Old Joe. It embarrassed me to acknowledge I really didn't know anything about him. He had said he'd never married but he must have had some family. Did he have brothers and sisters? What happened to him after Mamere passed?

That morning, I spied my new man out of the corner of my eye. When I turned to look at him, he vanished. He was very shy. But the next morning, he was back. He stood there looking at me. He looked hungry, and to be honest, kind of sickly. He was obviously homeless. I told myself sternly, "Look away. Don't engage. Don't get involved." But it was not in my nature to ignore a sickly creature.

The next morning, he was back and the look he gave me broke my heart. I could no longer pretend I hadn't seen him. I had to do something.

I went to a pet store later in the afternoon and bought cat food. Voices in my head said, "Don't do it. If you feed him, you'll be responsible for him forever." But I couldn't ignore him. The poor creature was obviously starving.

I looked for him when I got home but there was no sign of him. The next morning, I carried a bowl of cat food and a dish of water outside. I set them a few feet from the corner of the house and waited. He slunk around the house and warily approached the cat food before burying his face in the dish and consuming it all. He looked up at me as if asking for more. "Nope. No more today. It might make you sick." He looked disappointed and turned and disappeared back around the side of the house.

Every morning, he was there waiting for me to fill his dish. I gave him a little more food each day until I finally got to the amount the bag said he needed. "Tom," I said, because I had named him Tom, which was not very imaginative but appropriate since he was very obviously a Tom, "once we get you fattened up, I'm going to take you to the vet and have you checked out."

I didn't know how I was going to accomplish this. I never had a pet and Tom looked like he never had an owner. No doubt he was feral and would tear me to shreds if I tried to pick him up.

When I set out his food in the morning, I moved it a bit closer to my chair. Each day after he ate, he curled up to nap in the sun. He had begun to look a bit better now. Since he was no longer starving, he had the energy to devote time to grooming himself. He was an enormous orange tabby with four identical white paws, a white chest and belly. At least now I could see the white, which formerly had been dirt colored. I thought of Mamere's kitty, the King. This cat was not a king. Definitely a peasant. A homeless peasant.

We developed a routine. He'd come, eat his breakfast, wander over and plop down next to my chair. He didn't talk much but he was a very good listener. I'd tell him my plans for the day and point out interesting things in the marsh. He'd occasionally glance up and reward me with a meow.

To my surprise, one day he hopped up and curled up in my lap. I was a little afraid. Was he just lulling me into a false sense of security before lunging at my throat? His body began to rumble and I tensed, imagining the end.

"This is it! He's growling, getting ready to attack." It finally dawned on me he was purring. I tentatively moved my hand toward him and stroked the top of his head with my thumb. He pushed up against my hand and purred even louder. I smiled. I couldn't stop smiling. "He likes me! He really likes me!" I scratched him under his chin as he purred and pushed his paws into my thigh.

After a couple of weeks of feeding Tom, one of the women in the walking group asked if any of us had seen a feral orange cat around. "He showed up a month or so ago. Looks like he has rabies or some other communicable disease. I'm calling animal control to trap him."

"No!" I almost shouted. Then I laughed to tone it down. "I mean, no… you don't have to call. He's my cat. Name is… Tom. Tom Cat. Ha! I know he looks bad. He ran away for a while but he's back now." I was babbling and everyone looked at me oddly.

"Your cat? Are you sure we're talking about the same cat? This cat looks like he's been through a war or worse. I'm sure he is disease-ridden and covered with ticks and fleas."

"I know he looks bad. I need to get him to the vet. But don't worry, he's up to date on his shots," I lied. "Just needs a bath and he'll be good as new."

They all looked at me doubtfully. I smiled, forging ahead with my ridiculous story. The time had come. I had to capture Tom and make sure he got the required vaccinations. Especially rabies. And a bath would be a really good idea, but I thought cats hated water. How could they bathe him, I wondered? More importantly, how was I even going to get him to the vet?

I went to the pet store again and explained I needed a cat carrier for a reluctant cat. "They're all reluctant," the clerk chuckled. "But put a box inside and let the cat get used to going in and climbing into the box. Cats are crazy about curling up in boxes."

I got the carrier and a box. Tom sniffed around it for a few days and finally went in and curled up in the box. I could hear him purring from my chair. A few days later, after he went in and curled up, I leaned over and shut the door on the carrier. I expected him to go ballistic, bouncing off the sides and yowling, but he just continued to sit in his box. Maybe, just maybe, he wasn't a wild cat. Maybe he had been in a carrier before.

I took him to the vet and explained how I had come to acquire him. They took us in the back and the doctor reached in the top of the carrier, pulling Tom out. The vet looked him over carefully. Tom sat quietly, tolerating the exam.

"I agree Tom is not feral. He's too relaxed around people. Let's scan him and see if he has a microchip." I had no idea what the vet was talking about. He explained many owners and shelters microchipped animals so if they got lost, they could be reunited with their families.

"What an amazing idea," I said.

The vet waved a wand around Tom and got a beep. "He has a chip. Let's send the information in and see where this old boy came from."

I was bereft. What if Tom had a family already and they wanted him back?

The vet went to a computer and clicked on some numbers. "Here's his owner. I'll give them a call." He looked at me, worried about how I'd take this news.

What could I say? "Great. They've probably been looking for him for a long time. They'll be so happy."

He went to another room, and I sat there sadly stroking Tom. "You're going to go home, Tom. Just not to my home."

The vet came back, shaking his head. "Hmmm… that was interesting. I talked to some woman and she said, Tom, who she called Tiger, had been her mom's cat, but when her mom passed away, Tiger took off. I told her we had Tiger here at the clinic. She said she didn't want a cat and hung up. I bet she threw him out into the street and didn't know he was microchipped."

The vet looked at me. "If you want him, he's all yours. I got the name of her mom's vet before she got off the phone, so at least we can see what shots he's had and what he needs."

"That sounds wonderful." I couldn't keep the smile out of my voice. "Meanwhile, can we do something about his fleas?"

When I got Tom home, I took him inside and opened the carrier. He stepped out and looked around the house as if surveying his kingdom. A king after all. He jumped on the couch and settled himself in as if he'd lived there his whole life.

I couldn't wait to tell Joy and Hope about my new "man." They were happy for me. "I'm glad you have someone sharing your life with you," Joy joked.

"You laugh," I replied, "but it makes a huge difference. I have someone to talk to. Share meals with. And watch TV with. I always wanted a pet, but your grandparents were not interested. And with all our moving around, it probably wouldn't have worked out anyway. And your father wasn't interested in getting a pet."

Joy laughed. "Oh my God, yes! I remember when I was six and pestered you guys for a puppy and he said no—quite adamantly. I backed down to a hamster and he flipped out, wondering why anyone would willingly bring a rodent into their house." I grinned at the memory of poor little Joy trying to talk her dad into letting her have a pet.

"Finally, you got me that turtle." I imagined her rolling her eyes at the memory. "I honestly think it was plastic. I don't remember it ever moving. I quickly lost interest in my turtle and one day it was gone."

"I'm sorry, honey. Sorry for your plastic turtle. Now you're on your own, I recommend a cat. Tom is wonderful."

"That's great Mom. Really great."

I couldn't agree more.

28

Life is Good

FOR TWO YEARS, I LIVED happily in my new place, with my second-hand furniture and second-hand cat. The divorce and Chuck's sad death were behind me, and I was living my best life. My relationship with my girls was great and surprisingly, I enjoyed a new relationship with my parents. It had taken a lifetime, but I finally came to terms with my childhood issues.

Mom and Dad were both doing well. Dad had celebrated his ninetieth birthday the year I got my final divorce papers. He looked like he was in his sixties, well, maybe seventies. My mom, in her early eighties, looked better than me. Of course, she'd had those two little facelifts, but even without those, I wagered she'd still look amazing.

To celebrate their sixty-fifth wedding anniversary, Mom and Dad planned on throwing a huge party. I couldn't imagine being married that long. They held the event at the clubhouse of their senior community. Joy and Hope joined us for the celebration. It was wall-to-wall people. Apparently, Mom and Dad were the "it' couple of the senior set. Everyone at the party raved about John and Evie and how happy they were to be their friends. It made me happy for my parents.

At the halfway mark of the party, the band leader tapped on his mic to get everyone's attention and announced it was time for all of us to raise our glasses in a toast to the happy couple. Many people cheered as they toasted. Next, he said John and Evie would be dancing to the song they fell in love to. The band started playing. My father took my mother's hand and led her out to the floor, and they swirled around the floor. My mother's feet floated along not appearing to touch the ground while my father spun her. They were great dancers, moving together as one. But they had spent years perfecting their moves, so it was no wonder they danced so beautifully.

Joy whispered in my ear, "What's their song?"

"*I'll Get By.* That's what Mémé told me."

When Dad finished dancing with Mom, he led me out to the dance floor. Then he danced with Joy and Hope, who were charmed by his old-fashioned dance style.

Joy and Hope came to my house after the party since it was too far to drive home that night. They hadn't been to my place since my last birthday celebration. They walked around, admiring some of the things I had bought and refurbished. "You're getting to be quite handy," Joy said.

"I enjoy sanding, staining, and painting. I've learned a lot from books I've found at the library."

"Why didn't you do this before?" Hope asked.

"Do you think your father would have allowed me to buy junkie old furniture and bring it into his house and make a mess with dust and paint?"

We all laughed, knowing the answer to that question. "In hindsight, I wish I'd developed hobbies back then. It might have helped me feel better about myself if I had creative pursuits." *Instead of sitting around feeling sorry for myself.*

I introduced them to Tom, who glanced up. He regarded them with typical cat indifference before tucking his head under his paw and going back to sleep.

"He's not very interactive," Hope said.

"Maybe not, but he's nice to have around. Of course, your grandmother is appalled I took in a stray cat. She's convinced he's a carrier of all sorts of diseases, from rabies to bubonic plague, and no amount of papers from the vet will change her mind."

Hope shook her head, smiling. "I'm sure if Mémé had a pet it would be something sleek and gorgeous like a greyhound or a cheetah with a diamond collar." We all laughed at the image of their grandmother sauntering around the clubhouse with her pet cheetah on a leash. What would the other seniors think?

Joy asked me again for the name of Mémé and Opa's song. "I want to check out the lyrics," she explained. She typed into her phone. She started reading something and held up her hand to get our attention. "Interesting song. Not what you might call wildly romantic. *I'll get by as long as I have you…* And there's a bunch of stuff about poverty and rain and darkness. Kind of grim." Joy snorted. "It surprises me. I'd have thought Mémé's song would be something more… I don't know… passionate, or at least something that mentioned how beautiful and wonderful she was." We all laughed. "Not just a simple: I'll get by as long as I have you."

"It apparently summed up her feelings about Opa. All she needed was him to get by. I'm sorry to say I never asked her about it. She told me it was the first song they danced to the night they met. Maybe it had nothing to do with the lyrics."

"Did you and Dad have a song?" Hope asked and was immediately mortified for mentioning her father.

Reaching over, I patted her on the leg so she knew I wasn't upset. "No, we didn't. My first boyfriend and I had a song. *Can't Take My Eyes Off of You.* I still love that song. Unfortunately, music was another thing your father never developed an interest in."

Much later, as we sat on the deck staring out at the moon over the marsh, Joy said, "Recently, I was reminiscing about our childhoods. All these memories came back to me. You tried so hard to be a great mom with the forts, reading us books, and playing board games."

I smiled. I had made a difference after all.

"I loved it when Dad went out of town," she continued. "When it was just the three of us. Even when we were little, Dad spoiled every moment. He always seemed angry."

"I'm sorry." I couldn't think of anything else to say.

"Don't be, Mom. You seriously did your best to make sure we had a happy childhood and wonderful memories. When I talked to some of my friends about favorite childhood memories, they were all talking about trips to Disney, and the beach, and their parents buying a boat. I asked them if they had ever made blanket forts and read books by flashlights. They looked at me like I had grown up in a *Little House on the Prairie* episode. They were all sorry for me that a blanket fort was my best memory. I feel sorrier for them." Joy leaned back in her chair, smiling at the memory.

"Mom, you were the best," Hope piped in. "I'm sorry I was such an unappreciative little bitch. Teenagers care more about material things. It's kind of a non-stop competition with your friends to have the right clothes and the right shoes. It's social death to show up wearing the wrong thing."

"So true… kids can be self-centered. You don't really know what's important until you grow up a bit," Joy agreed.

"Yeah. When you're older, and you look back, it's those other things that create the best memories," Hope added.

"We could build a blanket fort tonight and sleep under it if you girls want to relive those happy memories," I suggested.

"I'm not sure it's a good idea for you to sleep on the ground at your advanced age, Mom," Joy said.

Throwing my napkin at her, I shouted, "I'm only in my fifties! I'm young. Look at Opa dancing and playing golf at ninety. You girls will be stuck with me for a very long time."

Despite the fact that we did not sleep on the floor, it had been a magical and wonderful night.

29
A Twist

A MONTH AFTER THE ANNIVERSARY party, my father had a massive heart attack while playing golf. His friends said he complained that he felt a little faint and needed to rest for a minute. He sat down while they continued to tee-up and when they turned back around, they saw him slumped over on the bench. His heart had simply given out. There one minute and gone the next.

Mom called me and said she was at the hospital. "Your father just had a heart attack. He's dead. I'm not sure why they even brought him here."

I was stunned. "Hold on. I'll be right there." Driving over as quickly as I could, I parked and ran around trying to find my mother in the huge building. Where do you go if the patient is already dead? I had no idea. Was he in the ER or had they checked him in? Someone finally directed me to the morgue.

There I found my mother at last, sitting outside a closed-off room. A man in a lab coat stood in front of her with papers in his hand. She didn't seem to be comprehending anything he said. Walking up quickly, I introduced myself. He mumbled the usual platitudes about being so sorry for my loss. I nodded, looking down at the papers.

"I just explained to your mother that we can hold your father's body," my mother winced at the word *body*, "for twenty-four hours, but then it needs to be picked up by a funeral home. Do you know if they had a place picked out?" He ended with a questioning look at me while handing me the papers.

"I don't think so, but I don't know." They'd picked out a cruise, not a funeral parlor. Bending down, I took my mom's hand. "Let's go home, Mom."

A friend had given her a ride to the hospital, so we didn't have to worry about leaving her car there. Parking outside her condo, I walked her inside. After settling her on the couch, I went to the liquor cabinet and poured her a shot of brandy. I poured myself one too. It seemed like the thing to do. She took a sip and shook her head as the liquor hit her throat. She grimaced and swallowed.

My mother, not surprisingly, appeared to be in a state of shock. They had been about to leave on a Mediterranean cruise. Dad's doctor had given him a clean bill of health and told him he'd probably live another ninety years. And then, just like that, he was gone.

"We need to find a place to make the arrangements for Dad." I didn't know how else to start the conversation. "Did you two talk about this? Have you picked a place? Or have any of your friends mentioned a place that does a good job?"

I winced. A good job? What kind of thing was that to say? Still, I thought at their age, many of their friends must have passed away already, so maybe there was a preferred place they all used. Maybe they sat around the clubhouse comparing people's funerals and discussing whose was the best.

"Yes." She took another small sip of brandy. "Your father wants, wanted, to be buried at the military cemetery in Fayetteville, outside of Fort Bragg. There are papers in his desk filed under B for burial. The army will take care of everything."

I settled Mom down for a nap and called the girls. They were still living together, so I only had to make one call. Hope picked up and I asked if Joy was there as well. Hope said she hadn't gotten in from work yet.

"I wanted to tell you both together," I started, "but this is the kind of news that can't wait. Your grandfather passed away today. He died playing golf. They said he had a massive heart attack, and there wasn't anything that could have been done to save him."

"Oh no," Hope said quietly. "How awful." She and Joy had become quite close to their grandfather in the last couple of years.

"I know. It's awful. It's the suddenness. We were all dancing and whooping it up just a month ago."

"How's Mémé?" Hope asked.

"As well as can be expected. She's still in shock. Not sure if she's wrapped her head around it yet."

A little later, Joy called. I told her the same thing I'd told Hope, adding I planned to go through Opa's papers and work out the details about having a funeral at a military cemetery per his wishes. We chatted briefly.

At dad's desk, I pulled out a drawer full of files. I looked under "B" for burial and found everything in perfect order. My father knew how to plan. Suddenly, my grief overwhelmed me. I'd been holding it at bay while taking care of Mom. Now tears and sobs erupted from the deepest part of me. Laying my head down on my arms, I cried until there were no tears left. Sitting up, I wiped my face with my hands before finding a box of tissues on Dad's desk.

I had finally developed a good relationship with my parents. Now my dad was gone, and I'd have no more time with him. Pouring another brandy, I went through the papers he had prepared.

That night, I stayed on the couch in the living room in case Mom needed me. The next day, I made calls. The military took care of everything, arranging for a burial with full military honors. Since the cemetery was two hours away, my mother wanted to have a memorial service at the clubhouse for friends who might not be able to attend the funeral. "Some of these people are quite elderly, you know," she told me. I wasn't sure if she was trying to be funny.

That weekend, we held a memorial at the clubhouse. The same people who had been at the anniversary party were there. My mom had rallied and told everyone this was a celebration of a life well-lived. "John wouldn't want anyone to stand around mourning him. He lived a full and wonderful life. So, let's kick this party into high gear." People stood up and told stories and jokes about Dad. I learned a few things and I'm sure the girls did too, including the fact he was a cut-throat card shark and a practical joker.

A week later, we were at the military cemetery. It was a beautiful day. A bright blue sky with wispy white clouds floating above the trees. "Perfect golf weather," my mother whispered in my ear, smiling. "Your father would be pleased."

We left the chapel, walking behind the caisson that carried the flag-draped casket. A soldier in a full-dress blue uniform led a black, riderless horse in front of the caisson. We were told the empty saddle symbolized a fallen leader. A pair of boots were turned backwards in the stirrups to represent a commander looking back at his troops for the last time. When we arrived at the gravesite, six soldiers carried my father's casket from the caisson to the grave and placed it on a stand. The chaplain said a few words about duty, sacrifice, and love of country. A volley of shots was fired, and a bugler played taps. The flag was folded and presented to my mother. "On behalf of a grateful nation," he said. My mother clutched the flag to her breast. The casket was lowered into the grave. There was not a dry eye among us.

They had a room waiting for us at the Officer's Club on post, where we had a wonderful lunch. Mom told us stories about how she and Dad met and how hard it had been when he went off to war. "I didn't think we'd ever be separated again," she said in a small, sad voice.

We drove home in silence.

I tried to see Mom more often. We'd get together for lunch or dinner or whenever she could fit me into her schedule. She wasn't lonely. Far from it. Her friends included her in everything they did. There were endless invitations to dinners, concerts, plays and other events.

Six months after my dad passed, Joy called to tell me she was moving back to Bensonville to complete her master's degree and eventually her PhD. "My plan, well my hope, is to get my masters and PhD then find a job teaching at a university. Teaching students how to be better teachers, which is my dream job."

I could hardly contain my excitement. My girl was coming home. She'd be right around the corner instead of a couple of hours away. "Is Hope coming too?" I asked. Hope had finally started taking classes at the community college in the same town where Joy lived and taught, though I got the feeling she wasn't burning her way through that endeavor.

"No. She's already signed up for classes next semester. She's moving in with her friend Tyler."

"Is he more than a friend?" I couldn't help asking.

"Not really my place to say," Joy responded, "but yes, he is more than a friend. They're quite serious, in my opinion."

I had met Tyler a few times when I visited the girls, and I liked him. He seemed genuine and caring. It made me glad that Hope had chosen wisely. It had been my biggest fear she'd pick someone like her dad and history would repeat itself.

Joy stayed with me for a week while she looked for an apartment, and I loved having her there. I had secretly hoped she'd move in with me, but I knew she had her own life and I needed to step back.

My life was even fuller now. I visited Mom during the week and on weekends. I also saw Joy some weekends and Hope and Tyler on others. I liked Tyler more and more with each visit, though I refrained from giving my opinion. I worried if I said I liked him, it might be the kiss of death.

Mom carried on valiantly, but an air of sadness enveloped her. If her smile slipped, I could see the sorrow in her eyes. "I wasn't meant to be without your dad." She sighed.

Mom tried in the end to be a better grandmother. It wasn't easy for her. She still gave the girls fashion advice and told them to fix their hair. "They're not little girls anymore," I said, trying to get her to understand her advice annoyed them.

She couldn't stop. She had become too set in her ways. I told the girls to grin and bear it. Mom was also scandalized Hope was living with a "man" without benefit of marriage. "Different world, Mom," I said.

"Why would a man marry you if you're giving it away for free?" she declared. I remembered that being one of the famous Evie pronouncements of the past.

"Because he loves you? Do you think Dad wouldn't have married you if you had sex with him prior to the wedding?"

She sniffed and looked away, refusing to answer.

A year after Dad passed away, I was on my way to my mom's when my cell rang. I answered even though it said "unknown caller" on the screen. "Is this Jane Jones?" a voice asked. I almost hung up since I wasn't interested in renewing my car warranty or getting involved in any other scam. I reluctantly allowed I was Jane Jones. The voice continued, "This is Mercy General. I'm calling to tell you your mother is in the emergency room. She asked me to call and tell you to meet her here."

My stomach clenched. I managed to squeak out a 'thank you' before hanging up. The emergency room? Why? Maybe she had slipped in the shower and stubbed a toe or something simple and the people at the Senior Center called an ambulance out of an excess of caution.

I drove quickly to the same hospital Dad had been taken to when he died and walked into the emergency entrance. It was deja vu all over again. The smells, the sorrow, the fear. "Please God, please God, please God," I said as I approached the information desk. The attendant looked up my mother's name in her computer and directed me to her room. My mother sat on the bed, looking lovely as always, even in a hospital gown.

"What on earth, Mom?" I rushed to her side.

"It's nothing. I felt a little short of breath, so my friend, Edith, insisted on calling 911. Total over-reaction. I'm perfectly fine. I'm in my eighties for goodness sakes! I'm entitled to feel a little faint on occasion."

The doctor walked in before I could respond. He looked down at his computer. A paperless world even in the hospital. "Mrs. Smith, there are a few things here I'm a little concerned about, but overall, you're in good health."

For a moment I thought about my father being given a clean bill of health right before he died. He listened to her chest and back with his stethoscope. "I want you to follow up with your primary care doctor. I'll send him my notes."

My mom thanked the doctor and got dressed. I drove her back to her condo. When we pulled up in front, I started to say something, but she quickly opened the door of the car and popped out. "See, I told you, I'm fine." She blew me an air kiss and walked quickly up the sidewalk.

A month later, I showed up at mom's for a planned lunch get together. I found Mom in the living room. I didn't smell anything cooking and wondered if she wanted to go out to eat. She had told me she really didn't enjoy cooking anymore.

"Hi Jane." She smiled, waving me in and indicating for me to sit next to her. She was nervous, and I began to wonder what was up. "Sit down… I have a bit of news to share."

30
And a Turn

SOMETHING IN MOM'S MANNER TOLD me this wasn't going to be good news. Had she had lost all their money in some stock market scheme or been conned into giving some shyster her social security number and bank account information over the phone? Now she was setting me up to tell me she had to move in with me because she was penniless. Was this going to be the story of Mamere and Louis Fontenot all over again?

I smiled, trying to be positive no matter what she might be about to tell me. "Don't keep me in suspense."

"Why don't you get us both a glass of wine first." Mom waved me toward the kitchen. I felt like a leaf being blown around by the wind. Wine for lunch? The bottle sat on the counter. Maybe this hadn't been her first glass of the day? I poured two glasses, handed her a glass, and sat in a chair facing her.

She took a sip and smiled at me. My anxiety ratcheted up while I waited.

Mom sighed and took another sip of wine. "There's never a good way to start these conversations… so… cutting to the chase… I had the follow up with my doctor, and I guess I'm not at the peak of health. I had a bit of a bout with cancer a few years back. Just some moles and skin things, not a big deal."

My anger meter shot through the roof. My mom had had cancer and never told me. I slugged back some wine to stop from yelling at her. "Mom," I said as calmly as I could manage, "why didn't you tell me this when it first happened?"

"You were going through your divorce from that jerk, and I thought you had enough to deal with. The doctors, at the time, were quite positive they'd caught it early and I would make a full recovery." She gave the Evie Eye Roll. "Easy for them to say. I seriously didn't think anything about it.

"Your father, on the other hand, became completely hysterical. So, for his sake, I did what the doctor recommended. And then your father up and dies!" She laughed bitterly. "Now it's back and the doctor isn't so positive this time."

"What are your options? What are you going to do?"

"Nothing," she said. "I can keep going to the doctor and having the things cut off, though apparently, it's metastasized. I am not interested in chemo. It's fine. I'm ready to go. I don't want to live without your father anyway. I always thought I'd go first, but it's probably better this way. Your father simply couldn't have managed without me. And all the single women here would have torn him apart trying to get him to marry them."

"Nothing?" I squeaked out. "What are you saying?"

"Jane, I'm eighty-some years old. I lived twenty years longer than my own mother did. I've had a fabulous life. I married the man of my dreams, and we stayed in love for sixty-five years. I had hoped to make it to our seventy-fifth anniversary and get a big write up in the newspaper. Well, ten years short. Still, sixty-five is quite an achievement. And we had a lovely party." She smiled sweetly at the memory.

I agreed. "Being in love for so long is quite an achievement. I don't think Frank and I made it to our fifth anniversary still in love," I said, feeling a little sad and a little angry. *Calm down, this is not about you*, I reminded myself.

"Yes. I was lucky. Met the right man. Made the right choice. And we lived the best life ever."

Over the next six months, I spent a lot of time at Mom's. During our visits, she informed me she hoped I hadn't been expecting an inheritance, since they had sunk all their funds into the Senior Center. "They said our funds covered our care from cradle to grave." She snorted. "Not quite from the cradle but the way it works is first you live independently in a town house and as you age, they provide more and more care up to life-support at the end." She sighed and gave a half-hearted eye roll. "Only problem, we had to make a huge buy-in which basically took every cent we had."

"Mom, don't worry, I wasn't planning on getting a big inheritance. Never gave it a thought." Which was true. My parents had always "enjoyed life" so I didn't think they were saving their money for me. I always compared their lives to the fable about the ant and the grasshopper. They were grasshoppers, not thrifty hardworking ants preparing for the future. "I'm quite comfortable. I don't need much. Or anything."

"We did this for you Jane, so we wouldn't end up being a burden on you in our dotage. Nursing homes cost a fortune. We thought this was perfect." She sniffed. "They made out like bandits on your dad and me. Your dad never made it past the townhouse and now all I'm getting is some nursing care. We gave them a small fortune. Unfortunately, there are no refunds or returns if you check out early and don't need all the services." Her eyes teared up for a moment. "I'm sorry, Jane."

"Seriously, Mom, don't be. I'm glad you moved here and enjoyed your lives. In some ways, maybe it's better not to have made it to the life-support phase," I said, hoping to cheer her up. "And the nurses come in and fix meals and take care of you when I'm not here."

"You're right. Probably better this way."

The next time I visited, Mom looked different. While still beautiful, it struck me she didn't have any make-up on, and her hair was combed back and covered with a wide headband.

"Mom! What's going on? Are you feeling okay?"

"Never better," she replied. "I'm so glad not to have to worry about making up each day and making sure my hair is coifed. I feel released from a lifetime of worrying about how I look." She laughed.

"You look beautiful." I leaned over and hugged her. "Always beautiful."

We spent most of our time talking about the past. Her past. And my dad's. She filled me in on the same family stories Mamere had told me, but now I heard them from her point of view, which was a whole different angle.

"I know you think I behaved badly toward my mom. I was angry with her for letting my dad treat me and Stefan so horribly. I knew Stefan killed himself because of the way my father treated him. My mother knew it too. She'd been my only ally and best friend, but when Stefan died, I twisted it in my mind to her not caring enough to stick up for us.

"Something in me died, too. I thought I couldn't ever care about anything or anyone again. When I met your father, I saw him as my ticket away from all of them.

"I felt so proud of my mom when she finally divorced my father, but she went back to him when he got sick and took care of him. It enraged me. I decided never to speak to her again. In our youth, we can be so judgmental. And when she married that gold digger, Louis, I thought she had gotten what she deserved."

Mom lay back on her pillow, exhausted.

When she woke up again, I was there, ready with something to drink or whatever she needed or wanted.

She sat up and I plumped her pillows. I handed her a glass of water and after taking a long sip, she said, "Jane, I want to apologize for not being the mother you needed." When I tried to dismiss her, she held up her hand to stop me. "You know it's true." I couldn't argue with her.

"In my defense, I didn't want children. I knew I wouldn't be a good mother. I only had so much to give, and I gave it all to your father. Your father didn't want children either. He never got over losing his sisters and brother. Finding his mother and the baby dead in bed completely traumatized him. He thought it was his fault, which is ridiculous. He couldn't have done anything. He was a child."

She stopped, indicating she wanted another sip of water. "My mistake was in letting you know you were not a welcome addition. I know you loved your grandmother, and I am glad you got to meet her, but she wasn't perfect."

My mother laughed. "None of us are perfect. Your Mamere was rather self-centered." She paused. "And the apple didn't fall far from the tree because that has certainly been my fault. Your father never saw any faults in me. He saw only perfection. And I tried to be perfect for him.

"I didn't want any distractions. You were a distraction. Plus, I wasn't any good at spreading love around. My heart was only big enough to love one person, and that person was your dad."

Mom shut her eyes and leaned back on her pillows. A few moments later, she began snoring softly.

I thought about Mamere telling my mom that her birth had been a huge disappointment to her father. I guess more than disappointed—disgusted. And about her telling me I wasn't wanted. At least I could say I had never done that to Hope. I never told her my decision to have another baby destroyed my marriage. That was on me. Not on her.

Mom and I had many talks over the next weeks. We talked about Dad. Their early years together, before my unexpected arrival. We talked about the girls. Her granddaughters who she hadn't taken much of an interest in until they got older. I mentioned Hope and Tyler were talking about getting married. "I'm sorry you won't be around to see the girls get married, have children…"

"Me too," she said. "But it's fine. It's not like I've been close to them.

Sadly." Mom looked pensive.

"I'm sorry you didn't find someone like your father to love. I blame myself for that too. Were you too needy for attention and love, I've asked myself? Is that why you settled for Frank, because you thought no one else would love you?"

"Don't blame yourself." I patted her hand. "I'm trying to move past blame. I've blamed everyone for the mistakes in my life. I blamed you and Dad for my miserable childhood." Mom winced and looked guilty when I said this.

"When things soured with Frank, I blamed him. I blamed myself for being such a whiney, wimpy loser. Now I'm living from this day forward. No more blame. When the girls start talking about Frank and the things he did, I try to shut it down. Look at what happened when you blamed your father and mother for the bad things in your life. Did anything good come out of it? You ended up cutting yourself off from your mother for years. It hurt her and you."

Mom quietly reflected on what I said. "I'm sorry now about how I treated her. You brought us back together. At least we were able to talk one last time and I got to tell her I loved her and was sorry for all the years I didn't visit."

When Mom fell asleep, I thought I had one thing at least to chalk up in my win column. I had brought Mamere and Mom back together, if only briefly. I knew it had made a big difference to Mamere. Now I was grateful that we had this time together to talk and say we loved each other.

During one of our last conversations, Mom told me how much she looked forward to being reunited with my dad, Stefan, and Mamere on the other side. I asked her if she thought she'd see her father there, which sent her into spasms of laughter. "That old bastard! I'm sure he's down below. Burning."

Mom took Mamere's solution to her problem. She had already said she did not intend to suffer. When the pain reached a level that it could no longer be controlled with medicine, she took all the pain medication she had left with a big glass of wine and quietly went to sleep. She waited for a night I didn't stay over. I guess she didn't want me to be the one to find her in the morning. The nurse called me early and even though her death wasn't unexpected, it still hurt.

We had another memorial service to conduct at the clubhouse and another funeral at the military cemetery, a simpler ceremony this time— no beautiful black horse, or a twenty-one-gun salute, or even a folded flag. Mom was back where she belonged. Next to Dad. It was another beautiful day with a bright blue sky. I looked at the clouds and thought of Mom and Dad happily reunited.

This time it was only the girls and me at the Officer's Club for lunch. Tyler offered to come, but Hope told him she wanted to spend the day with Joy and me. We shared stories about Mémé. I was sad that the girls hadn't been close to their grandmother. "I loved my grandmother, Mamere, and knowing her made a huge difference in my life. I wish you had a similar experience."

"She didn't make it very easy to love her." Joy sadly shook her head.

"Why did Mémé always act like she had a stick up her ass?" Hope asked.

Joy was obviously horrified, thinking I'd be hurt. "Hope! You shouldn't say things like that!"

I reached over and took both of their hands in mine. "Sadly, it's true. I'm not sure. She was very opinionated. Always. And your grandfather never called her on it. Of course, he thought she was perfect.

"In her defense, she had a hard childhood. She had a terrible father. She lost a brother she loved. Your grandfather had it even worse. He lost his entire family. Sometimes, we don't know the bad things that happened to people. Which is why you should always be kind, even to people who don't seem to deserve it." I smiled at them.

"She was never fuzzy or warm. She thought things should be just so. To her it was more important things were done properly than to worry about people's feelings." I reflected on that.

"I'm glad you weren't that way," Hope said after a while.

"Thanks. I tried not to be. Maybe I'm too much the other way. Too worried about how people feel."

"You can never care too much," Joy said softly. I contemplated her statement and silently disagreed. It was certainly possible to care too much. Especially when you put other people's needs and feelings over yours.

31
Jane the Orphan

*W*AS I AN ORPHAN? I had always been proud of being able to mark *living* when asked about my parents on medical forms. Now I had to check *deceased*.

It shocked me to realize I missed my mom. I never imagined one day I'd say those words. I missed talking to her on the phone every day. I missed our visits. I missed having lunch with her. I missed her telling me stories about her childhood. I discovered my mother had a wicked sense of humor and was a good mimic.

When I packed her things, I was surprised to find photos of me and the girls in her drawers. There were also little gifts that I had given her over the years that I thought she had tossed but were in with the rest of her precious things. The most surprising thing I found was drawings I'd done in elementary school. She had them all in a binder with the year written on the back.

As I grew up, she had become more of a friend. A role she preferred to mother. I had lost so many people I loved. Mamere being the first. My baby girl next and now my mom and dad both gone within the space of a little more than a year.

I missed my girls. I wanted to run to them and hold them and tell them how much I loved them. I wanted to remind them life was swift, and we needed to love each other as much as possible. Even though Joy lived in the same town as me, her studies kept her busy. And Hope had Tyler. I called as often as possible, sometimes simply to say, "I love you. Don't ever forget how much I love you." They tolerated my new obsession and always told me they loved me in return.

I had my friends. My walkers in my townhouse complex. My book club. My lets-do-coffee friends. My old roomies and former work colleagues. Those friendships weren't deep. We weren't "besties" as my girls described friendships when they were kids. I remember Joy once talking about a few of her friends, saying they were all her best friend. I tried to explain best meant only one. She thought about what I said, scrunched up her little face, and finally said, "Nope. They're all my besties." What do they say— out of the mouths of babes. I should have been more open to having lots of besties.

Still, I was determined to be happy and stay busy. I had my girls and Tom. What more could I need?

32
A Bunch of Guys and a Wedding

SHORTLY AFTER MOM PASSED, HOPE and Tyler decided to get married. When Hope called to tell me that Tyler had proposed, I was so excited. I remembered my mother telling me a mother always dreams of the day her daughter will marry. I didn't think my mother really spent any time planning my future nuptials, but I had imagined the day my girls would get married.

Hope wanted a traditional wedding with all the bells and whistles. She and Joy met me for lunch to talk about plans. First, we needed to find the right venue. Apparently, these places booked up as much as a year in advance. They made a list of places they wanted to check out. Then there was wedding dress shopping, bridesmaids' dresses, flowers, food, invitations, decorations—the list went on and on. My head spun considering it all. I thought about my simple ceremony at the courthouse and worried I wasn't up to the task. Which I wasn't. Thankfully Joy was.

Before the end of lunch, Hope dropped a bomb on me. Her plans for a traditional wedding included having her father give her away. I should have seen this coming. She was concerned about how I'd react to Frank being at the wedding. Not only being there but having a central role. I'd been quite surprised when they told me Frank had agreed to pay for a fancy wedding. Now I realized it was because he had a starring role. Even though he had always been tight with money, this would give him an opportunity to show off. He probably wanted to impress Claire and rub it in my face.

"I know you and Dad are not on the best of terms," Hope said tentatively.

I replied, trying to keep the bitterness out of my voice, "We are on no terms. The last time I saw him was during the fiasco at Chuck's funeral."

Hope winced. "I want things to go smoothly at my wedding. I don't want a scene with you and Dad getting into a fistfight at the altar."

I tried to give the Evie Eye Roll as best as I could imitate the master. "You know me better than that. Though I'd like to throw a glass of wine in Claire's face. I kind of always regretted not punching her."

"Mom!" Hope cried. "That's what I'm talking about!"

"Calm down. I'll behave." The thought of seeing Frank and Claire made my stomach clench. "I just wish I could show up on the arm of some gorgeous man, proving I moved on and found someone much better than your father." I smiled at the thought of Frank and Claire looking at me being escorted into the wedding by another man, whispering and wondering who he might be and how I had landed him.

Joy grinned. "You have a year or more to find him. These weddings take at least a year to plan. So, get busy."

We all stayed busy. We found the perfect venue. And the perfect dress. I cried when Hope came out in the most beautiful gown I had ever seen. Happiness transformed her. She wanted one of those sleek form fitting dresses but tried on a simple lace ball gown I picked out. I could tell from the look on her face this was the dress.

Save-the-dates were sent out. Invitations were designed and ordered. Bridesmaid's dresses were tried on and selected. Thankfully the wedding party was small, with Joy as maid of honor and Tyler's sister and one of Hope's friends as the only bridesmaids. I'd been worried there'd be some unmanageable number of people in the party, like eight bridesmaids. It was much easier to have three girls agree on a dress than eight.

After everything was signed and sealed and agreed upon and bills had been sent to Frank to be paid, Joy took me shopping for my dress. "You are the Mother of the Bride. You are also center stage, and we want you to look gorgeous," she said.

"I'd still love to look gorgeous on the arm of a gorgeous man." I grinned at her.

"You had a year to find someone!" she jokingly reproached me.

"You should have figured out by now finding good men is not my strong suit."

"Luckily for you, I found you the perfect guy."

I was momentarily speechless. "You found me a guy?"

"Yes, I did. And he is perfect. Age appropriate. And gorgeous, as requested. He's also Tyler's uncle, so he's part of the family."

"Where did you find this Adonis? And you're sure he's fine pretending to be my boyfriend?"

"He's excited by the idea. He recently got dumped by his lover and wants to help another injured person get their revenge." She grinned. "However, there is one thing about him you need to know."

Oh God, I thought. "What is this one thing? Is he a convicted criminal? Serial killer? What?"

"Mom, don't be so dramatic!" Joy laughed. "He's gay."

"Gay? As in likes guys? Not women?"

"He loves women, but as friends."

"I almost hate to ask… is he obviously gay? Are your father and Claire going to think he's a gigolo I hired for the night?"

Joy burst out laughing, and it took several minutes before she could continue talking. "I can't believe you even said that. No. He is not 'obviously gay,' whatever that means. Do you think Luke, my friend, is 'obviously gay'?"

I thought about it. "No. In fact, when you first introduced me to him, I hoped he was the one!"

"This guy looks like a regular guy except he's very good looking and a good dancer."

"Well, that's a dead giveaway. No straight man can dance."

We both burst out laughing.

❧

A month before the wedding, I rushed out of a coffee shop, almost colliding with a man coming in. We both apologized as we passed, and I stopped and turned to see him turning around too. We stared at each other for a moment.

"Jane?" the man said tentatively.

I looked closer. Oh my God. It was David. He looked good. Of course, his hair was gray, and he had a few wrinkles, but he looked trim and healthy.

"David? Is that you?"

"Yes," he said. "I can't believe I just ran into you here in town. I heard you'd moved away."

I started to answer, but he took my elbow, guiding me back into the coffee shop. "Do you have some time? I'd love to catch up," he said, as he led me over to a table. "Damn, what's it been? Forty years?"

Forty years and my heart still did a little flip flop when seeing him again. But it wasn't a gut punch.

"Yeah, almost that long," I replied, sitting down with my cup of coffee.

We said the usual, you look exactly the same and other lies people tell each other, though in his case it was true. I don't know how good I looked or if I looked the same. My hair had started to turn gray but thanks to Lady Clairol, I covered it. And thanks to good genes, I didn't have too many wrinkles.

We shared what had happened to us both since the last time we had seen each other. He was still (happily I assumed) married to Melissa. They had two sons. One a lawyer and the other one was "finding himself." I nodded. They didn't live in Bensonville anymore. After his father died of a massive heart attack at the age of sixty, David moved to another town and became a prosecutor.

"I always wanted to be a district attorney working for the people." he explained. "Dad shot that dream down. He said the money was in corporate law, which I hated. He was all about the money." I thought about my mom saying years ago David's father was a show-off. "I'm only back in town today and tomorrow. I'm helping my Mom. She's moving to a retirement home."

"That's great you still have your Mom," I said. "I lost both my parents in the last couple of years."

I told David I moved to Denton after I got married. Had two daughters. "My oldest lives here in town finishing her masters and my other daughter is getting married in a month."

I continued telling my tale. "Unfortunately, I'm divorced. It didn't work out. I moved back to Bensonville because there really wasn't anything for me anymore in Denton." I thought back and grinned. "I never liked Denton. My parents were still here. And I wanted to get away from my ex and his girlfriend."

We talked for about an hour, reminiscing about old times and catching up on new ones. He reached over and took my hand, saying, "This has been great. Sadly, I have to run. My mom's waiting. You know Jane, I've thought about you a lot over the years. I know I hurt you and it really bothered me. You meant a lot to me, but I was young and selfish. And my dad kept pushing me to get my degree and go to law school." He sat quietly for a moment, looking at his empty coffee cup. "I've tried not to do that with my sons. My oldest went to law school because he wanted to, not because I wanted him to. And I'm trying to be patient with my other son. I figure pushing will only push him away."

I didn't know what to say. Finally, I responded, "I guess things work out the way they're supposed to. I let the end of our relationship mess me up. I'm coming to grips with a lot of the mistakes I made over the years. My marriage might have been a complete disaster but my girls are wonderful, so I have no regrets."

We were both quiet for a moment when we heard "our" song, *Can't Take My Eyes Off of You*, playing on the café's sound system. Our eyes shot up and our mouths dropped open at the same time.

"Wow," I said, "what are the chances? I haven't heard that song in a million years."

"Me either." David smiled briefly before his smile faded and he looked a little sad. "I'm sorry." He looked like he wanted to say more but couldn't find the words.

"Don't be." I said, patting him on the shoulder. He stood to go, leaned over, kissed my cheek, and left. I touched my cheek and smiled.

When I got home, I told Tom I'd seen my old boyfriend, David. "My first love." Tom looked at me quizzically before turning back to washing his stomach.

"I know. Not very exciting news. Still, I feel good. Like I've gotten closure. I'm glad things worked out for him. He was a good guy."

Two weeks before the wedding, I went out to dinner with Simon, my date for the event. Joy thought we should get to know each other a bit before we pretended to be a couple at the ceremony.

I met him at a fancy downtown restaurant. I walked in and stood waiting for the hostess to notice me. I sensed a presence at my back and turned to see a handsome man smiling down at me.

"Jane?" he asked. "I'm Simon."

"Oh, my goodness. Joy was right. You are gorgeous."

He laughed. "Thanks." He gave his name to the hostess, and we were seated immediately.

We had a wonderful evening. Simon was everything any woman could want in a man. Attentive, funny, a good listener, and he had a great sense of humor.

"I guess it's true," I said at the end of the evening as he helped me into my coat.

"What?" he asked.

"All the really good guys are gay." I joked. "Why? It's not fair."

He laughed. "Not sure why that is. Sometimes I wish I was attracted to women. I like women. I like women a lot more than men most days." He grimaced. "Especially after my recent break-up. What a cad he was."

"Cad? Do people really say 'cad' anymore?"

"I just did. It's a great word. And he was."

We walked outside and he put me in a taxi. Kissing me on the cheek, before he shut the door, he said, "See you at the rehearsal dinner, darling. And remember, we are mad about each other. Simply mad."

The wedding was taking place at a vineyard a few hours away. The rehearsal dinner was planned for Friday night, and the wedding was the next day. The wedding party decided to arrive on Thursday so the guys could have a bachelor evening and the girls were going to have a last night together. The next day, we were scheduled at a spa for massages and mani-pedis. I tried to weasel out because the spa was quite pricey, and my funds didn't allow for such extravagances. I had begun to think I needed to start looking for a part-time job after the wedding.

Joy and Hope knew I couldn't afford the hotel and the spa, so they told me they were covering it all. "Consider it your next ten birthday, Mother's Day, and Christmas gifts. You deserve a special day too, Mom."

I enjoyed being pampered immensely. I decided if I ever had a second go-round at this thing called life, I would go for luxury and pleasure. Fat chance! I better enjoy this one day.

Cocktails were scheduled for 5:00 in a private banquet room at our hotel. At 4:30, I heard a knock on my hotel room door. I'd been putting the finishing touches on my make-up and looking at myself in the mirror for the hundredth time. The thought that I'd soon be seeing Frank and Claire made me ill. Nameless Dread curled around my insides.

"Who's there?" I called out.

"It's me, darling." I recognized Simon's voice. I threw open the door and in case anyone was walking by, I grabbed him and gave him a huge hug while pulling him into my room.

"That was quite the greeting." He smiled wickedly. "We're going to have a lot of fun tonight."

I burst into tears.

He looked stunned, and his smile slipped away into a look of concern. "That's not usually the response I get from either sex."

"I'm sorry, I'm sorry…" I sniffed, trying to wipe away my tears and succeeding in wiping off the makeup I had worked so hard on.

Simon took my hand and pulled me next to him on the bed. "You're worried about seeing your ex? Still hurt? Still angry? Still…?"

"Yes! It's absurd. It's been five years. I should be over it by now. I had hoped never to see him and Claire, that bitch, again. I guess that wasn't realistic given we have children together. I hoped he'd continue to be disinterested in their lives and I could go on happily avoiding him."

"Is it the ex or Claire that has you most upset?"

Simon was very intuitive. "Claire." I sighed. "She'd been my best friend and I loved her. No, adored her. She had been my confidante, my shoulder to cry on, and her betrayal was the worst thing ever. I couldn't stand Frank by then anyway, so no loss there."

I looked down at my hands and twisted my fingers together. The anger began to build again. "It's ridiculous it still upsets me so much."

Simon took both of my hands and held them up to his lips, kissing them softly. "Breath in. Breath out. These two are not worth your time. They should be embarrassed to see you. You are the better person."

I smiled up at him. "You're right. Why do I feel like I'm guilty and not worthy?"

"Tonight, we will make them jealous! Frank will wonder why he ever let you go, and Claire will look at Frank and think, why did I settle for this ugly old guy? Check out that hot new man Jane has!"

He put his fingers under my chin and lifted my face so we were staring into each other's eyes. "But first you need a major repair on that face, girl! And guess what? I'm an expert."

He was. When we walked into the reception a half hour later, fashionably late, I glowed. I looked better than I ever had in my entire life. Simon held my hand, smiling down at me. He did not overplay his role at all. He was considerate and attentive and so obviously besotted with me. "Did you ever act?" I asked. "Cause you're doing a perfect job as my lover."

He squeezed my hand and I looked up, smiling. When I turned away, I saw Frank and Claire not ten feet away. Frank had a bored expression on his face. Claire tried to look like we were still best friends and she couldn't wait to hug me.

Simon whispered in my ear, "It's now or never," while he pulled me forward.

Introductions were made. False declarations of "so nice to see you" and "how have you been" were exchanged. When I introduced Simon, I could see Claire eating him up with her eyes. I knew she was trying to figure out if this was the real deal or a charade.

"So where did you two meet?" Claire smirked, wondering what the story was.

Seeing her again momentarily flummoxed me, but Simon smoothly stepped in. "Tyler is my nephew and we met at a family gathering. I asked for Jane's number right then, but she was seeing someone else." Simon grinned convincingly. "When Tyler told me she'd broken up with that guy, I called immediately. We've been together ever since. Almost two years now, right darling?"

I nodded. "Best two years of my life."

Frank and Claire made some excuses and moved on. "Do you think we fooled them?" I asked.

"Yes! I even believed it." Simon chuckled.

At the rehearsal, my anger bubbled up again when Frank walked Hope up the aisle. "He was no kind of father to her and now gets to play a big role in her wedding."

"Don't give him power over you. This is Hope's day. Focus on her happiness."

I leaned over and kissed him on the cheek. "Good looking and wise. You're the complete package." He kissed me back. I continued, smiling up at him, "And tomorrow we get to check out that rumor that you're a good dancer."

"Oh, I will dance you off your feet."

Seating at the wedding got a bit awkward. Traditionally there is the bride's side and the groom's side. But where does the ex-wife sit even if she is the mother of the bride? Simon said, "You sit in the front row on the bride's side. You're the mother of the bride and you get the best seat in the house."

The usher walked me up first and I took the front row aisle seat. Simon joined me and sat to my left. A moment later, Claire walked up the aisle escorted by one of the groomsmen. When she got to the front row, she stopped and stared at me as if demanding I move over and give pride of place to her. I stared at her before nonchalantly turning away. My heart pounded so hard I thought it might drown out the organ music. She stepped past me and sat a few seats away from Simon.

The music swelled and Hope came down on Frank's arm. She was a dream in her white lace ball gown. Tyler wiped away a tear. After Frank replied to the minister declaring he was giving the bride away, he turned to sit down. He noticed I had claimed the best seat. He shot a blistering look at me before walking by and sitting stonily next to Claire. Simon took that moment to nuzzle my neck and whisper, "Ha, screw 'em."

The wedding was beautiful. Hope was beautiful. I blocked Frank from my heart and mind. Simon leaned over and wiped away my tears. I prayed fervently Tyler would love and cherish Hope. And he would make her laugh. Mostly, I prayed he would be kind. Kindness is underrated and in short supply in the world.

At the reception, we all cheered when the new Mr. and Mrs. Tyler Slate walked in. Once again, I had to bite back my anger when Hope had the first dance with her father and Tyler danced with his mother. Simon had his arm around my waist and tickled my side. "Smile darling. Remember that man and his concubine mean nothing to you." I laughed out loud. What kind of man says things like cad and concubine?

We had a fabulous dinner and champagne toasts. Fortunately, Frank's speech was short. I wanted to shout, "He really barely knows his daughter, which is why he doesn't have much to say." Remembering my promise to Hope, I kept quiet.

The band started up in earnest, since they had only been playing background music. As promised, Simon danced my feet off. I looked gleefully at Claire next to Frank. She tapped her feet and swayed in time to the music, obviously wanting to dance. I remembered she and Chuck had loved to dance together. Frank hated music and dancing. Claire only got to dance once or twice when some of the younger guys asked her. Even Tyler asked her to dance. I suspected Hope had suggested it to him.

Simon swung me into a tight embrace at the end of a song and whispered in my ear, "Methinks there is trouble in paradise. The soulmates look decidedly unhappy."

I glanced over at Frank and Claire and noticed her looking quite glum. Frank looked like he'd rather be anywhere than here. "As you said earlier, screw 'em," I whispered. Frank and Claire had never married. He probably didn't want to have to go through a divorce again and split his assets. Much easier to make a quick exit. He could change the locks on the doors and tell her, "Goodbye."

Simon and I closed down the party. We rode the bus back to the hotel. I snuggled next to him with my head on his shoulder. "What a beautiful wedding and what a great evening. Thank you."

"My pleasure. You are a wonderful person. You deserve good things."

I agreed. I did deserve good things. And I planned to get them. Though I wasn't a hundred percent sure what they might be or how to get them.

33
Hodge and A Job

AFTER THE WEDDING, HOPE AND Tyler moved to a different state. His job had given him a huge promotion so he couldn't turn the move down. It broke my heart they were moving so far away. I'd already begun dreaming of grandchildren and decided I'd move in next door when the babies started arriving.

Joy finished her PhD program and was offered a job teaching at Wake Forest, where she got her B.A. I was proud of her, though sad she was moving away again.

My mom was gone and soon my girls would be gone. I had a comfortable life in Bensonville. Still, something was missing. A real connection to another being. I had Tom, but sadly he was a bit selfish, like most cats. As long as I kept his bowl full of food, he was happy. He didn't need love and attention beyond the occasional scratch behind the ears.

Simon and I met up for dinner once a month and sometimes we went dancing. At our last dinner, he told me he thought he had met "the one." I told him to be careful. "I want to meet him to see if I approve," I said.

One evening, having nothing better to do, I checked out my Facebook posts to see if anything new was going on in one of my numerous groups—

Friends of the Library, Bird Watching Enthusiasts, Bensonville 411—when I saw a post from the local humane society about a dog that had been dumped off because his owner died and the family didn't want him.

"Kind of like you, Tom," I said as I read the post. "Thrown out into the streets. At least this dog got taken to the humane society and not just abandoned. People are awful." The cat looked up as if in agreement.

I looked at the pictures of the dog. I had never seen such sorrow and despair on the face of an animal. Possibly on the face of anyone. It was a rather odd face. I stared, trying to figure out the breed. This dog had a wide head, like a bulldog, though he also had thick fur and long dangly ears like a cocker spaniel. Not that I was much of a dog expert.

I momentarily considered adopting this poor soul, but I sternly told myself, no way. I did not need a dog. I asked Tom what he thought about getting a dog and he gave me a rather withering look. "I didn't think you'd be enthusiastic." I said, scratching him behind the ears.

On the way to the library the next morning, I passed the sign to the Humane Society. Funny, I never noticed the sign before. When I left work, I decided to swing by. He'd probably been adopted already, and I could go home happy.

I parked and walked in the front door expecting to find some gray, bleak concrete block smelling of death and misery. Instead, it was bright and cheerful inside, and the lady behind the counter immediately gave me a big smile and asked how she could help me.

"Ummm…" I wasn't sure what to say. I didn't even know the name of the dog I was inquiring about. "I saw a post last night on Facebook about a dog. I can't remember his name… something about being dumped here after his owner died? Brown dog with a white nose?"

"You must mean Duke," she replied with a huge grin.

"I guess so. Is he still available?" I hoped she'd say no. That he had been adopted by someone far more qualified than me.

"Yes, he is. It's your lucky day."

I hesitated. "I'm not really sure I want or need a dog, but he looked so sad. I felt sorry for him."

"Come back and meet him. He'll enjoy the company." The woman picked up an intercom and called for someone to escort a visitor to the back.

As I waited, I kept telling myself I did not need a dog. I knew nothing about dogs. This was not the time to get a dog.

The door opened and a young man waved at me to come with him. We walked down an aisle of bright, clean kennels with dogs barking and wagging their tails as we passed. When we got to the end, I saw a brown lump laying with his back to the walkway. No barks. No wagging tail.

"Hey Duke," the young man called out as he opened the door. "You have a visitor." Duke made no response. "Let me get a leash and walk him to the meet and greet room."

I nodded.

He bent down and slipped a leash over Duke's massive head. It was even bigger in person than on Facebook. Duke looked up and slowly got to his feet as the young man talked to him, trying to get a response.

"This way," he said as he walked past me. I followed him into a room and he took the leash off. "This is Duke." He smiled.

Never had a dog been so wrongly named. There was nothing noble or royal about Duke. He looked like a dog whose ancestry included dozens of dogs that should never have had anything to do with each other. He had the head and face of a bulldog. Enormous with a short snout. He had little piggy brown eyes and floppy ears. He had the body of a corgi, short legs but with a long curly tail. He also had long, unruly fur.

"Needs a bit of grooming," the worker said, "otherwise he's a fine looking fellow."

"Really? He looks like he's been put together from spare parts. Not even sure if he isn't half pig." I looked at Duke with a mixture of awe and horror.

The worker burst out laughing. "You could be right. Still, he has a good heart and that's the only thing that counts." He sat down and ruffled the hair on top of Duke's head, and Duke looked up with the sweetest expression. My heart melted. "Here, come over and sit with him. Talk to him. Give him a pat."

I sat down and reached out my hand to pet Duke, and he licked my hand and my cheek. The next thing I knew, I found myself back at the front desk filling out an application to adopt a dog. "I don't know what I'm doing," I said to the woman as I filled out the form. "I don't need a dog. I don't know anything about dogs. I've never had a dog. I have an old cat, but all he does is sleep and eat. Don't dogs require a lot more attention? Interaction?"

"You'll be fine. Our counselors will talk to you when you pick him up and give you all the information you need, and you can always call and ask questions if you need more assistance."

I left with a packet of information.

I returned a few days later with a new leash and collar, ready to claim my dog. The same young guy brought Duke out to me. He was a changed dog. They had spruced him up a bit with a bath and a clipping. He had a huge, toothy grin on his broad face and a pink tongue so long it almost dragged on the ground. He appeared to know he was going home. I bent down and put his new collar on and clipped on the leash. Duke wildly wagged his tail.

As I stood up, the woman behind the desk asked to take our picture. "We like to post pictures of our pets who've found a forever home." We stood together and they snapped a few shots. "It will be on Facebook tonight. We won't mention your name. You can share it if you like."

I was still in a state of shock. Why was I getting a dog? And if I had to get a dog, why this hodge-podge creature of unknown ancestry? It struck me that Hodge-Podge was what I should name Duke. I told the woman and she laughed. "It's perfect. We'll add it to the post. Hodge-Podge, formerly known as Duke, got adopted." Her facial expression changed, and she became quite serious. "I hope this works for you. I hope you don't bring him back. He couldn't survive being rejected again."

The pressure was enormous. There was no going back. We had to make it work. "Ready, Hodge? Ready for your new home?" He waddled out the door with me, wagging his tail enthusiastically.

Our first stop was the pet store. I wanted to get advice on what I needed for a dog. They had been quite helpful with all my questions about Tom. When we walked in, people turned and stared. I held my head up a little higher. "Pay no attention to them, Hodge."

The young clerk I liked came over. "I see you have a new friend." He bent down to pet Hodge. "If you don't mind me asking, what kind of dog is this?" This was the first time, but not the last time, I'd be asked that question.

"He's a long-haired Malaysian pig-dog," I responded.

"Wow. Cool."

Loaded down with supplies, Hodge and I went back to the car. I thought again I really needed to get a job. Pets were expensive.

Hodge hopped up into the passenger seat as if he had been riding with me his whole life. He looked out the window, grinning. Drool dripped on the door. I wondered how Tom was going to react to this newcomer. "So, Hodge, do you have any experience with cats?" Hodge looked over at me, drool now dropping on the seat. "Yes? Do you like them? I have a cat named Tom. He's pretty easygoing. I think you guys should do fine together." I crossed my fingers.

Hodge walked into my house and started sniffing around, investigating every nook and cranny. He eventually found Tom on the couch. Tom had been watching him closely since Hodge had walked in the door. Hodge had not noticed Tom at first. When he spotted Tom, his tail started to wag. He walked up slowly and stuck his face in Tom's space. Tom did not move but he let out a low threatening growl. Hodge backed off quickly. Luckily, I had bought him a dog bed because obviously Tom did not plan on sharing the couch with him.

Hodge changed my life in more ways than Tom had. Hodge and I started each day with a long walk. Unfortunately, my neighborhood walking group did not suit him. He liked leisurely walks in the park, with long stops to sniff at interesting smells. He also liked to mark every tree and post we passed. He preferred walking on soft green grass, not concrete. I didn't blame him. I liked the park too, though I missed the ladies. We also went for a long walk in the evening.

People often stopped and stared, and if they were bold enough, asked what sort of breed Hodge was. I always replied Hodge was a long-haired Malaysian pig-dog. I could tell some were wondering if I was pulling their leg, but others had the "wow-cool" reaction.

One day, returning home from the park, Hodge stopped at a café that had a water bowl outside for doggy visitors. He noisily drank until he emptied the bowl. I walked up to the door to let them know they needed to refill the bowl, and I saw a "Help Wanted" sign on the door. As I stood there reading it, the door swung open, and a woman came out, almost crashing into me.

"Oh my! So sorry. I didn't notice you there," she said, completely flustered.

"I'm sorry too. I wanted to tell you my dog emptied out your dog water bowl and then I started reading the Help Wanted sign."

She stared at Hodge. "Interesting dog. Let me refill the bowl." She took the bowl and filled it up from the faucet on the side of the building. She brought the bowl back and sat it down. Hodge tried to bury his head in it again. I pulled him back.

"You've had enough. Leave some for the next dog."

I started to walk away when the woman called out, "Are you interested in a job?"

I stopped and turned around. "I don't know. I've been thinking I need a job but I don't have any experience working in a restaurant."

"You don't need any. It's not like this is a high-pressure place. We're busy early in the morning with people stopping to get coffee and pastries before work. Then it settles down for the older breakfast crowd. There's usually a lull, which gives us a chance to catch up before the lunch crowd starts arriving. And that's it. We close at 3:00. Have a seat, and I'll get us some coffee and we can talk."

She came back and introduced herself as Susan and handed me a cup of coffee. Susan was the owner, manager, and head waitress. "I do everything but cook. Thank goodness, because no one wants burnt toast and runny eggs for breakfast. We have a wonderful short-order cook."

And kind of like getting a dog, I found myself with a job at the Morning Brew Café. At the age of sixty, my life was finally coming together. My own house, a cat, a dog, and a job.

I worked the late morning shift. I started when Hodge and I were done with our walk. Since I didn't get there until nine, I missed most of the early rush. I worked behind the counter, taking orders and making sure people's coffee mugs were filled while they waited.

It was a new experience for me and surprisingly, I enjoyed the job. I liked chatting with people, especially the regulars. I'd never been a chatty person so this was something new, which was exactly what I needed.

Susan let me bring Hodge to the café. He slept in the office until I finished my shift. I worked five days a week and still had a day to volunteer at the library. I didn't make a fortune, but it paid for cat and dog food, and every little bit helped. I had few other extravagances.

One Saturday, while I worked in my usual spot behind the counter at the café, Susan leaned over and whispered, "Oooh la la… Denzel is back." I looked up to see her staring over at a middle-aged black man sitting in a corner booth.

I thought for a moment it really was Denzel Washington because of her reaction. And while there were some similarities, I quickly figured out he was not the famous actor. "Why do you call him Denzel?" I asked.

"Look at him!" She fanned herself dramatically. "He used to be a regular here. He and his wife came every Sunday morning for brunch. Then they stopped coming. I didn't know if they had moved. Now he's back. Alone." She wiggled her eyebrows to indicate the significance of that statement. "I wonder if something happened to his wife."

Susan went back to work, and I busied myself filling up coffee mugs. The next time I glanced at the corner booth, it was empty.

Every Saturday morning, "Denzel" came into the café, ordered the same breakfast of scrambled eggs and toast with an orange juice and a large cup of coffee. I never served him because I worked the counter, so I had to admire him from afar.

34

Denzel AKA Moses

$\mathcal{S}$OME MONTHS LATER, HODGE AND I were walking in the park when Hodge spotted someone on a bench throwing bread to the ducks. Hodge pulled me over, hoping to get some of the bread. Hodge had an insatiable appetite.

As Hodge yanked me closer, the man from the café, Denzel, as I thought of him, glanced up at me and down at Hodge.

"Oh, my goodness. What is that? A pig on a leash?" He laughed, a rich, deep laugh which made me smile. It was the first time I'd heard his voice.

"This is a very rare breed." I pretended to be rather haughty about my prized dog. "He might be the only one of his kind. He is a long-haired Mongolian Pig Dog." I realized I usually said Malaysian, but I didn't want to correct myself. And I decided I preferred Mongolian.

"I bet he's rare, and I'm sure he's one of a kind." Denzel flipped Hodge a piece of bread, which he caught easily. "He's good at catching food."

Denzel looked up at me. "Do I know you? You look familiar." He cocked his head as if the memory might slide into place.

"I work at the Morning Brew Café. You've probably seen me there."

"Yes! That's it. Are you new there?"

"Pretty new."

He slid over to make room on the bench. I thought it would be rude not to sit down, so Hodge and I made ourselves comfortable.

We sat in silence. I began to feel awkward. I didn't have anything to say and apparently, he didn't either. I almost told him Susan, the owner, had me convinced he was Denzel Washington. I bit my tongue, thinking it might embarrass both of them.

As often happens, we began speaking at the same moment, laughed in embarrassment, and stopped talking again. Finally, he ventured a comment about Hodge, asking me where I had obtained such a unique creature. He did not use the word "dog" as if he still had some doubts about whether Hodge qualified as a member of that species.

I told him Hodge's sad story of abandonment and how I ended up adopting him, much against my common sense. "He's the reason I ended up working at the Café. He loves to meander through the park, and we exited out a new way and stumbled upon it. I noticed a help wanted sign on the door and got a job there."

Denzel laughed again. "Hodge is a very lucky dog. I've been a long-time customer of the Morning Brew since they opened. I used to go there with my wife for Sunday brunch. I stopped going for a while and now I go Saturday instead."

"Why doesn't your wife come with you on Saturday?" I asked and was immediately embarrassed to be asking such a personal question. Maybe learning how to chat mindlessly hadn't been all good. I blushed bright red and bent down to pet Hodge on the head, hoping to hide my mortification.

"Sadly, we are no longer together," he said quietly.

I looked up, staring into his face. He sounded so sad, I wanted to reach out and pat him on the hand. I wanted to say, "I know the feeling. I know what it's like to have your world upended."

He looked back with a slightly forlorn look and smiled. He had a beautiful smile. I noticed something familiar in that smile.

"You remind me of…"

"Denzel Washington?" He sat up straight and pretended to be showing off. "I've heard that many times before."

I laughed. "No. That wasn't who I was thinking of. Your smile reminds me of a man I knew many years ago. His name was Old Joe."

He looked crestfallen. "I remind you of someone named 'Old Joe'? You're not doing much for my ego."

I couldn't stop laughing. He tried his best to look hurt and wounded by being compared to someone named Old Joe.

"You should be proud. Old Joe was one of the finest people I ever knew. He and my grandmother were close friends, and the best summers of my life were spent with the two of them. He was a wonderful person."

"If he was wonderful, I will try to forgive you. I hope in addition to being wonderful, he was also incredibly handsome."

"I'm not sure. At eleven, I don't think I considered grown men in terms of how handsome they were. I have to admit, I simply thought of him as old. Ancient, in fact."

"Way to twist the knife." He grimaced, pretending to be deeply wounded.

"You don't look like him," I added. "You're about a hundred years younger, for one thing. But there's something in the way you smile that called him to mind. He had the most beautiful smile. It lit up his whole face" I sat quietly, remembering Old Joe. What a kind, decent man he'd been.

"Well, when a beautiful lady says I remind her of an ancient old man, it wounds my self-esteem." He tried to look sad, but I could tell he was suppressing a smile.

Beautiful lady? Had he called me a beautiful lady? That came out of nowhere. When was the last time anyone called me beautiful? Maybe Frank on our wedding day? Maybe David? I liked that this man thought I was beautiful.

"Also, I know Susan and the ladies at the café call me Denzel, which I take as a compliment." He grinned. "However, in case you're curious, my name's not Denzel or Joe, it's Moses, and before you even start, yes, I know what a cliché it is for a black man to be named Moses. Our parents sometimes don't think these things through."

"How right you are." I grinned. "My parents named me Jane. My last name was Smith. There could not be a less interesting name on earth than Jane Smith. And when I got married, I became Jane Jones. Not much of an improvement."

"I got you beat. My full name is Moses Elijah Johnson. Rather distinguished, especially if I was a prophet shouting in the wilderness."

I found it easy to talk to him. I hadn't had too many male friends in my life, other than Simon. More signs of my progress. I'm now able to talk to people, even virtual strangers.

I could have sat there all day on that bench looking at the lake, but I had to get ready for my volunteer stint at the library. Hodge had to be dropped off at the house before I could go, though he too would have been happily stayed at the park.

"I'm sorry I have to go. I hope I'll see you Saturday at the café."

"It's a date." He smiled.

Saturday, he sat at the counter instead of at his usual corner booth. "Decided to see what the view is like from up here," he said, as he sat on one of the high stools.

"You'll like it. Gives you a whole new perspective."

After he left, Susan slid up next to me, whispering loudly in my ear, "It appears as if you have made a conquest of the mysterious Denzel. First time he's ever sat at the counter." She arched her eyebrows at me in a questioning way.

"Oh, stop." I grimaced in mock anger. "I have not made a 'conquest' as you so dramatically call it. We happened to run into each other in the park and he was mystified or horrified by Hodge, and we started talking. I mentioned I worked here, and he probably didn't want to appear rude by sitting in his booth."

Secretly, I hoped he'd stick with the counter seat. I hated to admit to myself how much I enjoyed talking to him. I thought of Simon and how easy it was to talk to him and how much he made me laugh. With my luck, Moses was probably gay as well. On the other hand, he had been married. To a woman. Which was a good sign.

The next time he came in, he sat at the counter again and Susan wiggled her eyebrows at me, mouthing the word "conquest." I gave the best Evie Eye Roll I could manage and turned my attention back to my customers.

For the next month, Moses came in each Saturday, and we chatted as I ran around taking orders and filling up coffee cups. I didn't see him in the park, so we didn't visit outside of the café.

One Saturday, he didn't come for breakfast. I felt a little bereft and chided myself for feeling that way.

Halfway through the morning shift, Susan bumped up against me. "Have you run our Denzel off again? I'll miss looking at him."

I didn't respond and she picked up my mood. "Oh my goodness, Jane, are you already crazy for him?"

"Don't be silly," I said. "He's nice and I like him. As a friend. That's all. I have no interest in a relationship."

She smirked, obviously not believing me. I thought I'd turn the tables on her. "You seem quite infatuated. Why don't you get friendly with him?"

"For one thing, as you well know, I'm married. But you're not."

"Yes. Happily, not. I finally got my life on track after being dominated by my parents and my husband. Now I do what I want!" I laughed. "I don't answer to anyone about what I do with my time or how I spend my money. It's wonderful. Never knew life could be this good."

I could tell Susan was trying to decide if I was being truthful. "Don't you get lonely at night?"

"I was much lonelier when I was married. Nothing worse than being with someone who doesn't care."

Susan squeezed my arm and patted my shoulder before walking away. "I just wanted to be sure you're okay."

"And by the way, his name is Moses, not Denzel," I added as I turned back to serving coffee and breakfast.

Moses didn't come back to the café for the next month. I missed seeing him but I stayed busy and soon stopped thinking about him. One day, Hodge and I were walking in the park when Hodge practically yanked my arm out of the socket. He jerked me around and started pulling me toward a figure on a bench. Moses. Hodge ran up to him, licking and sniffing, trying to see if Moses had anything edible.

"Hi there." Suddenly I felt awkward and shy, wondering if he had stopped coming to the café because of something I had said or done. I still hadn't quite mastered this friendship thing.

Moses looked up from petting Hodge and gifted me with his beautiful, warm smile. "Hi, there back. What a pleasant surprise to see you here."

I sat next to him. "We've missed you at the café." I thought I'd be honest. "Susan especially misses her Denzel." I chuckled.

"I'm sorry. I've missed being there. I've been out of town, and I got behind at work and had to catch up."

"Where did you go? Was it for fun or business?" I immediately regretted this question. When had I gotten so nosy?

"I was visiting my son, so to speak." His smile faltered.

I wondered if the son had taken his mother's side at the end of the marriage and Moses had trouble maintaining a relationship with him. Like Hope had after Frank and I split up.

"Where does your son live?" I asked, thinking that was a benign question.

Moses looked down, staring at his hands. When he looked back up, his smile kept slipping on and off his face. I got worried.

He let out a long sigh. "My son is dead. This is the third anniversary of his death. I drove up to Arlington Cemetery to spend time at his grave. It's peaceful there. Quiet. All those heroes spending eternity together. Brothers-in-arms." A tear splashed onto his lap.

I gasped in shock and tears filled my eyes. I couldn't imagine anything worse in this life than losing a child. I had lost my baby years ago, but he lost his adult child. I reached out and took his hand. "Oh, Moses. I am sorry. How awful."

"I'm usually better about handling this," he replied. "But on the anniversary, all the memories flood back. His death is the reason my wife left me. No. That's an oversimplification. The end started long before he died."

"If you want to talk, I'm here. I don't want you to feel obligated to tell me," I said softly.

"Talking is good. I've kept a lot of it bottled up for too long. Blaming others for everything. Took me a long time to look at myself."

Damn. This man was living my life, like we were in a parallel universe. We both lost a child. Lost a marriage. Lost our way.

The alarm on my phone went off, indicating it was time for me to leave to get ready for my stint at the library. Moses waved at me. "I know you need to leave."

"No. I'll give them a quick call and tell them I can't make it today. It's not like the world will end if a few books don't get shelved. I want to hear the rest of your story."

And so Moses told me. "I was the son of a Baptist minister, from a long line of ministers. My father gave me the name of two giant prophets from the Bible because he assumed I'd be continuing the family tradition." Moses sat back, gazing at the sky for a while.

"I wasn't interested. I wanted to be a lawyer. A corporate lawyer, making the big bucks. I wanted to live in a huge house and drive a fancy European car."

That certainly reminded me of another man I had known. Maybe all men who come from humble backgrounds have dreams of becoming rich and successful.

"I did well in school. Went to the right college. Got into law school. I was on my way. When I told my father I had applied to law school, he was pleased because he thought I planned to set up a little store-front office next to his church in the poorer section of town and help 'the people.'

"I told him that was not my plan. I wasn't going to be a public defender or work for the little guy. I wanted to get rich. I'd never seen my father so disgusted. Rightfully so. He tried to hide his feelings, no doubt hoping I'd eventually see the light.

"I took my bar exam and passed with flying colors. I got several offers from major companies the moment I graduated. My hardest decision was which offer to choose. I wanted the one that would get me to the top of the heap the quickest.

"I got the job. Shot to the top. Married Adele, a beautiful, smart woman who was happy to live the country club life. My dream had come true. We had a child. A son. We were living the American dream. We named our son Magnus Benjamin Johnson. No biblical names for our son. He was destined for great things like I had been."

Moses stopped and stared out at the lake. He watched the ducks swimming around. Hodge sensed Moses was distressed and he snuggled closer and licked his hand. Moses looked down at Hodge, ruffling the fur behind Hodge's ears.

"I'm sorry," Moses said. "I feel like I'm unburdening myself and it's not fair to dump all this on you." He smiled slightly. "Our acquaintance is rather new. You're just so easy to talk to. I feel comfortable with you. It's as if you understand."

"We've both experienced hurt and loss. Maybe that's why?"

Moses nodded. "Our son became another adornment, like our big house and big cars. We were not good parents. I spent too much time at work. My wife, Adele, stayed busy with Garden Club, the Arts Commission, volunteer work, shopping, lunches with friends and whatever else rich women spend their time doing. We rarely had family dinners together or spent time doing things with Magnus.

"Our only involvement with Magnus was keeping pressure on him to excel at school. It was all about grades and the SATs and extracurricular activities that looked good on a college application. He wasn't a good student. Smart but not interested. He kept saying he didn't want to go to college. As usual, I paid no attention. I pulled some strings and got him accepted into my university on a probationary basis. I convinced them he was brilliant, he just hadn't found his groove yet. I patted myself on the back, proud of arranging my son's future.

"At his high school graduation ceremony, we congratulated ourselves on the fine job we had done. On Monday, he came home and told us he'd enlisted in the army. I thought Adele was going to faint. I couldn't speak, I was so furious. I kept sputtering about how could he do this to us. I think I even said, 'we've done everything for you and this is the thanks we get?' And he said, 'you never did a thing for me. It was all about you guys.' What he said was true, though I didn't see it at the time."

Moses sat quietly for a long time before speaking again.

"He left for boot camp. We hardly communicated at that point. Ben, as he demanded we call him, told us he had been accepted into Ranger school. We didn't even realize what an achievement that was. I swallowed my anger and went to his graduation. Adele didn't join me. She made some excuse about some committee meeting she couldn't miss. The cracks in our marriage were beginning.

"I'm glad she didn't come. Ben and I had some good talks over the weekend. For the first time ever. He shared how he appalled he'd been by our privileged life in a gated community. Life for him wasn't about climbing the corporate ladder and living in a big house and driving the most expensive car. He wanted to do something that made a difference."

I thought about Frank. Funny how he and Moses had the same life goals, though apparently Moses had a wake-up call. I didn't think that would ever happen to Frank. Frank seemed perfectly content with his choices, though it had alienated him from his family.

"I asked him, why the army? He laughed, saying, 'The shock value, Dad. I knew the army'd be the last thing you'd want me to do.' He wanted to slap us in the face. Ben said he considered the army a stepping stone. A good place to start.

"Turns out he was good at it. Rose quickly through the ranks. Got a lot of medals. Had several tours overseas. Before he left on his last tour, he told me he planned on getting out. Maybe becoming an aide worker or going back to school to get a medical degree. He had lots of plans. We talked a lot on the phone. Adele not so much. She was embarrassed when her friends asked what our son was doing. She could still barely admit he had joined the army instead of going to college.

"Ben never came home from his last mission. We were told he sacrificed himself to save his troops. They said he was a real hero, which only made Adele angrier. She ranted about why should she be happy because her son died a hero. He was still dead. Being a hero was another dumb choice." Moses winced at this memory.

"His last wishes were to be buried at Arlington with his comrades. Such a beautiful ceremony." His voice cracked and I could tell he was fighting back tears. My eyes filled too and spilled over.

"I know. My dad was in the army and had a military funeral. At the military cemetery in Fayetteville. Nothing like a military funeral." Moses nodded sadly in agreement.

"After the service, when we got in the car, Adele threw the flag into the back seat of the car. 'What good is a damn flag,' she yelled. 'Give me back my son you killed.' She was inconsolable.

"I took the flag and had it displayed in a box along with his medals, a photo of him in full-dress uniform, and a picture of his gravestone and put it in my office. It was a turning point for me. Each day I looked at that flag box and felt shame. Shame for how I had lived my life. I thought about my father, who devoted his life to others and could only ever afford a second-hand car.

"I went home and told Adele I planned to quit my job and put the house up for sale. She was stunned at first. Thought I must be joking. When she grasped I wasn't, she got angry. 'I lost my son and now I have to give up my house and my life too?'"

Moses paused for a moment. "We made it another year while I closed down that chapter of my life. She devoted her time to finding another rich guy to keep her in the lifestyle she had grown accustomed to. Which was fine with me. By that point, all we shared was a house and a country club membership.

"I moved on. To a job that gives my life meaning, if not much money. I opened that storefront law office and work as an advocate. I do lots of things, from working in soup kitchens to providing legal aid to people who don't have the knowledge or resources to help themselves. I feel I can finally look my son and father in the eye.

"Adele insisted on taking half of my retirement even though her current husband makes more than I ever did." Vindictive like Frank, I thought. "I got half the proceeds from our house sale. I live in a small apartment and take public transportation, and I've never been happier. All the stress of the rat race is behind me, worrying about things that really don't matter.

"My one indulgence is Saturday breakfast at the Morning Brew." He turned to look at me before adding, "Where I met a new friend."

I smiled back. A new friend. Someone called me a friend.

35

A Good Friend

WE FELL INTO A ROUTINE. We saw each other every Saturday morning at the café and every Wednesday at the park. I had finally found a man I could talk to. We bonded over our mutual losses—children and marriages. I was wary of anything deeper. I didn't want to fall for a guy on the rebound from a relationship. Being friends was fine with me.

The first time Moses came to my townhouse, he looked closely at my family photos hanging on the walls. When he noticed a photo of Old Joe smiling directly into the camera, he stared at it. "Is this the guy you said I reminded you of when we first met?"

I glanced at Old Joe's image. Bald head, thick glasses—not the handsomest man ever, but what a wonderful smile. "Yes. That's the one," I said, with love and affection for Old Joe.

"Handsome devil," Moses said with a smile playing at his lips.

"I don't know about that, but he was kind, which is more important."

"Agreed."

One day, Moses asked me if I wanted to go to the movies with him. "It's Denzel's latest," he added with a grin. "I know how fond you are of Denzel."

"Oh stop," I said, poking him the ribs. "I'm not the one who called you

Denzel. I called you Old Joe." He winced at the reminder.

We started attending other things together, concerts, museum shows, art shows, and other inexpensive events. Neither of us were flush with money.

Summer turned to fall and as Thanksgiving approached, I found out I'd be alone for the holidays. Hope and Tyler were going to his family's house. Joy had finally met someone, and they were going to his house so she could meet his parents. I couldn't wait to meet the guy who had captured Joy's heart. Both girls assured me I'd see them at Christmas.

When Moses found out I'd be alone for the holiday, he invited me to spend Thanksgiving with him at one of the local churches that put on a huge community feast. "We'll be serving meals to people who have nowhere else to go. It's a blend of lonely old people, people with addiction issues, and sometimes entire families who've fallen on hard times. It's always a mixed group and they're all so grateful."

This experience showed me what the Thanksgiving holiday really meant. All the guests were so appreciative of the food we served them. I overheard one man say this was the first hot meal he'd had in days. A young girl looked up at me as I loaded her plate and said, "I think this is what the first Thanksgiving was like. With the Pilgrims and Indians. They didn't know each other but they became friends. Like us." She smiled shyly.

Eventually, the last meal was served and the last dish washed. I sat down with Moses. "Wow, I'm exhausted. It was like a morning at the café on steroids, but I've never had a better Thanksgiving. This is the true meaning of the holiday." He nodded in agreement.

One morning after Moses had finished his breakfast at the cafe, I waved goodbye to him. "I'll see you later."

Susan slid up to me when the door closed. "I can't believe you haven't snapped him up or he hasn't snapped you up," she said. "You're perfect for each other."

"Please stop pestering me about this. Moses has not indicated he wants anything more than to be friends. I don't want more than that either. I've been burned by my failed relationships and so has he. We make good friends. We share interests and have fun together. It's enough for us."

"For now. Enough for now," Susan emphasized, before walking away.

I rolled my eyes and said, "God give me strength," channeling both my mother and grandmother.

At night sometimes, stretching out, I'd find Hodge or Tom curled up in bed with me. They were nice warm bodies, though I wondered if I was destined to spend the rest of my life alone in bed with just the two of them.

Christmas brought a visit from Joy and Hope and their guys, Tyler and Ethan. It was a bit crowded since I only had one guest bedroom, but they brought an air mattress and appeared happy with those arrangements.

My girls amazed me. They were so different than I had been at their age. I had been so indecisive. I spent my twenties waiting for someone to come into my life to give it direction. They were directing their own lives. It had taken Hope a little more time to get there, but she had turned out great. Joy always surprised me. She had been so strong from an early age, maybe because she had Hope to look out for.

The day after Christmas, Moses came for dinner. This was the first time everyone met. They got along nicely. The girls liked him a lot. The next day, Tyler, Ethan, and Moses went out to some sport event. I was glad they found something to do together that they all enjoyed. But I was even happier because that gave me time to spend alone with my girls. I thought Joy might have suggested a boy's day so we could have a girl's day.

As soon as we were alone, both Joy and Hope started giving me the third degree about Moses. "Mom! He's gorgeous. What's going on? Are you dating? Are you serious?"

"No! We aren't anything more than friends. He's been hurt a lot and so have I. We've bonded over that. He's opened up a new world for me."

Both girls looked at me quizzically. "Mom," they both said with a note of frustration, "you're only sixty. You have at least thirty or more years to live. Are you seriously planning on being alone the rest of your life because you had a bad marriage? He's perfect for you. You seem so happy together."

I sighed. "It's not like Moses has given me any indication that he is in love with me or wants anything more from our relationship. Honestly, I don't want to risk it. I'm more afraid of losing his friendship. Love can be difficult and it complicates everything. Why muddy the waters? I like my simple life. When I married your father, I gave up my independence. I had a job, a paycheck, my own apartment and while I wasn't wildly happy, I made my own decisions. Then I got married." I smiled ruefully.

I thought back all those years ago, regretting how I had basically handed my entire life over to Frank. "We were happy in the beginning. I was crazy in love and crazy happy. It was all I had ever wanted—to love and be loved.

"The first years were wonderful." I smiled at the memory. "Sadly, your father and I both had unhappy childhoods and becoming parents brought out a lot of things we'd never dealt with. I wanted a big happy family—the more the merrier! I'd probably have had ten kids if your father had agreed. I wanted to embrace his family and make them part of my life, but they were a strange bunch who were not interested in embracing me." I winced at the memories of meeting Frank's mom and family for the first time.

This was the first time I had ever mentioned Frank's family to the kids.

"We never heard any stories about Dad's family," Joy said. "I'm ashamed to realize we never even asked about them."

"They weren't worth talking about." I said bitterly. "Sadly, your father was embarrassed by them. Though honestly, they were awful. You met them when you were a tiny infant Joy, when we went up for your dad's mom's funeral, but of course you don't remember. After she died, your father never spoke to his siblings again. At least, not that I know of."

"That's sad," Hope said. "I can't imagine never seeing or speaking to Joy again." She looked over at her sister and they smiled at each other.

"But do you really want to be alone forever because you had a bad childhood and a bad marriage?"

"Yes. I do," I confessed. "I'm not good at picking men." I tried to do the Evie Eye Roll. "I've had zero success in my past relationships."

"You only had two! It's not like you've had twelve failed marriages."

"You have a point," I admitted. "In general, though, I'm not good with relationships. Took me all my life to become friends with my mom. And my one adult friend, Claire, totally betrayed me." I shook my head remembering the moment when they confessed all. "But it's fine. I'm finally over it. I should send her a thank-you note." I laughed.

They weren't ready to give up trying to convince me I should fall in love with Moses and we should get married.

Later, Joy asked, "Are you worried because of the race thing?"

"No," I replied, getting slightly annoyed at their persistence. "If I was thinking of having a relationship with Moses or marrying him, that wouldn't be a concern. I've always been an advocate of inter-racial relationships. Remember I told you guys I wanted Mamere to marry Old Joe way back in the day."

I glanced up at my favorite photo of Mamere and Old Joe laughing joyfully. Such pure delight. I thought about the fact Old Joe never married. Was he in love with Mamere? Was she in love with him? "I thought they were in love. I don't know if they were or if it was a fantasy of mine because in fairy tales, the boy and the girl fall in love at the end and live happily ever after." I grimaced, thinking what a joke that was. "Maybe they were simply friends and had no thoughts whatsoever of marrying. And who was I at the age of ten to decide how they should live their lives? Maybe they liked living in their own houses. Doing their own things."

"Kind of like us?" Joy grinned at me. "Trying to force you into a relationship when you're perfectly happy living on your own."

"Exactly!" I smiled and hugged them both. "Still, it's nice to know you care and are looking out for your mom's happiness."

36
Hodge and Me and Moses

IN THE WINTER, OUR SCHEDULE changed. After meeting at the café for breakfast, we'd walk Hodge in the park. Hodge adored Moses. He appeared to like him even better than he liked me, which hurt a bit. I reminded Hodge that I'd been the one who rescued him, but it made no impact on his love for Moses.

When it became too cold to sit in the park and talk, we often ended up back at the café for lunch. Moses started coming to my house on Friday nights. I slipped once and referred to it as a date night. He suppressed a grin. We discovered we had a passion for English mystery shows. We'd sit on the couch together with a bowl of popcorn. Hodge made sure our relationship remained platonic, since he always curled up between us. I was surprised Hodge wasn't pushing us together like everyone else.

"You know," I said once, looking at the two of them happily snuggled up, "I think if it hadn't been for Hodge, you wouldn't have even befriended me."

"Well, I do love this Pig. That's for sure."

"Hodge is not a pig!"

"Are you sure? Have you had a DNA test done? I'm definitely going for wild boar mixed with pot-bellied pig." Moses looked down adoringly at Hodge while he said this. Hodge looked back with his own look of adoration, his tongue hanging out, drool dripping on my couch.

"Oh, my God. You two should get a room," I said, though secretly I was happy for Hodge and Moses. They were good guys and deserved happiness.

Our lives slowly merged. Moses came in every Saturday for breakfast and after I finished my shift, I'd join him at his downtown office. Impressed with my financial work experience, he hired me to help people work up budgets or pay off loans, trying to get them back on their feet. Minimal pay for me but the work brought satisfaction on a different level.

I had to do a lot of research through the maze of federal regulations and agencies. "I'm too old to be learning all this stuff," I jokingly told Moses one day. "I thought I put it all behind me. Retirement is supposed to be fun."

"Isn't this fun?" he teased. "Mastering the art of government gobbledygook?"

"Not exactly." I wasn't going to admit it to him, but I enjoyed digging through the bureaucratic maze to help people. It was like solving a mystery.

We became an outreach team. On Sundays, we offered presentations to area churches about setting up soup kitchens and programs for the homeless and needy. There was always a request Moses needed to fill or to organize helpers for. He was amazing. No one could say no to him. I began to give speeches, too. Because Moses believed in me, I was able to stand up and talk without fainting or wetting myself.

"I know you worry about how people will react to you," Moses said, "but you're a natural. They respond positively to you because they can tell you are honest and sincere. You're genuine and people feel it."

There was that word again. The one Claire used to describe me so long ago. Genuine. I could embrace it now.

"I appreciate your confidence in me. Surprisingly, I'm enjoying it. I never liked public speaking, but I feel so passionate about what we're doing, it's easy."

The charity work took up more and more of my time, and I finally realized I had to quit working at the café. I didn't look forward to telling Susan. She'd become a dear friend. Unfortunately, we couldn't spend much time together outside of work because Susan had a loving husband and a large family waiting for her at home. Occasionally, at the end of a shift, we'd sit and talk for a half hour before she headed home.

I told Susan I needed to talk to her at the end of my shift. Moses stayed to support me, knowing it was hard for me to say goodbye. When we sat down, Susan looked from me to Moses and then back again. "You're leaving me, aren't you?"

I could only nod sorrowfully. "I knew it. I never should have introduced you to Denzel." She never stopped calling him Denzel, even to his face.

"You didn't introduce us," I objected. "If anyone can take the credit, it would be Hodge."

Moses laughed and Susan waved her hand, "Whatever. I'm reminded of that old movie about of all the gin joints in town you had to walk into mine. Only in this case, it's of all the coffee joints in town, both of you had to walk into mine."

I thought about fate and chance meetings and how our lives were affected by those encounters.

"I will always be eternally grateful for taking me on when I needed a job, given I had absolutely no experience." I squeezed Susan's hand.

"And I'm eternally grateful you're going to let Jane go, to help me do good works," Moses added. "Don't worry, you haven't seen the last of us! This will always be my favorite breakfast spot."

We ended up hugging and crying and kissing each other. It was all a bit over the top and overly dramatic. I left knowing I had taken another huge step forward in the evolution of my life and the new independent Jane.

Every morning, I met Moses at his little store-front office, and we'd plan our day. I continued to volunteer at the library, though now I headed up committees for book donations to under-served communities.

I squeezed in visits to see the girls whenever I could. Hope and Tyler were happy and talking about starting a family, which was exciting and welcome news. Joy and Ethan were quite happy as well, and I continued to hope they would get married.

The girls were pleased with the way my life had turned out. "Who'd have ever thought you'd become such advocate and volunteer in your golden years," Joy said.

Hope added, "I'm so proud of you."

"You're right. I never imagined one day I could stand up in front of a room full of people and speak without fainting. Or peeing on myself." The girls looked at me curiously. "Long story. Childhood incident. We'll save it for another time. If I had known the secret to happiness was in serving others, I'd have done this much sooner instead of hiding out in that big house."

I could tell they wanted to talk to me about Moses and our relationship, but they respected my feelings and said nothing. Or maybe they just thought us working closely together would seal the deal.

37

Another Wedding

ONE DAY, AN INVITATION ARRIVED in the mail. A beautifully handwritten note asking Moses and me to join Joy and Ethan for a wedding celebration at the city park in the town where they lived. I called Joy immediately. "Such wonderful news!"

"Yes. Just a simple ceremony with friends and family. I hope you're not bothered that you weren't involved in the planning, but this was spur of the moment. We aren't having any of that traditional stuff—no rehearsal dinner, no wedding party. Just us and the people we love."

"I'm just happy that you're happy and looking forward to seeing you get married."

Joy continued, "I'm sorry to say Dad and Claire will be coming too. I hope it won't be too painful to see him again. But he won't be part of the ceremony. I'm not having him give me away." She laughed. "I don't belong to him. So, at least you won't have to put up with him taking center stage."

"Thanks for the heads up. It's funny, I always dread seeing Claire more than your father. How silly is that?"

"This time, at least you don't have to worry about finding a date. You already have a handsome man to escort you. If Moses will come."

"If he's invited, he'll be there. I'll make sure of it."

"And bring Hodge too." I could feel Joy's smile across the line. "Show Dad you have a man and a pet and life is good."

When Moses came over later, I told him about the wedding invitation. "I hope you can join me. It would mean a lot to me."

"Of course," he replied. "I'm honored to be included."

When we showed up at the park the day of the wedding, I was overcome once more with the dread of having to see Frank and Claire.

Moses and I walked to a pavilion in the middle of the park, surrounded by ancient trees. The ceremony would take place under a grove of Magnolia trees. It was so Joy. Simple and beautiful.

Frank stood off to the side, looking out at the wide grassy meadow. He had not aged well since I last saw him. Had it only been three years ago? He looked gray and worn.

Without realizing it, I tensed up. Moses glanced down at me before following my gaze. "Is that the ex?"

"Yes. I don't see Claire, the woman he left me for. Maybe she's waiting to make a grand entrance, which would be her style."

"It doesn't matter where she is or that he's here. You're here for your daughter."

Another wise man like Simon.

Hope saw us and ran up to give us both a hug.

"Where's Hodge?" she asked, looking around.

"I decided not to bring him. You know he always causes a sensation wherever he goes, and I wanted this to be Joy's day." We both laughed.

She leaned closer and whispered, "Claire's not here. Apparently, she's left Dad. Ran off with the pool boy or the tennis instructor or someone from the country club."

"Poor Claire," I replied, shaking my head. "Still trying to grab that gusto.

I guess that explains why your father looks so miserable. Though honestly, they didn't even look happy together at your wedding."

The officiant, dressed casually in a white cotton shirt and pants, called out to everyone the ceremony was about to start. We all started toward the magnolia grove. There were no seats. We just stood under the canopy of bright green leaves and white flowers. The smell was intoxicating. A young woman started playing guitar. A young man joined her on the flute. Joy and Ethan walked hand-in-hand down through the middle of the guests. She looked lovely in a simple white dress with flowers in her hair. She carried a bunch of magnolia blossoms. A hippie wedding. I smiled.

After the ceremony, we returned to the pavilion where food and drink were spread out. Frank walked up to me to say hello which I thought was nice of him. Trying to act civilized at this daughter's wedding.

"Hello, Frank," I said, shaking his hand. Turning to Moses, I said, "This is my friend, Moses."

The two men shook hands, eyeing each other.

I thought about that bizarre incident long ago at Frank's mother's funeral, where his supposed dead father showed up and tried to rejoin the family. Now that Claire had dumped him, did Frank think or hope we could get back together and be a happy family again? No, that was ridiculous and not Frank's style. He'd never admit to having done anything wrong.

We exchanged a few more benign words and he walked off. Later, I found myself standing next to Frank at the bar. We glanced at each other. He said, "So, what happened to Simon, the guy you were with at Hope's wedding? I thought he was the one?" He said this in a rather snarky way, as if he suspected I brought men to these occasions to prove I wasn't alone. Which, I guess, had been true in Simon's case.

"Oh, we parted ways though we've remained friends. He's a great guy."

Frank sniffed. "Planning on getting married to this guy?"

I was taken aback by his rudeness. "Oh, I'm sorry. You've apparently misunderstood my relationship with Moses. We work together for a nonprofit agency. We represent the poor and disadvantaged in Bensonville. He's a lawyer who provides legal aid, and I do financial counseling."

"What on earth do you know about finances?" Frank sneered.

"I guess you forgot I used to be an office manager for a large firm before we were married. The annual budget and ledgers were all my responsibility. And that was before computers." I spoke slowly and deliberately, as if to a child.

He stared before turning away. I couldn't help myself and asked, "Oh, by the way, where's Claire? I wanted to say hello."

Frank stopped and mumbled something about a conflict in her schedule and she hadn't been able to come. Then he stalked off.

Later when I talked to Joy, I congratulated her and told her how beautiful the ceremony had been. "Simple and perfect. And what a gorgeous setting."

She hugged me. "We're all happily married now, Mom, and now it's your turn. You need to make a move on Moses. You will never find anyone better."

"I couldn't agree more," I replied. "He's a great guy, but we're just good friends. Even though we work well together and I enjoy spending time with him, at the end of the day I like going to my own home, putting on my ratty sweats, hanging out with Tom and Hodge and watching whatever I want on TV or reading a book or going to bed early. It's nice not to have to answer to anyone."

Joy shook her head sadly.

"Now, you promised you'd stop pestering me about this. Let's enjoy your day," Joy said as she hugged and kissed me.

Some months later, at the end of a long day, Moses turned from his desk and asked if I could lock up. He said he had an appointment and had to leave a few minutes early. It was an unusual request, since we always walked out together. I told him it was fine. I was straightening the papers on my desk and turning off my computer when I noticed him standing across the street, looking up and down as if waiting for someone. I wondered who this late appointment was.

I started shutting off the lights and when I got to the door, an expensive looking car pulled up. Moses got in. When the interior light came on, I saw an attractive black woman was driving.

It was like being hit by lightning. My cheeks burned. Who was this woman? Were they dating? Had he been seeing her behind my back? I was being completely ridiculous. I could hardly accuse him of cheating on me because as I had said repeatedly, we were friends. Nothing more. He could see other women. Date other women. He owed me nothing.

My stomach churned the whole way home. When I walked in the front door, Hodge waddled up and looked around behind me to see if Moses was there. I could tell by his posture he was depressed that his best friend wasn't with me. He stomped back to the couch and snuggled in the pillows with his back to me.

"Thanks a lot, Hodge. Just when I needed a friend. A warm greeting and a bit of love, this is what I get. My second rejection of the day." I changed into my ratty sweats and turned on the TV. I couldn't concentrate so I went to bed. If Moses got married, Hodge would be heartbroken. I might have to give him to Moses as a wedding present.

The next morning, I got up early and headed to the Morning Brew. I wanted to get there before the café opened for the day. I needed to talk to Susan. I needed advice. I needed a friend.

When I arrived, Susan stood behind the counter prepping the coffee machine for the day. She glanced up with a surprised look on her face and hurried over to let me in. She gave me a quick hug before dragging me inside. "It's good to see you. But this is a bit out of your normal visiting times. What's up?"

Before I could speak, she held up her hand. "Coffee first, then talk." She returned a moment later with two cups of steaming brew.

I sighed deeply. "I'm in need of advice. Some tea and sympathy."

"I'm more into coffee and a kick in the ass," she joked. "Hopefully I can help."

"You know how I always say Moses and I are just friends? That we are co-workers but that's all?"

"Yes. You've been spouting that crap for what—two years now?"

"It's not crap!" I almost shouted.

"Really? So why are you here? Did something happen?"

I was almost embarrassed to tell her I was jealous. "Last night, Moses met up with a woman after work and they appeared to be quite friendly. And I got to thinking maybe he's dating her. I felt like I'd been betrayed. Which of course is completely and utterly ridiculous because we aren't a couple." I looked down at my coffee, slowly adding sugar and cream. I didn't want to look at Susan.

"Jane, Jane, Jane." She exhaled a deep breath. "You try to act like you are past love. That you're happy with your single life and all you need is Hodge and your work and books and all the other things in your life, but trust your wise old friend Susan, we all want love."

Susan reached out and took my hand in hers. "We all want to love someone. To have someone love us. Do you want to spend the rest of your life alone? Don't you want to share your life with someone? You share most of your life with Moses and yet you keep him at arm's length. You lie to yourself, your daughters, Moses and me too, when you say you're nothing more than friends. It's like a badge of honor to claim you're past needing someone. That you can make it on your own.

"I see the way you look at Moses and I see the way Moses looks at you. He loves you. He's probably afraid if he says it, you'll take off."

I stirred my coffee, thinking. I did believe I wanted and needed to be alone. I wanted to prove to the world, and to Frank, which was of course completely ridiculous since we weren't even in communication with each other, that I was a capable person and could stand on my own two feet. And I had done it. But did I want to be alone for the rest of my life? That future seemed empty and bleak.

A tear slipped down my cheek and splashed in my coffee cup. "It'll taste salty now," I said.

"Oh, honey." Susan came around and sat in the booth next to me and hugged me. "You've done a great job showing the world that you are a strong, independent woman. You have nothing left to prove. Do you love Moses?"

"I think I might," I replied.

"Well, I hope it's not too late. I hope Moses hasn't decided he's not going to wait for you any longer and started dating. Tell him how you feel. Don't regret missing out on your chance for love. Do it now."

Susan and I hugged each other for a long time. Maybe I needed to start listening to what other people were saying.

❧❦❧

When I got to the office, I carried two cups of coffee from the Morning Brew. Moses was already at his desk, sorting through his stacks of files. He looked up, smiling. "Wow. What a treat. Coffee from my favorite café. Are you telling me you don't think our office coffee is good?"

I laughed, "No, it's adequate. But sometimes we all need a treat." I handed him a cup and sat in the chair next to his desk. I took a deep breath and plunged in. "How'd your appointment go last night? I noticed you got picked up by a rather fancy car. Going for a test drive?" I tried to keep my tone light and joking.

"Oh. I'm embarrassed you saw me. That was Adele. My ex. She wanted to talk about some papers she needed me to sign. I told her to drop by my office and she refused, saying she wouldn't be caught dead after dark in this neighborhood. I told her to pick me up and we could go wherever she felt safe and I'd sign."

I could hardly speak. He wasn't dating. He wasn't seeing someone behind my back. I closed my eyes. Relief washed over me.

It must have shown in my face. "Jane? Are you okay? You look flushed. I hope you're not coming down with something."

I opened my eyes and looked at his sweet face so full of care and concern. "No. I'm fine. It's just that…" Just that what? What could I say? Anything I said would no doubt make me sound like a teenager catching her boyfriend with another girl.

"Just what?" Moses prompted.

"I thought you were going out on a date with someone. And I was surprised how much it upset me. Not that I have any right, but feelings aren't really right or wrong, they just are."

Moses started laughing and laughing and I became irritated. "So sorry my distress causes you such amusement." I stood and headed to my desk.

Behind me, I heard Moses jump up. Then he grabbed my hand. "I'm not laughing at you. I'm just happy to know that the thought of me dating someone else made you jealous."

Turning around, I looked into his eyes.

"I've been wondering if you'd ever think of me as anything more than just friends, and you can't imagine how hard it's been for me to go along with that nonsense. Almost two damn years. If I'd only known the trick was to make you jealous, I'd have tried that a long time ago!"

He smiled and I smiled. "I fell in love with you the first day we met in the park. Well, maybe I fell in love with Hodge, but you guys are kind of a package deal."

"Hodge is easy to fall in love with," I agreed.

"And I don't want to be lovers, or friends with benefits or whatever the current terms are. I want us to get married. I want us to stand up in front of the world and say we love each other. What do you think? Do you think you might want to marry me? It won't be easy. The world doesn't always view mixed-race marriages favorably. Plus, we're both old as hell and people don't understand old people still have needs." He smiled wickedly.

I wasn't worried about the racial issue. I was worried about a guy seeing me in my birthday suit. Old bodies aren't very beautiful. I blushed. I could always keep the lights off.

I looked deeper into Moses' beautiful brown eyes. I ran my fingers along his face. "Yes," I said. "I will marry you. I will be Mrs. Moses Elijah Johnson. Jane Johnson. That is the name I want to spend the rest of my life with. But only if you kiss me right now, and it better be the best kiss I've ever had."

And it was.

Dear Reader,

This is a work of fiction but like all stories, it contains some elements of truth from my own life. My grandmother, Julia Rosa Boagni, was a true Southern Belle who married the town baseball hero and bad boy. My grandfather, Arthur Etienne Veltin, known as Toby, ran a nightclub and was probably a bit of a gangster.

My parents met during the war at my grandfather's nightclub and were married six months after they met. They stayed married and in love for the next sixty-six years.

Being an army brat is a fascinating life filled with many wonderful experiences, but it does have it's drawbacks. I was a shy child and found moving every year traumatizing. Luckily for me, unlike my character, Jane, I had my brother and sister with me to help.

And luckily, I also found a good man to marry and we have three amazing daughters.

I hope you enjoyed this book.

If you are so inclined, please leave a review on Amazon, Barnes & Noble or Goodreads. It's nice to get feedback from readers.

You can find me in a number of ways: my website pattiproauthor.com, Facebook (@pattiproauthor) and Twitter @PattiProcopi.

Or you can email me at Patti.pro@cox.net. I'd love to hear from you.

Acknowledgements

Thanks to my family, husband Greg, and my fabulous daughters Allie, Elena, and Leah for your love and support.

Thanks to my sister Joan who has been sharing this writing journey with me and is my constant cheerleader.

I would like to thank my critique group who I don't always agree with but they are always there for me and make my writing so much better: Peter Stipe, Dave Pistorese, Chris Pascal, Mark Green, Sonja McGiboney, Elizabeth Lee, and Caterina Novelierre. Thanks for reading each and every word.

Thanks to all my writing groups – Chesapeake Bay Writers, Virginia Writers Club, and James River Writers. I have met so many fellow writers through these groups. Networking and sharing the journey is so much fun.

And thank you once again to my wonderful editor and publisher Narielle Living of Blue Fortune Enterprises, who was the first person to want to publish my writings. My first novel, *Please … Tell Me More* was published in 2020, during the height of Covid. It was the one good thing I had to celebrate that year. This second novel is hopefully the start of many more projects. Look for the sequel to *Please...Tell Me More* in 2023, *Stop Talking*.

About the Author

Patti Gaustad Procopi is a former army brat who lived all over the world before settling in the small rural community of Gloucester, Virginia. Along with her husband Greg, they raised three daughters along with numerous cats and dogs. After retiring from working at two area history museums, Patti finally had time to do the things she always wanted to do, including writing the next great novel. Moving constantly made it difficult to make friends and form lasting relationships. Her writing is about those feelings of loneliness and loss, friendship and family.

In addition to writing, Patti fills her days photographing her beloved Ospreys raising their young, rescuing raptors for a rehab facility and researching her family's past on Ancestry. Patti and Greg hope to get back to traveling soon. Their bucket list is waiting.

Patti can be found on Facebook, Twitter, Instagram and Goodreads. Check out her website – Pattiproauthor.com. Patti loves to hear from her readers and is available to talk to book clubs and other groups.